Playing Dirty

Also by Kiki Swinson

Wifey
I'm Still Wifey
Life After Wifey
Sleeping with the Enemy (with Wahida Clark)

Published by Kensington Publishing Corporation

Playing Dirty

KIKI SWINSON

KENSINGTON PUBLISHING CORP.

DAFINA BOOKS are published by

Kensington Publishing Corp.
850 Third Avenue
New York, NY 10022

Dafina Books and the Dafina logo Reg. U.S. Pat. & TM Off.

ISBN: 978-1-60751-791-7

Printed in the United States of America

My children definitely mean the world to me, so I have to dedicate this masterpiece to them. We have weathered many storms, and God has brought us through them every single time. I am totally grateful for that. He is truly awesome!

To my editor, Selena James, I know I plucked your nerves throughout this entire project, so I have to thank you for your patience. Just know that I work better under pressure.

To my agent, Crystal L. Winslow, I know I plucked your nerves, too, but you and I have been working together for years now, so you're used to it (*smile*). Just kidding! Thanks for always having my back!

To all my readers out there, I love y'all so much! And thanks for making Kiki Swinson a household name.

From the Beginning

"Okay, Yoshi, it's your time," I whispered to myself. I ran my hands over my Chanel pencil skirt to smooth out the wrinkles. Then I turned toward the large bathroom mirror and checked my ass—along with my silver tongue and beautiful face, it was one of my best assets. I stood in the old-fashioned marble courthouse bathroom, making sure I looked as stunning as always before I made my way to the courtroom. My assistant had just texted my Black-Berry to tell me the jury was back with a verdict. The jury had only deliberated for one day. For a defense attorney, that could spell disaster. But that rule stood for regular defense attorneys—and I'd like to think that I was in a class by myself.

The trial had had its moments, but through it all I shined like a star. On the second to last day, I had all but captured the jury in the palm of my hand. I used my half-Korean background and my native Korean tongue to appeal to the two second-generation Asian jurors. My mother would've been so proud. As a proud Korean, she always wanted me to forget that I was half Black. She spoke Korean all the time. It had everything to do with the volatile relationship she had with my father before he packed up and left New

York to go back to his hometown in Virginia when I was only eight years old. Him leaving the family devastated my mother, but I was okay with it. I got tired of listening to them fuss and fight all the time. And it seemed like it always got worse on the weekends when he came home drunk.

That wasn't the life my mother's parents had in mind for her after they emigrated all the way from Korea to Brooklyn, New York. I'm sure they felt that if she was going to struggle, then she needed to struggle with her own kind. Not with some African-American scumbag, alcoholic, warehouse worker from Norfolk, Virginia, who only moved to New York City to pursue his dreams of making it big in the music industry. My mother, unfortunately, picked him to father me. When I got old enough to understand, my mother told me that as soon as my grandparents got wind of their relationship, they disowned her. But as soon as my dad packed his shit and left, they immediately came to her rescue and wrote her back into their will. They were so happy that nigga left, they got on their knees and started sending praises to Buddha.

I couldn't care one way or the other. I mean, it wasn't like we were close anyway. From as far back as I could remember, I pretty much did my own thing. After school I would always go to the library and find a book to read, which was why I excelled in grade school. After graduating from high school, I thought about nothing else but furthering my education in law. I had always aspired to be a TV court judge, so I figured the only way I could ever have my own show was to become an attorney first. So here I was defending my client, the alleged leader of the Fuc-Chang Korean Mafia, who was on trial for murder, bribery, and racketeering. Now I knew he was guilty as hell, but I pulled every trick out of the bag to make the jury believe that he wasn't.

"Ms. Lomax, the jury returned its verdict after just one day of deliberation. Are you worried?" a reporter called out as I made my way down the hallway toward Judge Allen's courtroom. A swarm of reporters surrounded me, shoving microphones in my face. I never turned down an opportunity to show up on television.

"A fast verdict is just what I expected. My client is innocent." I smiled, flashing my perfect white teeth and shaking my long, jet black hair. And right after I entered the courtroom, I switched my ass as hard as I could down the middle aisle toward the defense table. All eyes turned toward me. I could feel the stares burning my entire body. My red Chanel suit was an eye-catcher. It showed off my curves and it made me look like a million bucks. When potential clients approach me for representation, they are not surprised to learn that I charge a minimum of $2,500 an hour. They don't even blink when the figure rolls off my tongue. The way they see it, you never put a price on freedom, and with my victory rate, how can they lose?

Right before I took my seat at the defense table, I looked at my client, Mr. Choo, who was shackled like an animal and guarded by courtroom officers. He appeared cool, calm, and collected, unlike the men in black across from him. The prosecutors sat at their table and fiddled with pens, bit nails, and adjusted ties. They looked nervous and frazzled, to say the least. I was just the opposite. In fact, I was laughing my ass off on the inside because I knew I had this case in the bag.

The senior court officer moved to the front of the jam-packed courtroom, ordered everyone to stand, and announced Judge Allen. I looked up at Judge Mark Allen, with his salt-and-pepper balding head and little beady eyes. Mark is what I call him when he's not in his black robe. As a matter of fact, it gets really personal when he and I get together for one of our so-called romantic interludes. Last week was the last time he and I got together, and it was in his chambers. It was so funny because I let him fuck me in his robe with his puny five-inch wrinkled dick. He thought he was the man, too. And when it was all said and done, I made sure I wiped my cum all over the crotch of his slacks. Shit, Monica Lewinsky ain't got nothing on me. I wanted him to know that I had no respect for his authority or his courtroom. After I let him get at me, and I bribed a few of the jurors, all of the calls in the courtroom went my way. The prosecutors never had a chance. . . . It was amusing to watch.

The judge cleared his throat and began to speak. The courtroom was "pin drop" quiet.

"Jury, what say you in the case of the *State of Florida* versus *Haan Choo?*" Judge Allen boomed.

The jury foreperson, a fair-skinned Black woman in her mid-fifties, stood up swiftly, her hands trembling. " 'We, the jury, in the matter of the *State of Florida* versus *Haan Choo*, finds as follows: to the charge of first-degree murder . . . not guilty.' "

A gasp resounded through the courtroom. Then the scream of some victim's family members.

"Order!" Judge Allen screamed.

The foreperson continued without looking up from her paper. " 'To the charge of racketeering . . . not guilty. To the charge of bribery . . . not guilty. And to the charge of conspiracy . . . not guilty.' "

Mr. Choo jumped up and grabbed me in a bear hug. "Yoshi, you greatest," he whispered in broken English.

"Order!" the judge screamed again. "Bailiff, take Mr. Choo back to booking so he can be released." He had to go through his motions to set Mr. Choo free. I looked over at the prosecutors' table and threw them a smile. I knew they all wished they could just jump across the table and kill me. Too bad they hadn't taken what I had offered them after the preliminary hearing. Both assistant district attorneys were new to the game and overeager to take on their first high-profile case. Out of the gate they wanted to prove to their boss that they both could take me on, but somebody should've warned them that I was no one to fuck with. With a smile still on my face, I strutted by them and said, "Idiots!" just loud enough for only them to hear. Then I threw my hair back and continued to strut my shit out the courtroom.

After I slid the city clerk's head administrator ten crisp one-hundred-dollar bills, it only took about an hour to process Mr. Choo's release papers. Money talks and bullshit runs the marathon! And before anyone knew it, Mr. Choo and I were walking outside to greet the press. He and I both were all smiles, because he was a free man and I knew that in an hour or so, I was going to be $2 million richer; that alone made me want to celebrate. But first, we needed to address the media. Cameras flashed and microphones passed in front of us as we stepped into the sunlight. Mr. Choo rushed to the huddle of microphones that all but blocked his slim face from view. "Justice was served today. I am innocent and my lawyer proved that. I no crime boss, I am family man. I run my business and I love America," he rambled, his horrible English getting on my nerves. I waited patiently while he made his grand stand and then I took over the media show.

"All along I told everyone my client was innocent. Mr.

Choo came to the United States from Korea to make an honest—" *Bang, bang, bang, bang, bang, bang!* The sound of shouts and then screams rang in my ears. Then I heard someone in the crowd yell in Korean, "You fucking snitch!" The shots stopped me dead in my tracks; my words tumbled back down my throat like hard marbles, choking me. I grabbed my arm as heat radiated up to my neck.

"Oh shit, I'm hit!" I screamed. I dropped to the ground, scrambling to hide . . . and saw Mr. Choo, his head dangling and his body slumped against the courthouse steps. His mouth hung open and blood dripped from his lips and chin. Before I could figure out what to do next, someone snatched me up from the ground. I didn't know where we were headed—my thoughts were on my throbbing arm and my racing heart. Then suddenly my vision became blurry and the world went black.

My career changed after Mr. Choo's trial. Shit, after having almost lost my damn life, I would not accept anything less than the best.

After the shooting, the law firm of Shapiro and Witherspoon was thrown into the media spotlight like never before. I became known as the "ride-or-die bitch attorney" that would take a bullet to get a client off. I became the most sought-after criminal defense attorney in Florida. Sometimes I didn't know if that was good or bad. But one thing was sure, my life changed and my appetite for money and power grew more and more intense. I started living each day as if it were my last.

Years ago, I never thought I would have turned out to be the way I was today. When you look at it, I had become a heartless bitch! I could not care less about anyone, including my own damn mother. Even when having a nightcap with my flavor of the night, I never let my feelings get involved. Once I put the condom on him, I reminded myself that it was only business and that my client's freedom was on the line, so everything worked out fine. That's how I kept men in line. After the shooting, I vowed that my heart would remain in my pocket forever.

Baller Status

My life was great. Hands down, I was really doing it big. After my brush with death, I was propelled into the firm's million-dollar club. Yes, I did say million-dollar club—a club at the firm that was usually reserved for prestigious White men. But I broke through that glass ceiling. I had become a giant and I was continuously growing.

After the incident and the media rush, I was promoted to junior partner at the firm, which sent my bank account swelling. I was waiting for senior partner, but this would do for now. I purchased a split-level penthouse for $5.2 million, right in the heart of Collins Avenue. I had a beautiful view of Miami Beach. At the firm, I was given one of the best offices in the building—an executive suite. My office was like a second home, complete with a dressing room and a granite-tiled full bathroom. I could sleep there if I wanted. There were a lot of haters at the firm after that.

My reputation spoke for itself. Not only did I have a 98 percent acquittal rate, most of my clientele were rich, I mean fucking wealthy—and most, if not all, were high-level crime heads. I wasn't representing any petty thugs or hand-to-hand street hustlers; they could never afford to pay even my retainer. Trust me, I had my shit together and I couldn't be touched, because I maintained a license to practice law in New York, Arizona, Florida, and Nevada—not bad for a thirty-four-year-old daughter of a Korean immigrant. I was single, but I got my fair share of dick. I was married to dead presidents; I didn't need a fucking man locking me down or trying to share my dough. And I damn sure didn't need any kids. Speaking of which, I had my brush with almost becoming a mother; but I got rid of that fucking baby so fast, it wasn't even funny. I wasn't about to let a baby slow me down. I had a lot of shit going on, so a newborn baby did not fit into that equation. Not only that, the asshole I was pregnant by had a wife, so that would not have worked anyway. I am not into sharing someone else's husband and calling the bastard my fucking baby daddy. Come on, now, how does that shit sound? Ridiculous, if you ask me, so I wasn't about to take myself through that unnecessary drama.

Shit, I was Yoshi Lomax. Wherever I went, I commanded attention. Everyone and their mother knew who the fuck I was. And it wasn't because I was a fucking beautiful woman; it was because I was a TV whore. I was one bad bitch and I knew it. I'd learned as soon as I got to the firm of Shapiro and Witherspoon that I could either work hard or work smart. Needless to say, I chose to work smart. I'd see these little lawyers running around doing tons and tons of research for a case, but I said the hell with that! I mean, what the fuck was the point? I'd rather go to the judge, DA, or police officer, and offer them a big payoff in exchange for my client's acquittal. And if they're attractive enough to fuck, I'd throw in a quickie or a one-nighter, depending on how high the stakes were. Speaking of which, half of everyone I had working on my team preferred to fuck me over the cash, so I'm like, hey, that works for me. Shit, I didn't mind keeping the cash in the bank. I was all for it. And since that was how the game was played, I played my cards very well.

* * *

I stood on the balcony of my Miami Beach penthouse and inhaled the fresh scent of the ocean. It was the middle of January and I watched the sun rise; the hint of orange and streaks of purple that laced the sky and glinted off the sea's horizon made me feel good inside. The seventy-degree air was brisk and blew open my silk and lace La Perla bathrobe. I flinched as the air brushed across my rock-hard nipples. I started to rush to close my bathrobe but decided to let my perfect C-cup breasts catch the sunrise.

I turned and peered through my glass patio doors just in time to see Paul stirring in my bed. My stomach turned. I hated his fake tanned body and his jet black greasy hair. A fake-ass Al Pacino is what he looked like. I watched him stroke his dick, getting it ready for yet another round with me, which was something I was totally dreading. Not only was his fuck game on zero, this guy's dick was a mess. If Viagra wasn't on the market, he would be up shit's creek without a paddle.

Paul Shapiro was my egocentric boss at the law firm of Shapiro and Witherspoon. He wielded his power like an ax, chopping down anything that got in his way. When I first arrived at the firm, fresh out of law school, I could not get a break to save my life. Although I had been assigned some of the most challenging cases and had an almost perfect acquittal rate, I still could not get the respect I deserved. My praises were minimized to meager bonus checks and a pat on the back. It seemed like I couldn't break into the good ole boy network that dominated the firm's culture. Hard work was a curse at Shapiro and Witherspoon. I learned that lesson very quickly.

After I rebuffed thousands of sexual advances, sleeping with Paul was not a decision I made easily. My career relied on it. I finally obliged and gave him some ass, but I had other things in mind when I did it . . . like making partner. Well, you know what Malcolm X said, "By any means necessary!" I was a true believer in that shit, especially if it meant keeping me in the most expensive jewels, designer clothes, cars, and vacations. A few minutes of sweaty fucking meant a lifetime of money, jewelry, cars, and trips. It also meant making my mother proud. She'd worked like a slave cleaning up after people—just like Paul—to send me to college and law school.

I walked inside and flashed a halfhearted smile at Paul. "Listen, I have a meeting with a new client, so we have to cut this short," I lied.

"What, you gonna leave me and him high and dry?" Paul asked, pointing to his hard dick.

I sighed. "Look, Paul, I have a meeting," I said dryly, walking into my master bathroom. I clicked on the twenty-seven-inch flat-screen TV that hung over my Jacuzzi tub; I wanted to drown his voice out. I was also trying to get up the gumption to tell his silly ass that our fucking sprees had come to an end.

"What client you meeting with on a Saturday?" he yelled from the bedroom.

"It's a new guy that contacted me. I have to look up his name," I lied again, thinking quick on my feet. I actually had a lunch date with my best friend, Maria. Maria Hernandez had been my best friend since college and she also happened to be the director of the Drug Enforcement Administration's Miami field office.

Paul walked up behind me, his dick sticking straight out. He grabbed my bare breasts and rubbed his dick up and down my ass.

"Paul! I said I have to go. Now you can stay and let yourself out, but I have to go!" I screamed, frustrated with his constant bullshit.

"Yoshi, you sure have been acting different lately," he complained.

I paused for a moment, thinking that there was no better time than now. "Look, Paul. I don't think we should do this anymore. I am starting to feel funny at work," I said flatly.

"What are you talkin' about? No one is looking at you. If they are, it's because they are jealous," he replied, grabbing at my robe.

I jerked away from him. "Look, this whole thing isn't working for me anymore. All this back-and-forth fucking, here at my place or on top of your desk in your office, has gotten old, so it has to stop today. All I want to do is my job and continue making the firm money," I said forcefully.

Paul's eyes turned dark and he furrowed his eyebrows. "You don't wanna fuck me anymore, huh, Yoshi?" he asked, clenching his jaw.

"Paul, don't get mad. I just think we both should focus—"

"Fuck you, Yoshi. I made you junior partner and it wasn't because of your damn work, so don't let your head get too fucking big! Remember who the fuck I am," he growled, his dick shrinking back down to two inches. He was clearly turned off.

"Paul, don't take it personal. I just want to do the right thing," I lied, throwing on a phony smile. I was tired of fucking his whack ass, and to top it off, he did not know how to eat my pussy right. I was totally fed up with coaching him, so it was time to hang up the towel. Not only that, junior partner wasn't good enough for me, especially when he kept promising to make me senior partner. If Paul thought he was going to keep fucking the shit out of me for that little-ass promotion, then he had another thing coming.

"I hold your career in my hands," he began, "so don't ever forget where you came from!" He stormed out of the bathroom and began gathering his things.

"Trust me, I know where I came from, but since you're on some threatening shit, you need to also remember that I know what type of shit you're into. So just in case you want to get cute and start slicing away at my benefits around the office, don't forget I've got your wife and your friends at the IRS on speed dial," I said.

Paul was back in that bathroom like a bat out of hell. "You fucking bitch! Don't you ever fucking mention my business again. Do you hear me? That shit will get you killed," he threatened, and then he didn't say another word. His ego was crushed and I knew it. Get me killed? Yeah, right! What a joke! Paul was a fucking punk trying to act tough, like he was Tony Soprano or somebody. I laughed right in his face and he looked at me like I was crazy.

I knew that after I crushed his fucking world, he was going to leave, and I was right. Immediately after I turned on the shower faucet, stepped into the tub, and turned around to close the shower curtains, he walked out of the bathroom. So I proceeded with my bathing, and when I was done, I turned off the water, slid the curtain back, and stepped down onto the bathroom rug. As I was about to dry myself off with the towel, I realized that it was completely quiet, so I wrapped the towel around me and stepped into my bedroom to see if Paul had left altogether. Sure enough, he was gone. But he left a note and five crisp one-hundred-dollar bills on my nightstand. So I rushed over to my nightstand and picked the note up:

BITCH, YOU WILL ALWAYS BE A WHORE TO ME,
SO HERE IS YOUR PAYMENT FOR THE
LOUSY FUCK LAST NIGHT.

Reading his note gave me an instant migraine. I couldn't believe Paul was so ignorant. But then I realized how pompous he was, so I had to laugh at his immaturity.

I heard a vacuum switch on, letting me know that my housekeeper had arrived.

"Ophelia!" I called out.

"Yes, Ms. Lomax," Ophelia answered, almost instantly standing in my bedroom doorway.

"Here, take this money and go do something nice for yourself," I said, handing her the five hundred dollars.

Her eyes lit up. "Oh, my God, Ms. Lomax! What is this for? I don't get paid this week," she asked, surprised.

"It's a gift. Now take it and go treat yourself to something really nice," I said. She took the money from my hand apprehensively, surveyed it, and scurried out of my sight. That was my nice deed for the week. Those were few and far between.

As I began to get dressed, I thought about that stunt Paul had just pulled. I began to laugh all over again. I mean, did he really think I would keep his petty-ass cash? I would rather give that shit to a bum on the street before I kept it. Didn't Paul know who I was? I had just picked up two big clients, one of which was Killer Dee, the most popular rapper in Miami. He got picked up on a gun charge and had his people call me. Then there was Mr. Dicaprio, the lieutenant captain of the most notorious Sicilian crime family in Florida. Nevertheless, his case would be over in no time because the feds got him charged with some bogus conspiracy shit. That's what I was all about: big names, rappers, crime bosses, and the Mafia. That's where the real money was.

After I got dressed, I picked up my BlackBerry to send Maria a text and I noticed that my private file folder was open.

"What the hell is this?" I questioned. My heart began racing. I couldn't remember if I had left my file open. It was super private. That is where I kept all of my special contacts at the DA's office, judges, and, more important, records of my exchanges between myself and my clients. I knew it wasn't wise to keep that kind of stuff on paper, but I always thought it needed to be kept just in case I ever needed to refer to it for my own protection. "I must have left it open," I whispered to myself. I knew Paul wouldn't have the balls to go through my BlackBerry, or would he? Those thoughts raced through my mind the entire drive down to meet Maria.

Dealing with
Heavy Hitters

I rushed into me and Maria's favorite spot after grabbing the ticket stub from the valet driver. I had important things to discuss with Maria today, and it would definitely be worth it for her. She was so damn knowledgeable about shit going on in the streets, which was why it was a must I had her on my payroll.

"*Hola, mami,*" I squealed, as I grabbed Maria for a hug.

"*Hola, mi amor.* Your Spanish gets worse and worse each year," Maria joked, smiling and returning my embrace. We hugged for a few minutes and exchanged our customary peck on each cheek. And, as always, we surveyed each other from head to toe to check out what we were both wearing. It was what we had been doing since college, a habit of sorts, but we both knew there was no harm intended.

"I love the new hair." I complimented Maria's new bob haircut. Maria was a beautiful caramel-colored Latina. Although she was Mexican, she had the ass and face of Jennifer Lopez. Maria also had a taste for the finer things in life. Every time I saw her, she had on a designer bag. Today she carried the new Chanel Coco Cabas bag and I was loving it. I made a mental note to go cop one right away.

"*Sí,* it was time for a new look," Maria replied, flashing

her stunning smile. Maria was one of the few people in the world I felt I could trust. She was also thirty-four, stood five feet six inches, and was very sexy. She and I had been friends since our early days in college. Maria—just like me—was never given shit for free. Her parents were first-generation Mexican immigrants and they, too, worked for scraps while trying to give their children a better start.

Maria and I always remained loyal to one another. I had helped her through college—basically, I did all of the school work and she helped me through the rough times in my life. To be more specific, she helped me kick a small cocaine habit I had developed my first year in school. She sat up with me for two weeks straight while I went cold turkey; and she always reminds me of how that withdrawal almost killed my ass. Since then, we always had each other's back. Maria always promised me that she would repay me one day for helping her through school. She would've never made it through college without me, and that would have meant letting her parents down. I never told Maria, but I felt the exact same way about her. If she hadn't helped me kick that fucking cocaine habit, I never would've made it through college or law school, which would have meant letting my mother down, too.

Maria and I took our seats at our regular table inside the beautiful, upscale Oceanaire Seafood Room on Miami Avenue. We were comfortable at that restaurant. The entire waitstaff knew us, and also knew not to disturb us after we ordered and got our drinks and meals. Maria and I usually had important business to discuss. I was there today to tell her that my assistant, Donna, had informed me that Sheldon Chisholm, one of the most notorious gangsters in the Miami area, had contacted my office looking to retain my services. I had not returned his calls yet because I wanted to get Maria's opinion first. She and I usually ran things by each other that way. Maria knew the kinds of people I defended, and she also knew the kinds of things I did to get them off. Believe me, she wasn't an innocent bystander, either. Maria had made her fair share of dirty dollars as well.

"So, what do you know about Sheldon Chisholm?" I asked as I took a sip of my Washington Apple. Maria looked up from her appetizer, surprised.

"Why do you want to know about him?" she asked, although she already knew the answer to her own question.

"Don't I always tell you not to answer a question with a question?" I joked, chuckling.

Maria laughed, too. She caught on real quick.

"Well, from what I know, Sheldon Chisholm was born in Haiti, dirt poor, came from nothing," Maria began as we sipped our drinks. "He lost his entire family in a drug deal gone wrong in the early '80s, and that was the start of his reign of terror. He worked his way up in the mysterious Haitian Mafia, and has since become the number-one heroin supplier in all of West Miami."

I listened intently. Behind every word Maria said, I heard dollar signs.

"He's a very flashy Haitian, with a penchant for violence. He is nothing to play with. Not only that, he is a fucking millionaire with very little conscience or patience. He will kill a newborn baby over ten dollars," Maria informed.

"Do you know anything about his case?" I asked. She looked at me strangely, like she knew I was going to ask, but also like I better have some cash for her if I was asking.

"Yes. It's being handled by agents in my field office. From what I've been told, his driver was pulled over for a traffic violation, and when his license was run, it came back suspended. That gave my people probable cause to search the vehicle, and when the vehicle was searched, my agents found a trunk filled with kilos of one hundred percent uncut heroin. They say it was at least sixty-five million dollars in value. He's out on bail now."

"Damn, that's a lot of drugs."

"Yes, it was. But I've seen more."

"So, would it be hard to get rid of?"

"You just say the word and it is as good as gone," she told me, and then smiled.

I smiled back at her because I knew everything was going to work in my favor and we both were going to be a couple of million dollars richer after I made the deal with the Devil, which was Sheldon Chisholm himself. Everybody may be scared of this guy, but I wasn't, because I knew he needed me. Me and Maria held his fate in our hands, so I knew he wouldn't try to pull any of the stunts on us like he'd done with other people. That wouldn't be wise on his part. I hoped he had enough sense to realize that. After I counted all the zeros in my head that I would be receiving from him, I smiled once again at Maria and then held up my glass.

"Let's make a toast to success!" she said, raising her glass almost simultaneously.

I pressed my glass against hers. "Success!" I added; then my thoughts shifted elsewhere. "Hey, wait. Who is the Assistant U.S. Attorney on the case?"

"Relax, girl. Because of the media implications, Brad Carlton is taking it himself. . . . No assistant on this one— the U.S. Attorney himself," Maria said, like she knew the deal.

"Shit, today must be my fucking lucky day. I'm going to play the lotto when I leave here. Maybe I can get richer," I said, letting out a gut-busting laugh. I was feeling more confident about Sheldon Chisholm's case already, so I planned to contact him right after lunch. "Well, on a lighter note, I told Paul we couldn't fuck anymore," I said, changing the subject.

"What?" Maria asked, raising her eyebrows.

"Yes, and he went crazy," I replied, telling her about the note and his little threat against my career. We got a good laugh out of it. "Paul is harmless," I said, trying to convince myself that breaking off our little affair wasn't going to have a horrible backlash.

After Maria and I ate ourselves to death, I picked up the tab. Before I stood up to leave, I handed her an envelope with twenty thousand in cash in it. "Here's a little something to get things rolling on Sheldon's case."

Maria took the envelope and stuck it in her handbag. "Thank you very much," she said, and then stood up.

Right before I stepped away from the table, I embraced her and then we said our good-byes. "Call me later," I said.

"I will," she assured me; then we parted ways.

I left the restaurant with a lot on my mind, mainly how much money I could potentially get for representing someone like Sheldon Chisholm. I got excited inside. With the connections I had, I was already confident I could get him off, which meant if I could give him a guaranteed acquittal, I could get him to give me any amount I threw at him. I mean, we were talking about his freedom here. And something like that can cost him anywhere from five to ten million. And since I knew he had money to burn, I might just hit him in the head and charge him the latter. He wouldn't miss it. From what Maria told me about this guy's organization, they were supplying 35 percent of the Eastern Seaboard, and that little bit of dope the DEA seized from him was just a tear in a bucket for him. So you see, I've got a potential gold mine if I play my cards right, and from where I am sitting, I could definitely come off with a royal flush if I keep pulling from the deck. I can't see it any other way. So let the games begin.

After I left Maria, I was driving down Washington Street, and a call came in on my BlackBerry. I looked down to see who it was, but the screen of my phone read "no caller ID." I started not to answer it, but then I figured it might be one of my clients trying to call me collect.

"Hello," I finally said, and sure enough the recorded prison system message came through loud and clear. So I waited to hear the name of the inmate, and when I heard the voice, I immediately accepted the call.

"Miguel Santos, is that you?"

"Yes, *mami*, it's me. I'm so glad you answered my call."

"What's going on? What do they have you down there for now?"

"They are trying to pin this murder on me."

"What murder?"

"They're trying to say I executed this Mexican dude and his family a couple of nights ago."

"Oh yeah, I heard about that."

"Yeah, it's been all over the news, but I didn't have anything to do with it."

"Where were you on the night it happened?" I asked.

"I was at home."

"Was anyone there with you?"

"No."

"Do you have a bond?"

"No. The magistrate denied it."

"So, what do you need me to do? Because we can work this thing out a couple of different ways."

"Don't worry about getting me a bail hearing. I was

thinking more on the lines of you taking my case and working your magic so I can get out of here for good."

"Well, okay, that can be arranged. But, you know, I'm going to need my retainer fee before I make any phone calls or file any motions."

"How much is your retainer?"

"Come on now, Miguel, do you have to ask?"

"It's been—what?—four years since I had you as my attorney?"

"Believe me, Miguel, nothing has changed but the gas prices." I chuckled.

He chuckled a bit himself, but it sounded like it was forced. And then his laughter stopped. "Well, umm, I was wondering if you could do this case for me as a pro bono. You know, since I helped you out and referred a lot of people to you throughout the years."

"Are you having some kind of financial problem?" I didn't hesitate to ask. The mere thought of him asking me to take his case for free damn near sent me into cardiac arrest.

"Yes, things are looking bad for me right now. I've got a lot of gambling debts floating around out there. But as soon as you get me out of this mess, I can get you the money with no problem," he insisted.

I paused for a second, because I didn't want to come off as a self-righteous bitch. But, on the other hand, I realized that there was no need for me to beat around the bush with him. There was no way in hell I would take his case without payment up front. I don't do that shit for anyone. It doesn't matter to me how much money you paid me in the past. I can't live off memories. So, if you don't have the cash at the door, then we have nothing further to discuss. "Miguel, I am so sorry! I don't do pro bono cases. But if you tell your judge that you're financially indigent, then I'm sure he will

assign you a court-appointed attorney. I wish you the best!"
I told him, and then I politely disconnected the call.

After I laid my phone down in the passenger seat of my
car, I replayed the entire conversation in my mind. I mean,
how could he get up the nerve to call me with that bullshit?
And then, on top of that, tell me he had gambling debts,
like that was going to make me feel sorry for his ass! Come
on now, give me a fucking break! He's a fucking loser with
a capital *L,* and I can't help him. If he knew what was best,
he'd lose my damn number really quick.

Monday Morning

I started prepping myself for Sheldon's case before I even called him back and before he officially hired me. I mean, there was no doubt he would hire me and I wanted shit to be in place for the case. For the price I was going to charge Sheldon, I had to guarantee him an acquittal, just like I did all of my clients. So, you know, the gears in my sinister little brain immediately started working after I spoke to Maria, thinking up my strategy for Sheldon's acquittal. Once I found out that Brad Carlton was working the case, I knew everything was going to work together in my favor.

I called up Mr. Carlton—the federal United States Attorney himself. Brad and I had a mutual understanding and a long-running business relationship that included the occasional personal touch. I liked Brad a lot, but Yoshi Lomax was not settling down anytime soon—so having one man, no matter how much I liked his ass, was out of the question. The phone was ringing and my heart skipped a beat. I had to get my game face on.

"Hey, you," I purred into the receiver of my cell phone.

"Ms. Lomax . . . I knew you'd be calling me sooner or later," he answered, sounding amused. I could tell he had a big fucking smile plastered on his fine-ass face.

"I'm sure. So, when do you want to sit down and talk?" I asked, knowing that he knew just why I was calling.

"You're calling me, so you tell me," he continued.

"I'll tell you what. Let me get back with you after I check my itinerary."

"What time should I be expecting your call?"

"Give me a couple of hours."

"Sounds good. I'm looking forward to our meeting."

"I'm sure," I said in a cute but sarcastic way. But the thing was, I needed to see Brad as soon as possible to get the details together for Sheldon's acquittal.

"I'll be waiting," he assured me, and then we ended our call.

It didn't take me long to go through my itinerary, stored inside my BlackBerry, and figure out I could squeeze Brad in right before I went into the office. I called him right back.

"Hey, are you busy right now?" I asked as soon as he answered his cell phone.

"No, I'm free for at least another hour."

"Where are you?"

"I'm at home wrapping up this paperwork so I can head to the office."

"Can I come by?"

"Sure. Come on."

"Okay, I'll be there shortly," I replied, and then I busted a quick U-turn and headed over to his condo. Being a political appointee, Brad set his own rules, so him working at home was nothing strange. I whipped my shit down the road and I got to his house in record time. I checked my makeup in my visor mirror and noticed that nothing was out of place. I was the shit, if I did say so myself. I wore very little makeup and I was still stunning. Clear skin was what most women would die for, and I had it—so, you know, a lot of bitches hated me. I loved being hated! It kept me on my toes.

Brad opened the door before I could knock. He was a fucking trip. "You and those fucking cameras!" I said, and chuckled. "You're more paranoid than a damn crackhead," I joked, smiling and kissing him on his cheek.

"What was that?" he asked, referring to my peck on his cheek. He let me in, and as soon as I passed him, I could tell he was watching my ass.

"You can't ever seem to keep your eyes off my ass!" I smiled wickedly.

"That's because it's so perfect and round." He smiled.

I tapped him on his shoulder and said, "Come on, Brad. Let's focus, please!"

I grabbed a hold of his arm and escorted him into his study, where we always had our meetings. And when we walked inside, I took a seat on one of the chairs placed in front of his desk. "Ready to talk business?" I sparked up the conversation.

"What's on your mind?" he asked after he took a seat in the chair behind his desk.

"I need to know where we stand with the Chisholm case," I replied directly.

He let out a sinister laugh. "I'm gonna let you make that call," he said, blatantly rubbing his dick to let me know what he had in mind. He kind of pissed me off because right now I wasn't in the mood for the "fuck for favor" program. Lately I'd been paying my own way, so the clothes stayed on, unless I was in one of my horny states of mind. And today was definitely not the day.

"Brad, I've decided not to lay on my back for favors anymore. I'll pay for the shit I want," I remarked, throwing a small stack of cash on top of his desk. I wanted him to know my new stance; it wasn't all about me fucking and sucking him off, it was more about me taking control and getting my fucking way. Because on some real shit, no one was going to ever think Yoshi Lomax actually needed them. I didn't need a motherfucker; in fact, it was more like they all needed me.

"I never said you didn't pay," he replied, looking at me slyly and picking up the money, pretending like he was weighing it.

"Don't worry, it's enough to pique your interest."

"Yeah, it feels like the right amount," he said, smiling. I could see the excitement in his eyes. He knew that the money I'd just laid on his ass was just a small portion of what was to come if he could guarantee me Sheldon's acquittal.

"Don't play me," I said, and before I could fully finish my sentence, Brad was all over me like a bee to honey. He removed the Louis Vuitton hair clip that was holding my hair in a neat ponytail and shook my hair loose. I knew he loved my hair. He had told me once that for a Black man, to fuck an Asian woman was like a dream. He'd said that all Black men fantasize about it. What the fascination was, I had no idea, but I guess fantasizing about White girls had gotten boring, since they were so easy for Black men to get now.

Unlike Paul, Brad was packing a nine-inch dick, and had a chiseled body, beautiful teeth, hands, feet, and legs. I didn't think he had any imperfections. His skin was smooth like a bitch's. I think he got facials and manicures or something because there was no other way he could naturally be so fucking perfect.

"Look," I said, moving his hands back. "I'd love to fuck you right now, but I'm really pressed for time." I was lying.

Truth be told, I wasn't in the mood for his dick or anyone else's. All I wanted to know was, would he be behind me on this case.

"You know I got your back," he said, trying to pull me into his arms.

I allowed him to hold me in the embrace, but that was where it stopped. "Do we have a deal or what?" I pressed the issue.

Brad looked at me with uncertainty. He knew I was one slick-ass bitch, but I never let him know the depths I would go to to get what I want. "What's in it for me?" he wanted to know.

"Just name your price."

"You're not wired, are you?" he asked, patting me down around my back and sides.

"Don't insult my intelligence. Believe me, if I wanted to bury you, you would've been in your grave a long time ago," I replied sarcastically.

"Well, then, tell me who else have you brought in with you?"

"No one. You are the only one I've contacted on this case."

"I find that hard to believe when the DEA are the investigators and your friend Maria works with them."

"What you're saying makes perfect sense. However, if that be the case, don't you think I would've just gone to her and canceled you out altogether? I mean, why try to go through you when I could've killed the evidence from the source who gathered it all?"

"Well, I guess you're right. But I still believe that you've got Maria in on this somewhere."

"Trust me, I don't tell Maria everything," I lied.

"Well, alright, you got this one. But the next case is mine."

"Okay, deal!" I said with excitement, then I broke away from his arms.

"Hey, wait a minute—before you run out of here," he said as he watched me grab my handbag and car keys.

"What's up?" I asked.

"You got to promise me one thing."

"Sure, what is it?"

"Don't fucking embarrass my people," he instructed, still sounding a little unsure about our newest deal.

"I thought you were taking the case yourself?" I asked, a little worried.

"I was, but I don't want any part of your little ass in court. I will make sure it goes away, even if I assign it out to an assistant," he assured.

"Don't mess this up for me. I got a lot of shit riding on this acquittal."

"Yoshi, it's gonna be alright. Calm down."

"I'm calm. I just don't want any bullshit!"

"Everything is going to be taken care of."

"It better!" After I gave him the "don't fuck with me" look, I patted him on the shoulder and told him to have a wonderful day. He looked at me like I was crazy. And what's so funny about that was, most men were starting to give me that same look. So, I asked myself, was I crazy? Maybe, maybe not. But I did know that I was crazy about money, and now that Brad had given me the green light, it was on.

I let the heat waves from the hot Miami air blow through my hair as I whipped my Mercedes down Collins Avenue. I pulled up at a red light, and as I looked out onto the crowded Miami streets, my cell phone rang. My heart skipped a beat when I looked at the number that flashed on the screen. It was Luis Santana, one of my former clients.

After the Choo trial, Mr. Santana was the first of many crime bosses clamoring to hire me. I took his case because he was offering the most money. There was actually a sort of bidding war for my services. Santana had won when he showed up at the firm with his checkbook in hand. Paul walked his ass into my office VIP-style; it was an offer Shapiro and Witherspoon could not refuse. Mr. Santana was a relatively easy client to please; all he wanted was an acquittal. I delivered my part of the bargain with ease. I had gotten him off on all of the usual charges—conspiracy, racketeering, murder, and criminal enterprise, and he had paid me well. I'd taken a retainer of $75,000 from him, and for the victory, an additional $500,000. He had been cleared of every single charge, and, trust me, the prosecutors were trying to hang Santana's ass out to dry. In Mr. Santana's case, I was just the bitch he needed, or else his ass would've been up the fucking river without a paddle. Once the jury I'd bribed returned the "not guilty" verdict, Mr. Santana was overjoyed; he had grabbed me into a bear hug right in the courtroom and yelled that he was forever indebted to me. Those damn Cubans were so loyal. I wasn't complaining because I loved the attention. He continued to tell me how great I was for days after the trial.

"Hello?" I picked up my cell.

"Ms. Lomax, *hola*," Mr. Santana replied. His Cuban accent was so damn sexy. I wouldn't lie to myself and say I wasn't the least bit attracted to him. He was a good-looking man, well-kept, and rich as a motherfucker. If he wasn't my client, I probably would've fucked his brains out right after the trial. But I had to draw the line somewhere . . . or did I?

"How are you, Mr. Santana?" I said, low and slightly seductive. It was a habit; whenever I spoke to men, I put on a seductive voice. I had learned to do that as a child.

"I'm fine, beautiful! Did you get my gift?" he asked.

"Which one?" I chuckled. He had sent me flowers, a David Yurman bracelet, and six bottles of champagne right after the trial ended.

"The one I sent today," he said.

"Where did you send it?" I asked, puzzled. I hadn't received anything new.

"To your office," he replied.

"I'm on my way there," I said, getting excited.

"Okay. Please call me when you receive it," he said.

"Will do, and thank you so much," I said.

"You are most certainly welcome," Mr. Santana said, and disconnected the line. I raced through the streets like a bat out of hell. I loved receiving gifts; it was almost like having a good orgasm for me. Anything that was free was for me.

I pulled my car into the employee parking garage and headed for my spot. I slowed down and cursed to myself when I saw that someone had parked their car in my spot. "What the fuck," I grumbled, rushing out of my car to get a good look at the car that was improperly parked in my spot. As I approached the front of the car, I saw a huge pink bow tied to the hood. My heart started racing. I grabbed a white card from the windshield and read it aloud, "For a job well done." My heart was pounding through my chest now. I took a good look at the beautiful candy apple red Aston Martin. This car cost $200,000! I knew Mr. Santana was happy to be free, but damn! There was another card inside the envelope. It was an invitation to a "freedom celebration." This would be the second celebration Mr. Santana had indulged himself with.

"He was really happy with me," I whispered.

I parked my Benz in a visitor's spot and raced upstairs. There was paperwork that needed to be filled out in order for me to make the luxury vehicle my own. Besides, I needed to hurry and get some paperwork for an upcoming trial I was preparing for; I also needed to get ready for the freedom celebration. Shit, I could definitely use a party right now, I thought to myself. Good things came to those who worked hard.

I rushed off the elevator and headed straight for my office. As I made my way down the hallway, I caught the stares of my coworkers.

"What now?" I mumbled to myself.

"Hey, Yoshi, I heard you bought a new car," Eric Bretner called out. He was an overweight, bottom-of-the-barrel loser of a lawyer. Eric and I had started around the same time; on our first day he'd whispered in my ear, "You'll never survive here." Ha! I had to laugh at that shit now. I had surpassed his ass ten times over! Boy, was he such a fucking hater.

"Yeah, with all the bonuses I received from my ninety-eight percent acquittal rate this year," I retorted. Eric turned red in the face and flipped me the bird; I did the same in return. I was amused by fucking with him. I knew if he could be alone with me for ten minutes, he'd like to torture and kill me. That's how deep his hate ran for me. As I rushed past Donna, my assistant, she jumped up from her desk and stepped in front of me.

"Uh, Ms. Lomax, uh . . . ," she began. She looked all strange in the face.

"What, Donna? Move out of my way, I have no time today," I huffed, trying to go into my office, annoyed with her crazy behavior.

"There is something . . . ," she began. I pushed past her and entered my office. Donna was right on my heels. "There is something I wanted to tell you," she finally finished, all out of breath. It was too late. I almost dropped everything in my hands. My eyes widened and my mouth dropped open. I was at a loss for words. It was him—really him. I had to blink a couple of times to make sure. But all and all, I kept my cool.

"Good morning, Ms. Lomax," he said, his deep baritone and his heavy accent dancing in my ears. He was not attractive, but his appearance sure had sex appeal. It was him in the flesh—the notorious Sheldon Chisholm. His face had been plastered on every news channel for the last few days. He was the hot topic this week.

"Mr. Chisholm, what a pleasant surprise," I said calmly, even though my heart was leaping beyond my chest. I quickly pulled myself together. *Never let 'em see you sweat* . . . that was my mantra, and had been for years.

"I'm sorry for dropping by unexpectedly, but I'd been calling and leaving you messages, but you failed to call me back. So I guess you left me no choice but to come by and see you in person."

I placed my things onto my desk and then I walked over and extended a handshake. "I do apologize for not returning your calls, but, believe me, I was going to give you a buzz today."

"Well, that's good to know, but since I am already here, can we get down to business?"

"Sure," I said, and took a seat behind my desk, while Donna stepped back out of my office.

Moments later, Sheldon reached into his blazer and pulled out his indictment papers. He was not trying to waste time, and I could tell just from his immediate action that he was not a patient man. Sitting in my chair and paying close attention to Sheldon, I hadn't noticed the other two guys standing against the back wall of my office, so I immediately surveyed them. Both wore dark shades and were all in black; they just looked ominous. Along with Mr. Chisholm, they gave me the chills. I couldn't let that small matter come between the lucrative deal I was about to get into, though. So I dismissed my feelings altogether.

"I see you are a man who doesn't waste any time," I said, sitting up in my leather-bound swivel chair. I took the documents from his hand.

"I really need to know if you are going to take my case. I don't have time to play," he said, revealing no expression on his dark, wide, and flat face. I couldn't stop staring at the huge, raised keloid scar that ran from his chiseled jawbone down the side of his neck. Somebody had sliced his ass up real good. His chin was square, with a dimple smack-dab in the middle of it, and his lips were huge. I'd never seen skin so dark. . . . He was so black, he was almost blue. Even his hands had small healed scars on them. Sheldon looked like he'd had a rough-ass life. Aside from that, he was sharp. His hair was cut perfectly, not one line out of place, and his jewelry looked very expensive. The huge diamonds in his ears and on both of his pinky fingers blinded me each time the sunlight from my office window glinted into them.

"Well, Mr. Chisholm—"

"Call me Sheldon . . . ," he blurted out, cutting me off midsentence.

"Okay, Sheldon. You have to give me a minute to review my schedule," I explained. I didn't want to seem too eager to take his money . . . I mean, his case.

"I'm sure you can fit me in," he said demandingly, pulling an envelope from his blazer pocket and tossing it onto my desk. I knew it contained money. He threw it on the desk, as if to say, "Money ain't a thang."

"What's that?" I asked, acting naïve.

"That's *your* retainer. I've heard about you, Ms. Lomax," he said, peering at me over his tortoiseshell Versace shades.

"I hope you've heard good things," I replied, looking down at the envelope, dying to tear it open.

"I did, and that's why I need you to jump on board and tackle this case of mine so you can bury those sons of bitches that arrested me!"

"When is your next court date?" I asked, even though I'd already known.

"My preliminary hearing is four days from now."

I sighed heavily. "That's not a lot of time to do anything. I am working on another huge case as we speak," I said; then my voice faded as I went into deep thought. "Unless I pay my staff to work with me day and night on it, but . . . ," I said, as if I had just come up with the best idea ever. I did this, hoping he would take the bait. I wanted him to believe that it would be impossible to do the quality of work I do in that short period of time without an added bonus.

"But what?"

"Well, I was thinking that if I did take your case, I would have to get my staff to start on your paperwork today, plus pay them overtime to stay on the clock after work hours. I mean, we are talking at least twelve to sixteen man-hours a day nonstop—if you want a guaranteed acquittal."

Saying the word "acquittal" was music to Sheldon's ears. His face lit up. "So you're saying that you can guarantee me an acquittal?"

"Yes, I can," I said, jumping the gun. "But it would take me and my staff working all those hours to go through your case to find every loophole there is and to poke holes through them."

"What will it cost me to get you and your staff to do that?"

"To retain me is fifty thousand, and I take that in cash. And depending on the severity of the case my hourly rate starts at twenty-five hundred, again, in cash. And to have my staff work side by side with me beyond normal business hours will cost you an additional nine hundred an hour. The firm will send a separate bill for the staff fees."

"I don't care how much it costs. I just want to be a free man after this is over."

"And you will be after I work my magic."

Sheldon put a huge smile on his face. It was evident that he was happy as hell. So as he stood up he said, "Well, I guess this means you're hired."

I didn't respond. I just smiled, trying to play it cool because all I could think about was all the money he was going to be throwing my way. And to think I was going to be paid $2,500 an hour in cash, while the firm sent a bill for nine hundred dollars an hour, which is actually the firm's billing rate on a case like this. I'd be getting cash up front and the billing. I was one bad bitch!

"That's one hundred grand right there. Bill me the rest," he said, and then he and his boys walked out of my office.

"No problem," I said as I watched him leave.

Right after he walked out, I called Donna into my office.

"Yes, ma'am," she said.

"Take this indictment and make Mr. Chisholm a file, complete with the standard motion of discovery forms and the motion to suppress."

"So you're gonna take his case?"

"I already have," I said, and then I dismissed her.

Immediately after she left, I grabbed the envelope from my desk and tore into it. . . . The curiosity was killing me. I found two banded stacks of one-hundred-dollar bills . . . each band read, *one hundred thousand*. Sheldon paid well already! I smiled and thought about what I'd do with my new cash and my new car. As I sat wondering, Donna came back into my office.

"Ms. Lomax, another potential client called to hire you

today. His name is Lamont Whitehead, but he raps by the name Crazy Eight," she said.

"Wait, didn't he just lose his recording deal?" I asked, with my face crinkled up.

"That's what the tabloids are reporting," Donna replied.

"Then tell Crazy Eight to lose my number because he can't fucking afford me. I defend only millionaires. Ballers, not crawlers," I spat.

Donna turned and left, without a word. I sniffed my new cash again. "Ahhh, the smell of success."

Not too long after Sheldon and his crew left my office, Paul's silly ass came strolling into my fucking office. I immediately cringed at the sight of him, and then I threw on a fake smile.

"Good to see you! How is everything?" I asked, knowing damn well I could not have cared less.

"Ah, don't give that bullshit-ass 'good to see you' line. Tell me what's going on with the fellow who just left here," he demanded as he stood over the top of my desk.

"What? You didn't recognize him?"

"Of course I did. Now, are you representing him or not?"

I smiled and said, "Did he walk out of here with a smile on his face?"

"Stop the bullshit, Yoshi! Are you representing the guy or not?"

I sighed heavily. "Yes, I am, Paul."

"I know you like to bill your clients the firm's rate plus your random ego fees. How much are you charging him?"

"Enough," I said without giving that bastard any solid numbers. Shit, that's personal if you'd ask me.

"Well, you just make sure you get that guy a victory! I

would hate to see you fuck his case up and his people come back through here and kill everyone in sight."

I burst into laughter. "Do you know who I am, Paul? That would never happen. And you can take that one to the bank and cash it."

"Yeah, okay. Don't get too cocky. Remember, there's always a chance that your case can fall right out of your lap."

I laughed louder. "Not one of mine."

"Okay! We'll see," he said, and then he walked back out of my office.

Immediately after Paul carried his hating ass out of my office, I got on the phone and called Maria. She sounded like she was in her car when she answered her phone.

"Girl, you will not believe it when I tell you that Sheldon Chisholm just left my office." I didn't hesitate to tell her.

"Is it official? He's your client?"

"You damn right!" I said, sifting through the stack of one-hundred-dollar bills.

"How much did he lay on you?"

"Let's just say that I would be able to drive off the lot with a Maserati for me and you, and still have a huge piece of change left over."

"Well, I guess that means I can get a raise," Maria hinted, then chuckled.

"I don't know about that, but I'll tell you what, if you continue to get me what I need, then you'd definitely keep your job." I chuckled right back at her.

"Oh, Yoshi, you are such a tight ass! You know I'm good for a five percent raise. You saw the new house I just bought. You know I'm going to need it."

"Granted, your house is beautiful, but I didn't tell you to go out and make a huge purchase like that. Shit, a five percent raise ain't gonna help you. Your ass needs a man!"

"Well, find me one!" she replied sarcastically.

"You don't want me doing that, especially with all the thugs I know," I said, and laughed. "Fucking around with me, you'd probably be dating a wealthy-ass criminal. And I know you don't want that, especially since they won't have a pension plan."

"I see you are full of jokes today."

"Got to be when you're working around assholes like Paul," I said, changing the subject. "Speaking of which, do you know that this fat fuck just waltzed in my damn office and asked me why Sheldon Chisholm was in my office? So, in short, I told the nosy motherfucker that he was there to pay me a retainer so I could represent him in his upcoming trial. So then he asked me how much I was charging him."

"What did you tell him?"

"I didn't tell him shit. Paul knows that he's not privy to that information."

"So, what did he say after that?"

"He just got frustrated and started talking about how I needed to be careful—"

"Careful about what?" Maria cut me off.

"Girl, I don't know. He was kind of talking off the wall, if you ask me. But, believe me, I cut his conversation short and got him out of my office really quick."

Maria laughed once again. "I know he wasn't too happy about that."

"No, he wasn't, but I'm sure he's gotten over it by now."

"So, what's on your agenda for the rest of the day?"

"Well, first off, I am getting out of here. And then I am going home to freshen up for a party I was invited to later on tonight."

"Whose party?"

"One of my old clients."

"You aren't going to get enough of hanging out with your old clients until something bad happens."

"Come on now, Maria. What could possibly happen?"

"Do I seriously need to answer that one?" she replied sarcastically.

"Alright! Alright! You've made your point. Let me assure you that I am only going to this party to show my face, pass out my business cards to a few potential clients, have a couple of drinks, and then I am out of there."

"Well, you be careful."

"I will."

"So, when are we going to hang out and go to a club or something? You know I'm getting tired of sitting at home, my head buried in paperwork."

"We'll get together this weekend."

"Okay, well, call me tomorrow and let me know how your night went."

"I will. Now have a good one."

"You do the same," Maria told me; then we hung up.

Time to Celebrate

After stashing half of my personal retainer from Mr. Chisholm and picking myself up a bottle of the most expensive champagne I could find to celebrate my new client, I headed home in my new Aston Martin. The freedom celebration awaited my presence, and I was going to make it spectacular. I made it home in enough time to relax a bit before my night out to celebrate. When I turned the key and entered my penthouse, I was met by Ophelia. She was cleaning all of my luxury European furniture, fine art, and china with a feather duster. I smirked to myself. It made me feel good to have a servant. I picked up the mail she'd left on the front table for me. Nothing of interest.

"Ophelia, have the valet pick up my Benz from the office. The keys are in my purse, and the car is parked in the visitor's spot nearest the entrance. Oh, and please run me a nice hot bubble bath." I could have done it myself, but why do that when I was paying her ass?

"Yes, senora," Ophelia replied, dropping what she was doing and rushing toward my master bathroom. She always moved right away when I requested something; she knew I had very little patience.

"Oh yeah, and could you also fetch me a cup of hot mint tea?" I asked. I loved to see her rush at my beck and call.

"Would you like the tea at the bath side or right away?" Ophelia asked.

"Um . . . I'll have it in the bath," I replied as I headed for my massive bedroom. "Oh, Ophelia, can you lay out several party dresses for me and several pairs of shoes? I will choose something after my bath."

"No problem, ma'am," she answered in a low tone.

I took off my clothes and left them right in a pile on the floor for Ophelia to pick up. I looked in the mirror at my beautiful shape, and my five-seven frame was perfect. My waist was tiny like a doll's, which was from my constant gym activity. I sometimes wondered if it was a sin for one person to love herself this much. After admiring my beauty for a while, I stepped into the bathroom. Ophelia had done just what she knew I'd like. She set the tea at the side, ran the tub lukewarm, with just the right amount of bubbles, and lit the entire bathroom with candles. This was the life. The atmosphere was serene and I loved it. I climbed into the tub and let my muscles relax. I soaked in my oversized Jacuzzi tub for more than thirty minutes, sipping tea from my finest china. I felt like a queen, but time was ticking and I had to get ready.

Picking out a dress was a job—so many beautiful designer things to choose from. I finally settled on one, but it wasn't easy. I turned around and around in front of my floor-length mirror, checking my ass over and over again. The slinky black spaghetti-strapped Roberto Cavalli dress I'd chosen fit me perfectly; my tiny waist and long legs had me looking like a model. Driving around Miami, I often got mistaken for Kimora Lee Simmons. I'd even gotten a free dinner one night after I hadn't denied being her to the waiter— he was convinced I was the sexy Asian female mogul in the flesh.

I clamped my Charriol diamond pavé earrings onto my ears and swung my head back and forth. My loose curls danced around my face and I slid one back behind my ear so that the earrings showed. I topped my outfit off with a brand-new pair of Christian Louboutin open-toed stiletto sandals and a Marc Jabobs clutch.

"Ophelia, have the valet bring my car to the front, please," I called out. Then I whispered to myself, "Okay, Yoshi, do it, girl." Mr. Santana better be ready for me tonight. He was so used to seeing me in suits in court, I might make his head spin tonight. "Fuck his wife," I whispered. I was so wicked. I laughed into the air.

"Ms. Lomax, your car is here," Ophelia notified me. I looked at my diamond-encrusted Cartier watch. . . . Perfect, I was running on schedule. I took one last look at my stunning ass before I left. Ophelia watched me either in admiration or in hatred.

As I took the elevator downstairs, my phone rang. It was Paul. He had been calling me and leaving me all kinds of threatening messages since he left my office earlier. This motherfucker was really insane. On one of the messages, he'd said, "Yoshi, you have gotten really cocky these last couple of years. But remember, I hold your career in my hands. You are nothing without me." Was he seriously that sprung over some pussy? Well, since it was my pussy, he had to be, I guess. With all the dirt I had on Paul, he'd better not fuck with me.

I ignored his call and his message as usual and I rushed out of my building to my waiting Aston Martin. The valet smiled at me and I did the same in return. As he opened my car door, he said, "If I wasn't the one who had driven that hot car of yours around here, I would've sworn you were about to be carried off on a white horse by a prince." I loved attention of any kind. Flattered, I flashed my perfect white teeth at him.

"Don't tempt me—one day you might just see me being carried off on a white horse," I said jokingly. I got into the car and looked up at him. When he closed it, I reached for his hand and touched it. He looked at me and I could see him blushing. I placed a one-hundred-dollar bill in his hand and continued on. I knew I had made his fucking night. A hundred dollars was nothing to me, but I knew it might've meant a month's worth of groceries for him.

The car was the right accessory for my look. It drove like a dream. I mean, the tires hugged the road and it felt like I was in a spaceship, riding on air. When I pulled up to the Panama nightclub, the crowd outside was outrageous. There had to be more than two hundred people outside alone, so I could only imagine what inside was like.

"I should've invited Maria," I said out loud. I didn't want to be lost in a sea of unknown people. A valet approached my car and I slid out. All eyes seemed to turn to me. As usual, I flashed a sexy smile and walked toward the front door. I was held up by security, but I pulled Mr. Santana's personal invitation out of my bag and the velvet rope was immediately moved out of my way. I felt like the only VIP.

The inside of the club was decorated beautifully with all red, white, and gold. I'd learned from living in Miami that Hispanics always loved those colors. There were bouquets of bloodred roses on each table and gold glittery accents all around. It looked more like someone was getting married. A jazzy-sounding Carlos Santana tune blared from the speakers and the Latina were eating it up. I struggled my way through the hip-swaying, foot-tapping crowd, trying to make my way to the VIP room. Finally, after a million "excuse me" and "watch it" asides, I was at the door. A tall, skinny man dressed in all black guarded the door.

"Hi, I'm here on the request of Mr. Santana," I screamed, yelling over the music.

The man looked at me from head to toe. "Your name?" he asked stoically.

"Yoshi Lomax," I screamed in reply. He immediately moved.

"Shit, now that's first-class service," I said to myself, feeling good as hell.

Sauntering my sexy ass into that VIP room felt like walking a red carpet. In fact, the carpets were red. The room was decorated just like the rest of the club, and the gold accents gave everything a rich feel. I looked around for Mr. Santana. I didn't see him. But I did see a whole lot of gorgeous—and I do mean *gorgeous*—Latina women. These women looked like supermodels and they were dressed to kill. I suddenly began to feel a little self-conscious. After looking at them, I no longer felt like the belle of the ball. Then I noticed that I was receiving my fair share of stares from the well-dressed men in the room. All of a sudden my high confidence came rushing back. "Never doubt your beauty, Yoshi," I said to myself under my breath. I guess I was the different kind of beauty in the room.

They were all Latina and kind of looked the same. I was Asian and Black, so I looked way more exotic than they did. I walked toward the bar. I was going to get my own party started. Before I made it all the way to the bar, I felt a hand on my back. I whirled around in surprise.

"Yoshi, I'm so glad you could make it," a soft voice whispered right in my ear. I could tell from the smell of that sweet-ass cologne that it was Luis Santana.

I seductively turned my body toward his voice. "I would not have missed it for the world," I said back.

"You look amazing," Mr. Santana said, grabbing my hand and leading me away from the bar.

"Wait, I wanted to get something to drink," I told him, still allowing him to hold on to me.

"Don't insult me. You don't drink from the bar," he replied. We walked hand in hand toward the back of the room. As we approached, I could see a table with bottles of high-priced liquors on it—Perrier-Jouet, Johnnie Walker Blue King George V, and Moët Gold Label were just a few. I also noticed the women. The red suede couches were filled with exceptionally beautiful women. They sat and posed like statues. Mr. Santana still held on to my hand. We approached a woman dressed in a red sequined dress—one I could swear I saw Halle Berry wear on the red carpet.

"Adrianna, this is Yoshi . . . the woman I owe my life to, and, Yoshi, this is my wife, Adrianna," Mr. Santana said, rolling his *R*'s as he introduced me to the beautiful woman.

"Nice to meet you," she replied dryly, eyeing me up and down.

"Same here," I said, just as dryly. I wasn't going to show any signs of intimidation, but I did take my hand out of his. It was just rude to hold another woman's hand and introduce her to your wife.

"Sit down and make yourself comfortable. This is all for you. . . . You made it possible, so indulge yourself," Mr. Santana said, opening his arms wide to show me that all of the food, drinks, flowers, cakes, and candles were a result of my hard work. I took a seat on one of the couches and he sat right next to me. His wife got up and walked away. Maybe she was used to him being rude as hell and inappropriate with other women. As I looked around, that is when I noticed it. A silver platter sat on the table in front of me, piled high with cocaine. I hadn't ever seen that much coke in my entire life. My hands immediately got sweaty and my head started to spin. I had not gotten high since my whole addiction ordeal in college. Maria would've killed me if she saw me sitting like a queen in front of a silver platter filled with my chemical archenemy. My stomach began to churn and I felt like I would throw up right there on the spot. There was one difference between me and Maria—she was disciplined and could say no to things. I wasn't that strong . . . never have been. I could excuse myself and run the fuck away, but then I reasoned that I would lose other rich client referrals from Mr. Santana. So against my better judgment, I sat there, stiff, like a beautiful porcelain statue about to be cracked. For some reason everything in the room seemed like it had been stopped, and my heart thumped loudly in my ears, drowning out the salsa music. I wanted to scream. There weren't many things that I couldn't handle, but my addiction to cocaine was something that could get the best of me. As strong-willed as I was, that shit always made me weak, no matter what the circumstances.

"So, how is business?" he asked.

"Business is good," I replied as I became mesmerized with the mountain of coke in front of me.

"Got any other crooks like me off lately?"

I gave him a shylike smile and said, "Come on, now, you're not a crook. You're just an honest businessman who works extremely hard to get what he wants."

He burst into laughter. "Good answer! Good answer!" He then took a sip from his glass.

I took a sip from my glass, too, and then I put my focus right back on the pile of coke. But Mr. Santana quickly redirected my attention back to him. "So, what big clients are you representing now?" he continued.

I thought for a second and then I said, "Well, I haven't had any clients as big as you. But I have taken on this fellow by the name of Enrique Hernandez and this Black guy named Eugene Wallace. One of them was charged with drug trafficking, and the other one was charged with gun possession. They are not as rich and powerful as you, but they can hold their own."

"I'm sure, but I want you to be very selective about what clients you take on. You are very special to me, and I would hate for you to get caught up in another scandal like that one you got mixed up in behind Mr. Choo."

"Come on, Luis, I'm a big girl, so I am going to be fine," I began to say. "Speaking of which, I had this Haitian fellow by the name of Sheldon Chisholm come by my office requesting for me to represent him on a drug charge."

"So you're going to represent him?" he asked strangely.

"Of course I am."

"Do you think it'll be worth it?"

"There is no doubt in my mind," I told him.

"Be careful," he warned me.

"I told you, I'm a big girl," I said, and then I took another sip of my drink and diverted my attention back to the pile of cocaine.

"I see you keep eyeing the richness of my product," he said.

"I've just never seen so much at one time," I told him.

And before I could get out the words "No thank you," he lifted the platter and a small, pretty gold-metal straw-looking contraption right to my face and offered it to me. Shit, when I snorted coke in college, I'd steal straws from McDonald's, cut them up, and use them. Now, here I was being offered a golden straw. I guess you could say a golden straw for a golden opportunity. There was no reason for me to take that straw. I'd already gotten paid by Mr. Santana; it wasn't like my career depended on him or anything. My logical brain told me that the white powder that shined so beautifully from that tray could ruin everything I'd worked for; my logical brain also said, "Yoshi, run as fast as you can out of this fucking VIP room and never have contact with Luis Santana again." But the pressure from the part of my brain that said, "Yoshi, you can handle this. You are in control. Just take a dab and you can shake it off. This might land you some rich motherfucking clients"—well, that section made me smile, pick up that golden straw, and sniff an entire line of cocaine.

"Aha! I knew you were a pro," Mr. Santana exclaimed, taking his turn.

Now I really couldn't hear anything except my heart racing like crazy. My head lolled back and forth, and the rush from being high again made my pussy wet. I remembered how much of a fiend I was for this feeling, an escape from everything. The demons of my present and my past. I could hear Maria in my head saying, "Yoshi, what the fuck!" But the feeling I had right now could not be matched. It was like good dick on a rainy day, or like the best chocolate cake when you have your period and were craving chocolate. I looked out into the smoky, crowded room and noticed bodies moving close to one another. It was then that I noticed men kissing on necks, women feeling crotches, and mouths pressed together. The party suddenly seemed like one big orgy to me and I wasn't excused. The drugs had me feeling hot and horny; I wanted someone to press their dick up against me. I had busied myself with fucking old judges and nasty-ass Paul for so long that I'd forgotten what it was like to fuck a real man and be attracted to him at the same time. Luis Santana was a sexy-ass Cuban. His dark skin and wavy hair were attractive, not to mention that fucking accent that drove me wild. I was suddenly compelled to look down at his crotch, and the bulge seemed to be staring back at me, like maybe the dick was calling me.

"More?" Mr. Santana asked, passing the silver platter back in front of me and breaking my train of thought.

"No, I'm good," I said, barely able to get the words out. My mouth was dry. I wanted to drink a gallon of water. I also wanted to feel him near me; I felt an overwhelming urge to fuck him.

"C'mere," he said, grabbing onto me. He kissed my neck and slid his hand down my back to my ass.

"Wait!" I said, pushing him in his chest. Didn't he know I was his fucking lawyer and not one of these bitches in here? I didn't want to seem too eager.

"Yoshi, I've been wanting you since I saw how you worked that courtroom. You looked so sexy when you railroaded those fucking DAs. That shit turned me on. And I couldn't help but think about you day and night. I told my wife about it and she wants to get in on the action, too," he said, and that is when I noticed his wife sitting next to me on my other side. At the same time she placed her right hand on my left breast and gently ran her fingers over my nipples. My head was really spinning now. I really wanted to leave, but my body and my weakness for the drug wouldn't let me. I had let out a beast, but I had to get it under control.

"Hold up . . . ," I said, reaching for the platter despite my resolve. Just this one time wouldn't hurt. I sniffed another half of a line. I hadn't gotten high in so long, I thought that if I took at least a half of a line, it would probably put me in the mood to hear what Mr. Santana was throwing my way.

"That's it. That is how you do it, Yoshi," Mr. Santana whispered in my ear. Suddenly I felt excited. I wanted to jump up and dance. That coke had to be laced with some other shit. For real, I felt like dancing and dancing. I stood up and started moving my body. It was like I was a puppet on a string and someone else was controlling my movements. I swayed my hips seductively in front of Mr. Santana and Adrianna. I didn't care. My long, shiny hair flowed in the smoky room. I threw my arms up to the music, which I really couldn't even hear that well. I was clapping and Mr. Santana stood up to join in my wicked mating dance. He rubbed his dick across my ass and my pussy thumped. I looked down at Adrianna, who was still sitting on the bench. She smiled. For some reason, her smile seemed more evil than inviting. With the drugs completely in control, I bent down and kissed her. It wasn't the first time I had experimented with a lesbian encounter. During my drug-haze days in college, I had all-out fucked a girl named Candy . . . just for drugs. Was I doing the same thing again? Although I had a reputation to uphold, I couldn't care less who was watching me—and little did I know, I was being watched.

Adrianna invited me into her mouth with no resistance. Our tongues flicked together and I grew extra excited now; my inner thigh became damp with my own vaginal secretions. My pussy was definitely ready for a dick now. Adrianna squeezed one of my nipples as her husband held on to me from the back. I could feel the gropes and kisses all over my body, but I could not defend myself. I was all in, but my mind kept telling me: "Yoshi, you got this shit under control."

"Let's get out of here," Mr. Santana whispered in my ear.

"I can't. I gotta go. You have done enough, really," I said with my mouth—although my actions told another story. Now as I moved my body, I made sure to slide my ass on his rock-hard dick.

"Look, I have a hotel room at the Mandarin Oriental. You can rest up. We don't want you crashing your new car," he joked, chuckling.

"I'm good," I assured him, but he would have none of it.

"No, Yoshi, you're coming with us. We are harmless," he demanded, grabbing my hand again and leading me toward the exit. I felt like a little kid, I couldn't get my mind clear enough to make my own decisions. I followed Mr. Santana and his wife to their hotel room that night, and for the low price of the best coke I'd ever had, I unwittingly sold my soul to the Devil. And for that very moment, I had the time of my life.

Mr. Santana and Adrianna both had me feeling intoxicated. It felt like I was trapped in a web of lust, especially after Adrianna started licking every inch of my body while Mr. Santana watched. The whole experience of having this woman give me foreplay was unbelievable. It was a moment of ecstasy. *"Uhhhh!"* I screamed, biting down on the bed's pillow as she teased the tip of my clitoris while I crouched down on my knees in the doggy position. I rode her face until I released every ounce of juice I had left in my body, and soon after, Mr. Santana was pounding the hell out of me with his dick. I couldn't tell you if he had a condom on or not, that's just how fucked-up I was. I do remember him trying to fuck me in my ass, but I wasn't having that. There's not enough money in the world to make me want a man to do that shit. So I gave him the thumbs-down and he pushed himself inside my pussy.

Thank God our little fucking spree didn't last more than a couple of minutes. After about four or five strokes, his dick erupted like a fucking volcano. And when I looked back to see his facial expression, he looked like he was mad at the world. I asked him what was wrong. And he told me that he was upset because he came too fast. I immediately dismissed that dumb-ass remark because I found that men say that same shit all the time. To me, it's just a lame-ass excuse to cover up the real truth that they were just mere minute men. It's just that simple.

After our little escapade I rolled over in the bed and watched him and his wife as they both exited the room. And before I even realized it, I was out like a light.

Dealing wit' My Demons

I couldn't tell you how I got home, but it had been two days since the party and it had been the awakening of my cocaine addiction. They say old habits die hard. Or in my case, they never do.

I vaguely remember Ophelia calling the office to let them know I'd be out sick. After that, everything for me was moving in slow motion. It felt like my life was sand, dripping grain by grain through a broken hourglass. I was sick as a dog, throwing up and shitting. Not using cocaine for so long, and then trying it again, had fucked up my stomach. I had been willing myself to stay inside, because all I'd thought about since the night of the party was getting high. I was ignoring all my calls, especially the twenty I'd gotten from Maria. During her last voice mail she said if I didn't answer, she was coming over. I'd promised myself that I had to take the next phone call that came in. I was too ashamed to speak with anyone. I had made a complete asshole out of myself. I thought maybe Maria would be able to tell something if I spoke to her. I had to buy myself a few days. I promised myself that I was not getting high anymore and that I would pull myself together. After all, I am Yoshi Lomax.

* * *

Dozing in and out, I finally jumped out of my sleep and caught an instant headache. Sunlight streamed through my glass patio doors and beamed directly on my face. I could barely open my eyes, my head hurt so bad. I finally looked across my bedroom and noticed that my party clothes were rumpled in a pile, still in the same place I'd pulled them off. I guess Ophelia wasn't trying to come into my room to clean it up, with me sleeping for days. Or she was probably avoiding me. I knew she thought I was crazy, because she had never seen me behave the way I did the morning after the party. I felt like crying as I thought about how embarrassing it was the morning I came home from my night with the Santanas.

The morning after the party, Ophelia had woken me up. My mouth tasted like paste, and my head spun in circles as I struggled up off the floor. It was as if she and I had noticed at the same time that I was butt-ass naked except for my heels. Although she didn't say a word, the look on her face— one of disgust and shock—had said enough. After she helped me up, it was like paranoia had taken over my mind. I had run around, looking all over my penthouse, frantically wondering who was in my house, wondering how I had gotten there butt-ass naked. I was thinking that I had to have fucked somebody . . . or else I would have on some sleepwear.

Ophelia had asked me several times if I was okay, while I was in my frantic nutty-ass state. She watched me like I needed a fucking psychiatrist. I don't think I ever answered her. Just like in the past after I got high, I was paranoid as hell. I continued to run through my house looking for God knows whom. Ophelia kept asking me if I needed a doctor. After searching my place and not finding anyone, I had raced into the bathroom. I looked up at myself in the huge vanity mirror and what I saw staring back almost broke me down. My eyes were puffy, my hair disheveled, and worst of all, I had huge purple hickeys all over my neck and titties.

"What the fuck!" I screamed. I couldn't remember shit. I dropped to my knees and started crying. Ophelia knew me so well; she didn't try to comfort me. She just walked me to the bed, helped me into my favorite Victoria's Secret soft pajamas, and left me alone.

My thoughts of that horrible night were interrupted when I heard my BlackBerry going off. I picked it up and it was Donna, my assistant. I pressed the ignore button. I couldn't possibly go into the office looking and feeling the way I did. I scrolled through my messages and there were about fifteen messages from Donna. The last one said: TODAY AT 1PM IS MR. CHISHOLM'S PRELIMINARY HEARING.

"Oh shit, I forgot all about the preliminary hearing!" I screamed, even though it was just a brief formality. The preliminary is only for the judge to get acquainted with the attorney and the DA on the case and to set an actual hearing date, but I wasn't up for that shit. My head was thumping like mad and I had to be in court at one o'clock. If I wasn't so fucked-up after Mr. Santana's party, I would've remembered. It was not like me to forget my high-profile clients' court dates or meetings with prosecutors. I hurriedly called Donna and told her to reach out to any of the court clerks I had on my payroll to ask them to push my time back. If Brad was going to live up to his word, I probably wouldn't have to worry. However, I hadn't heard back from him on the status of the case, so I knew I had to appear in court and go through the motions. Besides, I had agreed to a trial acquittal with Brad, not an all-out dismissal of the charges, so I had to do a little bit of work. I needed to pull myself together. I called for Ophelia and asked her to lay out some court clothes for me. I jumped in the shower and let the hot water stream over my body. My skin was sensitive and it felt like someone was pricking me with needles. I told myself that I needed one more quick snort of coke and I'd be fine for court. I hurried and got dressed. Although I had only forty-five minutes before I needed to be in court, and I had not even spoken to my client, the addict in me told me that I could go to the West Side, find some coke, and still be in court on time.

Ophelia had called down to have my car out front, but when I got down there, the valet had pulled up in my Benz and not the Aston Martin that I had received from Mr. Santana. *Where the fuck is the other car?* I thought, willing myself to remember. My mind drew a blank. I didn't have time to worry about it right now. I hopped behind the wheel of my Benz and peeled off. Shit! There was so much fucking traffic. Living in the heart of South Beach was sometimes annoying. I couldn't believe that just moments ago I wanted to get my fix. I was better that that—I had a life and a demanding client, and coke could not fit in the picture.

The courtroom was packed and I rushed in to find Sheldon sitting at the back waiting for me. He looked angry and so did his two goons. Just as I noticed him, I noticed Maria.

"Shit!" I cursed under my breath. There was no way I was going to get out of this fucking courthouse without her giving me the third degree about where I'd been for the past couple of days.

"Mr. Chisholm, sorry I'm running behind schedule," I said, flashing a smile. Although, in my assessment I looked like shit, I knew I was still beautiful. Ophelia had picked out a navy blue Anne Klein suit for me, and I had thrown on a simple pair of black Michael Kors slingbacks. I looked sophisticated, yet businesslike, not my usual flashy self.

"I pay you to be on time," Sheldon griped as soon as I walked up. He had no change in his facial expression and looked as ugly as ever, but he was definitely still blinging. Why he would come to court so flashy, I had no idea. I was too tired and preoccupied to even scold his ass.

"I'm aware of that. It won't happen again," I assured, rolling my eyes. "Let's talk," I said to him, pointing toward the hallway. His docket was going to be recalled. I had that in the smash, I was sure. Maria watched me leave the courtroom. She didn't budge, she was waiting.

I spoke with Mr. Chisholm and explained to him that the purpose of the preliminary hearing was to determine whether the prosecutor had enough evidence to justify further criminal proceedings against him. Sheldon was tense as I spoke. I tried to put him at ease with my words, but it wasn't working. I explained to him that after the prosecution presented its evidence, I would respond with a motion to dismiss the case and that it would be up to the judge whether or not there was probable cause to send the case to trial.

"What are my chances?" Sheldon asked seriously, the same unmoved expression on his face.

"Good," I assured, confident that Donna had ensured that the case was on the docket of a judge I knew *personally* and that Brad was going to come through like we'd discussed. I assured Sheldon again that I was going to make a motion to dismiss his case today based on the fact that he had just been a passenger in the car and was not aware there were drugs hidden inside.

"Sounds good," he replied. With that, we both headed back inside the courtroom.

Back inside, we waited. I couldn't keep my mind off getting high, Maria couldn't keep her eyes off me, and Sheldon kept his eyes on everyone.

The judge finally called Sheldon's docket number. When I looked up and saw Judge Williger, I instantly got happy inside. I just knew I was good money. I had fucked him a few times and paid him as well. He knew he could expect big things from me—especially if the calls went my way in the courtroom.

"Your Honor, I'd like to make a motion to dismiss, on the grounds of meritless arrest," I yelled out.

The judge looked at me over his wire-rimmed glasses. "Motion denied," he grumped. Judge Williger didn't even give me a chance to explain the reason for my motion.

And right at the time when I was about to make my rebuttal, the prosecutor jumped up excitedly. "We move for an immediate trial," she yelled. It was a prosecutor I didn't recognize. Clearly, Brad hadn't spoken to her or set me up to have a prosecutor who knew the deal. Either that or Brad wanted the case to go to trial so he could take me to the bank. I was fucking pissed to no end. Where the fuck was Brad Carlton? If he was there, I probably would've walked right up to him and slapped him right in the fucking face. He'd told me he was going to assign the case to an assistant who would make sure we moved past this shit. I had a bone to pick with Mr. Big Dick—that was for sure. I made a mental note to check his ass.

"Trial date will be set for thirty days from today," the judge said with finality.

"Wait, Your Honor, I—I . . . ," I started, moving uneasily behind the defense table. I could feel Sheldon's eyes on me, the heat of his glare burning my ass to bits. Out of the corner of my eye, I could see him flexing his jaw like he wanted to bite my fucking head off.

"Counsel, you and your client are dismissed. On to the

next docket," the judge interrupted me, banging his gavel, and looking at me as if to say, "Get the fuck out of my courtroom." He had totally crushed me and my ego. Williger seemed like he wasn't fucking with me, which was strange. I had just had him on another case, and he threw the case right out. I looked around, confused and slightly embarrassed.

While all things couldn't always go my way in the courtroom, I certainly expected it to go smoothly when it was supposed to be all set up that way, and when I'd reached into my pocket to make sure of it. I expected to lose motions to dismiss with judges I didn't know, but not with Williger. What the fuck! It seemed like something was really up.

As Sheldon and I moved toward the exit, I could feel Sheldon walking so close to me, he was damn near on my heels. Once we got outside the courtroom, he moved his huge, ugly face close to my ear. "Are you alright?" he asked.

"Yes, I am fine," I told him as I tried to muster up a serious but confident expression.

"You sure? Because they just walked all over you back there."

"Oh, that was nothing," I replied, and waved my hand like I was dismissing that little stunt the judge and the prosecutor pulled on me.

"Well, I sure hope you do better at trial."

"Oh, don't worry, I've got this thing in the bag," I assured him.

"Good, because I can't go down. And I want you to remember I am paying you to make sure of it," he growled with his thick accent. It was very clear that he didn't want another stunt like this pulled at the major showdown, and I understood. I got an instant headache, and I literally felt like I had stepped into very unfamiliar territory.

Now as I watched him and his two bodyguards walk

away, I felt like he was taking my life with him. That alone gave me an uneasy feeling and I didn't like it one bit. So, to keep my head level, I had to remind myself about my pot of gold at the end of the tunnel. And as soon as that registered, I was back to normal.

When I turned around to leave, I noticed Maria. It would've been inappropriate for her to approach me there in the courthouse. She was DEA and I was a defense attorney; we were on totally different sides of the fence. No one outside of our immediate circle knew that we were best friends; we kept it that way purposely. I used the fact that she wouldn't dare come up to me right there in the courthouse to my advantage. I immediately raced for the elevators, and when I reached the first floor, I bolted out the back of the courthouse, heading for my car in an almost dead run. I started fishing in my purse for my keys before I made it to the car. I wanted to get out of there as fast as possible; talking to Maria was not on my agenda for today.

As I walked up to the car, I noticed that Maria was standing right there. I can't figure out how the fuck she got there so fast—this bitch acted like a ghost sometimes, seriously. I guess in this case she was a woman on a mission. She'd told me a long time ago that it was her life's mission to repay me for helping her through school, and she took on the task of keeping me straight and clean. It was a task that she took dead serious. At this very moment she didn't look too pleased, and I didn't want to look her straight in her face. If anyone knew me well, it was her. She didn't look too happy to see my ass, and I damn sure wasn't happy to see her right now. This bitch could read me like an open book. We both knew that.

"Where have you been?" she asked sternly, her arms folded across her chest.

"I went to visit my mother," I lied, avoiding eye contact.

Maria knew I never went to the nursing home to visit my mother. I sent plenty of money, but I couldn't stand to see my mother in her condition. Alzheimer's had all but claimed what was left of her frail body. I was ashamed of her, and I couldn't stand to see her in her current state.

"Bullshit! I know that's a lie, and you know it!" she confronted me. Maria knew better than anyone how selfish I was. She also knew how I acted toward my mother's condition. Therefore, saying I was visiting her was the worst lie I could have ever come up with, and I knew it as soon as the words had rolled off my tongue.

"Maria, I don't have to lie to you," I replied calmly.

"Well, you're doing it," she shot back. Then she leaned in toward me. "Come on now, I know you've been frolicking around with those fucking criminals you hang out with. It wouldn't surprise me if you got pissy drunk and fell out smack-dab in the middle of the floor. Then one of Santana's henchmen carried your ass up to the nearest bedroom and took advantage of your ass."

I gave her a half smile. "Yeah, right! That would never happen. I'm too classy for that type of shit. And besides, you know me well enough to know that I don't fuck the help. Maybe Santana, but not one of his flunkies!"

"Oh, so that's who you were laid up with these last couple of days?"

"Are you fucking kidding me?" I snapped.

"Well, it must be true, because you are getting a little too defensive."

"I'm not getting defensive, I'm just a little tired."

"How was the party anyway?"

"It was okay." I tried to downplay it.

"Somehow I find that hard to believe. So spill your guts and tell me how it really was."

"Look, I'm dealing with a lot right now. You could at

least ask how I was doing before giving me the third degree," I complained, quickly changing the subject, fidgeting with my keys.

She sucked her teeth. "When have I ever asked you how you are doing?" she replied sarcastically. "We talk to each other damn near every day and that question never comes out of my mouth."

"Oh, fuck you, Maria!"

"Please spare me with that nonsense," she answered, softening her tone and scanning me, trying to probe with her eyes. I knew just how to play it off with her. I wasn't about to let her look in my face for a long time. There was but so much makeup could hide.

"You wanna do lunch?" she asked, already knowing the answer would be no.

"Nah, I gotta go to the office. I got work to do. You saw what just happened," I explained, getting myself out of going to lunch with her. If I was around her a second longer, she would definitely know I had gotten high.

"Yeah, I was really surprised at Williger," she replied.

"That's alright. I'll get Judge Allen on the trial and it'll be another Choo or Santana for me," I confidently assured her as I began to walk away.

"Look, don't disappear again on me, bitch, or I'll come get your ass," she said jokingly, clearing the air between us. I was glad she gave up on her interrogation of my whereabouts. I hated to lie to her right to her face, but sometimes she left me no choice.

"I won't," I assured her before I slid into my car. And right when I was about to pull away, she ran toward my car and stuck her head in the driver's-side window.

"Oh yeah, and stop fucking all of your clients and get some sleep. You look like shit! And besides, I know you don't want to end up with a bad rep!" she said.

Her words hit me right in the gut. I wondered if she knew something or if she was just joking. You never could tell with Maria. I gave her a halfhearted smile and I pulled out. She had said I looked like shit, and that was the first time she'd said that in years. Well, little did she know, I felt like shit as well. I had to get myself back on track. I called Ophelia on her cell phone and told her to get my valet ticket from my Marc Jacobs clutch and give it to the valet I'd given that huge tip to and tell him to retrieve my Aston Martin from the Panama nightclub. With that off my mind, I was ready to get down to business.

Out of My Comfort Zone

The very next day Maria begged me to come over to her house. So after work I hopped in my car and drove over there. She lived in a posh, new neighborhood next to Lake Cabbas. The homes here had to be in the neighborhood of $800,000 to $1 million. The only people I could imagine living out here were judges and high-level executives. I, on the other hand, wouldn't be caught dead living out here. It reeked from the smell of family life and children running around in the streets on their fucking skateboards. I can't deal with that type of lifestyle. (I was far from a wife and a soccer mom, so I've always left the two-story homes with manicured lawns to Maria. I just cross my fingers that one day she'll find her knight in shining armor who will fuck her to death and give her a couple of kids.)

Upon my arrival she greeted me at the front door. She was wearing a pair of sweatpants and a T-shirt. "Thanks for coming by," she said.

I stepped across the threshold and extended my arms to give her a hug.

"Wow! You smell good! What is that you're wearing?" she asked.

"Agent Provocateur," I said, making my way through

the foyer. "It was something I picked up from Neiman Marcus a few weeks back."

"Good choice," she replied; then we both walked into the living-room area of her home.

"What's up with the workout gear? Whatcha just come in from working out?" I asked as I took a seat on the sofa.

"Yes, I did. Our whole task force had to do a drill today. And guess who had to tag along?"

I chuckled. "You, huh?"

She sighed heavily. "Yes! And that shit liked to have killed my ass. I've never been worked so hard in my life."

"I thought you said basic training was hard."

"Yeah, it was, but when you haven't worked out in a drill exercise in a while, then you're bound to feel fucked-up," she explained as she headed over to the bar area stationed in the corner of her living room. "Want a drink?" she continued as she fumbled with a couple of glasses.

"Yes! Make me a martini, please."

"You want it shaken or stirred?"

"Shaken, please."

"You got it," she said as she started making the martini precisely the way I wanted it. "So, what's new?" she continued as she fished around in a bowl of olives with a toothpick in hand.

"It's the same ole thing, different day."

She walked my drink over and handed it to me. "Well, a couple of my agents got a big case that's about to go down, and the guy that they're about to bust has money coming out the ass! He has real estate in South America and in upstate New York. The word around the office is he's running five hundred kilos through the ports once a week. And that much coke coming into the docks without being tampered with leads me to believe that this guy has a lot of people on his payroll. So there will be a lot of people going down when this whole thing blows up."

"Who is this guy? What's his name?"

"Juan Alvarez."

My mouth fell wide open. "Wait a minute, are you talking about the Juan Alvarez who owns the night club La Cienda? The drug lord from Ecuador? The motherfucker who had his daughter killed because she married one of the Gomez brothers?"

"He allegedly had his daughter murdered. He beat those charges, remember?" Maria corrected me.

"Whatever! Same damn thing!" I interjected. "So you're telling me that this guy is about to go down?"

Maria nodded her head, and all I could see were dollar signs. "Well, when is it going to happen?"

"I can't say because it's confidential. But I will say that as soon as we bring him in, I'm gonna let you know, so you can be the first one on the welcome wagon."

"Well, can you tell me if there are any informants who'd kill the case for me if I decided to pick it up?"

"There are a few, but they aren't credible. You'd be able to eliminate them at the preliminary hearing."

I took a sip of my drink. "It sure feels good to have contacts on the inside, but I just can't figure out how you guys are going to catch him with his shipment. Normally, men of that caliber don't come within ten miles of their shit."

"I know, but word has it, a lot of his product had been disappearing after it comes through the docks, so he told his right-hand man he's going to show up at the pier to make sure that his product gets through without any interruptions."

"Wow! This shit sounds like I'm watching a fucking *Scarface* movie or something."

"It's going to look like one when my boys take his ass down."

I smiled. "You like that cowboy-and-Indian shit, don't you?"

"My adrenaline pumps when I talk about it. That's why I wished I were back on the streets."

"Girl, please get over it and leave that cop-and-robber shit to the men! All you need to do is sit back and get all the information you can get, so you can get paid. That's it," I told her, and took another sip of my martini.

The conversation about Mr. Alvarez lasted for another five to ten minutes, and then we started talking about Sheldon Chisholm. I didn't have much to say about him, but Maria had a lot to say. I sat back and listened. Pretty much everything she said, I had already known, so a lot of the shit she was saying kind of went in one ear and right out the other. I was more interested in that drug bust that was about to go down. Yeah, it would be good to get the cold hard cash and the publicity for representing him, but who's to say that he didn't already have counsel on payroll? And if he did, then where did that leave me?

Unless I intercepted their whole operation by informing Mr. Alvarez that he was about to be taken down. I knew damn well I could get a million in cash for that type of information. And if that be the case, I'd be able to get more money in less time than if I had to represent him. What a sweet deal that would be. But then I figured, what would that do for Maria? She would be devastated if she knew I crossed her. But then, too, how would she find out?

I was sure Mr. Alvarez wouldn't tell her, but after I let the cat out of the bag that he had an informant in his midst, shit was going to really hit the fan. I just hoped he would play it cool and keep things under wraps, because I couldn't have my name mentioned in any form, shape, or fashion. Maria would shit on me for real! Not only that, she could lose her fucking position if it was leaked that I got the information from her. But then again, shit happens. It's a dog-eat-dog world out here and people were going to look out for themselves. I guess I was going to have to follow suit and do what I needed to stay in this game. Right now, I was trying to stay on top, and if that meant fucking people over to do it, then so be it. Maria would just have to understand.

Two martinis later I called it quits and headed to my car. Maria tried to get me to stay longer so she could talk me to death about how she was tired of not having a man, but I wasn't up for that sob story tonight. I had to get out of there because I was on a mission.

On my way home I tried to figure out a way I was going to get in contact with Mr. Alvarez without Maria's agents finding out. I knew it would be hard, considering they had him under surveillance. However, he did own a nightclub, and I was sure the agents didn't have that place all wired up. It would be too hard, considering how noisy it was in there. I was sure the phones were tapped, though. So the best thing for me to do was to make my way inside the club and, hopefully, be able to have a chat with him while no one was around. As difficult as that might sound, if there's a will, there's a way.

After leaving Maria's house the night before, I could only think about how I'd be able to strategically plan the perfect time to approach Mr. Alvarez. I knew time was of the essence and that I wouldn't be able to drag this out any longer. Government agents worked odd hours—so who knew when they would execute their plan of attack? I wasn't about to take any chances, so I finally decided to put on a provocative dress and strut my stuff into his club. The only thing I would need to worry about was how to break the news to him. That was my only concern.

"Ophelia, I need you to run me a bubble bath," I yelled.

"Okay, ma'am," she replied, and then I heard her run off to my bathroom.

I had no idea what I was going to wear, but I knew what image I wanted to portray. "Sexy" and "glamorous" were the only two words that popped in my head, so I searched for a dress that would give me that exact look. After sifting through at least one hundred dresses, I finally ran across the perfect one. It was a black Carolina Herrera off-the-shoulder faille dress. It stopped right above my knee, so it would look dazzling with my four-inch satin Jimmy Choo pumps and the clutch bag to match. I knew the crowd would stop and take notice of me the moment I stepped foot inside the club, which was exactly what I wanted to accomplish.

My bubble bath was warm and the suds from the bubbles felt like silk on my skin, so I lay back and relaxed in it for at least twenty minutes. When the water started getting cold, I climbed out of the tub and headed back to my bedroom to get dressed.

"Ophelia, have the valet fetch my Aston Martin, please. And tell him that I'll be down in five minutes," I yelled.

"Okay, ma'am," she replied, and then she disappeared.

Once I had everything in place—my attire, my hair, and my makeup—I sprayed on my favorite fragrance and exited my home like I was Cinderella. Maria called me while I was in transit. I started not to answer her call, but I knew she'd keep ringing my phone until she got in touch with me. I exhaled right before I said hello.

"What are you getting into tonight?" she inquired.

"Oh . . . nothing," I said, trying to sound like I was relaxing.

"You sound like you're dead tired," she commented.

"I am. But I can't let that stop me from working."

"Whatcha working on? One of your cases?"

I sighed. "Yes, I am, and I'm getting a headache, too."

"Why don't you step away from it tonight and come out with me so you can clear your head? Then tomorrow you'll start over fresh."

"No, I don't think that'll be a good idea. I've got work up to my neck, so the best thing for me to do is sit my ass right and continue doing what I started."

Maria sighed. "Alright. I guess you know what works for you. But if you decide you want to hang out, give me a call."

"I will," I assured her; then we hung up.

I only had a couple of blocks to drive until I reached Juan Alvarez's club. My heart was beating like crazy, but I didn't let that stop me from continuing on with my mission. As I pulled up curbside in front of the club, the valet driver met me and took my keys in hand. I greeted him with a seductive smile and carried on about my business. The line for Mr. Alvarez's club wrapped around the building, but I was not about to stand in it. I was too glamorous for that shit, so I entered inside through the VIP entrance. I had to pay the guy two 100-dollar bills before I was given the green light. It didn't matter, though, because that little bit of money was just a penny in the bucket compared to what I was about to earn.

After I walked into the club, I had to climb a flight of stairs that led to the VIP room, which overlooked the entire club. It was really nice and a sight to see. Everyone who had tons of money was in the VIP section. I recognized a couple of the faces, like the infamous Valdez brothers. There were three of them and they were all very handsome. Plus they were notorious for the enormous amount of power they had. The entire family owned a massive amount of hotels and other real estate in Miami. Hailing from Colombia, they also owned massive cargos of cocaine, too. No one in any government agency had been able to bring these guys down. They had been under a microscope for a few years, I'd heard, but no busts had been made.

Another familiar face walked by me and my heart dropped. It was Juan Alvarez in the flesh, dressed in a black Armani suit. I played it off and smiled as he turned around to get another look at me. I braced myself and tried desperately to look like I fitted into this whole scene. He stopped in his tracks and walked back toward me. "You look very stunning!" he complimented me.

"Thank you very much," I replied, and extended my hand.

"You look very familiar to me," he said, squinting his eyes, simultaneously jogging his memory.

"You've probably seen me on TV"—I helped him—"I'm Yoshi Lomax, attorney-at-law."

"Oh yes, how are you?" he asked, grabbing my hand a little firmer.

"I am fine!" I said. "I just wanted to get away from the office and come out so I could enjoy myself for once."

"Well, you picked the right place!" he said. "Have a seat over here at the table with me and my guest." He escorted me over to a table lined with a few members of his entourage and a couple of sleazy-looking women.

I took a seat at the very end of the table, and Mr. Alvarez took the chair next to me. It was evident that I was going to be his special guest, because immediately after we sat down, he poured both of us a glass of champagne. "Drink up. We are going to have fun tonight!" he insisted.

I took a couple of sips of my champagne and immediately started feeling the vibes in the club. The salsa music was blasting through every speaker the club had mounted on the walls and in the floors, and everyone seemed to be enjoying themselves. It was apparent that everyone was there to get fucked-up and take one of these bimbos home afterward. I was there for a totally different reason. I had a motive. And my motive was to get paid. So I began to gather my words together, so they would come out of my mouth right. While I was in deep thought, Mr. Alvarez started up a conversation with me.

"So, how's business? How long have you been an attorney?"

"Business is good. And I've been an attorney so long, I've lost track of the years."

"What's your acquittal rate?"

"Let's just say that I have never lost a case." I got cocky.

"That's good to hear! Do you have a business card?"

"Why, of course I do," I eagerly said, and whipped one out of my clutch and handed it to him.

He stuffed it in the inside pocket of his Armani jacket, then said, "Let's make a toast to us."

"What's the occasion?" I wondered aloud.

He and I held our glasses up to each other. He said, "Let's make a toast to freedom!"

He and I tapped our glasses against one another and made the *ding* sound, saying the word "Freedom" in unison. It felt really good to sit there in the presence of this man and become cozy with him. I felt like he and I were on the verge of something really special. I'm not speaking from an intimate standpoint, because I was not the least bit attracted to him. Okay, granted, he's a fairly attractive man. He kind of reminded me of the actor Sean Connery, with the salt-and-pepper thing going on. But I was up to my neck when it came to fucking these tired old men. All I wanted to do was make this deal with him and keep it moving. That was it.

Two hours had passed and I could see that everyone around me was ripped. The sleazy whores were falling all over each other, making themselves look very cheap. I stayed close to Mr. Alvarez, but I was also able to hold my liquor a lot better than these women, who were making complete spectacles of themselves. And when Mr. Alvarez had gotten tired of the show they were putting on, he had two of his men escort their asses downstairs. I laughed my ass off on the inside, because that was surely a sight to see.

Amid all the loud music, drinking, and laughter that was going on, I noticed that one of Alvarez's men tapped him on his shoulder; then he leaned over and whispered something in his ear. I was literally killing myself to hear what he was saying, but, of course, I couldn't manage over all the noise. And then all of a sudden, Alvarez leaned over toward me and said, "Excuse me, Ms. Lomax, but I have some business to take care of, so I am going to have to call it a night."

My heart started thudding like crazy, because I didn't know what was going on. I couldn't let him leave without telling him what I knew. But the way things were looking, I didn't have enough time. "Ah, you're leaving so soon?" I whined. "I was just starting to build a connection with you."

"There will be another time," he assured me. "I have your number, so I will be in touch."

As he began to lift himself up from his chair, I grabbed him by the arm. "Please don't go," I begged.

He smiled. "I'm sorry, beautiful, but I have to. Don't worry, though, you'll see me again."

"You don't understand. I came here tonight to warn you

that the DEA is onto you because someone in your organization is feeding them a lot of information about you. They know how much coke you bring in once a week from South America, and they know that you're going to be at the docks when your next shipment is brought in."

Looking very alarmed, he sat back down. "Who is the traitor?" he demanded.

"I'm sorry, but I don't have a name. But I do know that whoever is your lieutenant is the informant. And I also know that whichever day you step foot on that dock, they will be waiting for you," I continued; then I looked around to see if anyone was watching me.

"How did you get this information?"

"I'm sorry, Mr. Alvarez, I can't tell you who my source is. But I can tell you that they are definitely reliable."

"Indeed they are," he said; then he buried his face in the palm of his hands.

I didn't want to say another word. It became very clear to me that he needed some time to think, so I sat back in my chair and waited for him to say something.

Fifteen seconds later he lifted his head and looked around the room. He motioned for one of his men to come to him. And as soon as he approached Mr. Alvarez, he leaned down toward him, and that's when Mr. Alvarez whispered into his ear. Several seconds later the guy left the room and headed downstairs.

I immediately became uneasy and wished that I had not said anything. But it was too late, I had already let the cat out of the bag. Now I had to wait and see what happened. Nervously sitting there, I got up the gumption to speak. "What's going on?"

"I told my driver to fetch my car," he replied.

"You're still leaving?"

"Yes, I am, but I want you to know that you have given me some very valuable information. And I assure you that you will be compensated for it."

"But I don't understand what you mean," I said, trying to play dumb.

"Let's just say that you've saved my life, along with millions of dollars, and for that, I must repay you. So tomorrow I am going to have someone bring something very special to your office."

"You don't have to do that," I said, knowing damn well that's exactly what I wanted.

"Stop it! I insist," he said, and stood back up from his chair. He grabbed ahold of my hand and kissed it.

I smiled and said, "Please promise me that you'll never mention that we had this conversation."

"You have my word," he told me, and then he made his exit. And just like that, he was gone. Vanished behind a set of black doors. I sat there and had myself another glass of champagne. I made a toast to myself about the power move I'd just made. And after I finished gulping down the last drop, I set my glass down and left. The entire drive back to my house, all I did was smile and wonder about the special gift Mr. Alvarez was going to have delivered to me. I knew it couldn't be anything other than money. The question was, how much was he going to toss my way? And since I hadn't thrown any figures at him, it could be anything. But knowing the magnitude of revenue he had at his disposal made me believe that it would be half a million or better. Time would tell, though.

Dodging the Bullet

My BlackBerry started ringing and it startled the hell out of me. I looked over at the alarm clock on my nightstand and realized that it was 6:00 A.M., so I immediately wondered who the hell could have been calling me at this hour. I picked up my phone and looked at the caller ID. Maria's name was beaming out at me like headlights on a car. I had an idea what she was calling me for, so I hesitated to answer. But then I realized that if I didn't answer, she'd know that I had something to hide. I pressed down on the call button and said hello in the groggiest voice I could muster.

"Yoshi, wake up. We need to talk," she demanded. I could tell she was pissed.

"What's the matter?" I asked.

"Please tell me you didn't blow the whistle on my agents' investigation?" she begged.

"What are you talking about?" I asked, playing dumb.

"I am talking about the Juan Alvarez case."

"What about it?" I asked, continuing to act like I had no idea what she was talking about.

"His case went bust on us this morning. And we can't locate our informant anywhere," she said.

"Tell me what the hell does that have to do with me?" I countered.

"Yoshi, you were the only person who knew outside the agency."

"So you're accusing me of blowing your agents' investigation?"

"I'm only asking. You were the only person I told."

"Come on, Maria, you've known me for a long time now. You know I wouldn't betray your trust like that. What you need to do is talk to your agents, because this sounds like an inside job to me." I tried to sound as convincing as possible.

"No way. My men wouldn't do that. They've worked over five hundred man-hours in a two-month period to crack open this case, and then to have it blow up in smoke like that . . . no, I just can't believe that."

"Well, Maria, I don't know what to tell you—"

"I need you to tell me the truth," she interjected.

"What the hell do you think I've just done? Maria, I am an attorney! Not an informant. And besides, I didn't know the specifics anyway. Remember, you kept all that information to yourself."

"Yeah, but you knew who we were after."

"So what! That doesn't mean shit!" I snapped.

"Look, Yoshi, I'm not trying to get into a fight with you."

"You should not have called me with that bullshit then. You've really insulted my intelligence."

Maria sighed; then she said, "Cut it out, Yoshi! No one could ever do that."

"Are you done? Because I am ready to go back to bed."

"Yes, I am done. But I must inform you that if we ever find our informant and he utters your name, just know that life is going to look very dim for you."

"Wait a minute, Maria. Are you fucking threatening me?"

"If you had any involvement in sabotaging my agents' investigation, then, yes, I am threatening you."

"I am appalled that you would think that I would be capable of doing something like that. I mean, what could I gain from it? Absolutely nothing. I make my money representing clients in a courtroom. I'm not into anything other than that. So, whenever you do find out who blew the whistle on your agents' case, feel free to call me back and give me an apology. I'll be all ears." I indignantly ended the call.

After I hung up, I laid my phone down on the nightstand and turned back over in my bed. Deep down inside I felt bad, because I never wanted to double-cross Maria. She and I had been friends forever. She was like the sister I never had. But when I looked at it from another angle, I had to come to terms with the fact that I came into this world by myself, and that's the way I was going to leave. So, to hell with her and her threats! Shit, I was trying to get paid by any means necessary!

I finally rolled out of my bed around 8:30 A.M. so I could shower and get dressed. After I had my usual cup of hot tea, I headed straight to the office.

I got my usual stares when I entered the building, but I wasn't expecting to be greeted by Paul first thing in the morning. He was acting very weird as I walked by him. I threw on a fake smile and said good morning.

"We need to talk," he said as he followed me toward my office.

I looked back at him. "What's wrong with you?" I asked.

He waited until we both walked into my office and

closed the door behind us. "Are you involved in any type of illegal shit?" he questioned.

"No, I am not! And why would you ask me something like that?"

"Because there were a couple of agents here a while ago asking a ton of fucking questions about you!" he roared.

"What agents? And what kind of fucking questions were they asking?" I felt really nervous on the inside. I had instantly gotten sick in the stomach, but I played it cool in front of Paul.

"The DEA, that's who! And they wanted to know everything—from what time you come to work in the morning to what time you go to the bathroom to take a shit!"

"I don't understand. I mean, why would they be coming here and inquiring about me? I haven't done anything illegal."

"You better hope not. Because I let them go all through your office."

"What! Are you fucking kidding me?" I screamed. "Why the fuck would you do that?"

"They had a search warrant, so there wasn't shit I could do about it."

"Did they take anything?" I wondered aloud as I looked around my office, scanning everything to see what was out of place.

"No, I didn't see them take anything. But they looked through your entire file cabinet, your computer, and your planner."

I slammed my fist down on my desk. "That's bullshit, Paul! They can't go through my shit like that!" I protested.

"Yes, they can, when they have a search warrant."

"On what grounds, though? What fucking judge gave them a search warrant to go through my shit?" I continued to roar.

"I'm not sure. But whoever it was felt you had something they were looking for."

I sucked my teeth. "Well, if I had it, I'm sure they would have walked out of here with it."

"Look, I'm not trying to get in a debate with you. Just keep your fucking nose clean, because I'm not going to tolerate any more of these episodes with agents walking into my firm. It makes me and the other partners look bad."

"You're always thinking about your image."

"And I should," he replied sarcastically, and abruptly left.

I walked over to my office door and slammed it shut. I knew this whole thing had something to do with Juan Alvarez, so I was pissed. And to know that Maria had something to do with it made my blood pressure skyrocket. I knew she was only doing her job, but I can't handle that type of heat, especially here on my job. I guessed I was going to have to handle her ass with a long-handled spoon. I'd still be her friend, but from a distance. And since the heat was on me, it wouldn't be hard at all to keep her away from me, which made me wonder if they knew she and I were friends.

Yeah, she had to have told them something, or else they would not have pursued me. Oh well, whatever she told them would definitely have to be proven. And since I dot all my *i*'s and cross all my *t*'s, they were going to have to do better than what they were doing right now. I should call Ms. Maria and tell the bitch, "Thanks for everything." But, nah, knowing her, she'd be waiting, so I would not waste my time. I'd get her ass back by totally giving her the silent treatment. She hated that, so that was exactly what I intended to do. Other than that, I was going to live my life and step my game up just a little bit more.

After I sat in my office for about an hour and mulled

over the fact that agents had been searching through my personal files, I got a knock on my door. I was very agitated at this point and my tone expressed it. "Who is it?" I roared.

"Ms. Lomax, it's me Donna," my assistant said. "I have a package for you."

"Come in," I ordered her.

She walked into my office and set the manila envelope down on my desk. "This just came in," she told me.

"Who is it from?" I asked, hoping she'd be able to tell me before I found out myself.

"There's no return address on the envelope," she replied.

"Alright. You can leave now. Thank you," I told her.

After she exited my office, I ripped open the package. But before I pulled out the contents, I told myself that this had to be from Mr. Alvarez. He assured me the night before that he was going to have his people send me something the very next morning. So this had to be *that something*. . . . At least that's what I hoped. I took a deep breath and stuck my hand inside the envelope. Inside of it were two pieces of paper, so I pulled them out. "Oh shit!" I uttered unconsciously. In my hand I held a fucking cashier's check in the amount of $5 million and a handwritten note that read:

You have done a very great deed!
And it will never be forgotten.

I almost passed out. I mean, I wasn't expecting this. Shit, I was banking on half a million, not five. But, hey, I won't complain.

Before I stuck the check inside my handbag, I kissed it about ten times. This was the quickest five million I'd ever made. And to know that I did it without stepping one foot inside a courtroom made me one happy camper. Maria wasn't too happy with me, but I couldn't care less what she or any-one else thought about me. I knew one thing—after I was done with Sheldon's case, I was going to Virginia to visit my father's side of the family.

I had always wanted to be close to them, but my mother never allowed it. She thought we were too good for them. Okay, granted, a lot of them had struggled throughout their entire lives but, hey, some people were just not as fortunate as others. That was no reason to look down on them.

I hadn't spoken with any of them recently, including my favorite cousin, Carmine. I was sure everyone was doing well, considering we lived in a wealthy country and the op-portunities around us were endless. So I would pay her and the rest of my family a visit as soon as I get the first chance.

I ended my day at the firm somewhat earlier than usual. The cashier's check was burning a hole through my hand-bag, so I had to get to the bank to make a deposit. And that's exactly what I did.

Getting the Surprise of My Life

Days had passed and I hadn't talked to Maria once. It was Saturday, but it didn't matter to me because it was my day off and I made it my business to treat myself to a day at the spa. I needed it really bad after what I'd been through these last few days. After I got dressed in my Christian Dior strapless sundress, I slid on my Roberto Cavalli shades and headed downstairs to the lobby.

Once I was outside, the valet driver had my Aston Martin parked out front with the AC pumping. As I walked over to get in, the valet smiled at me, like he usually did.

"You seem pretty happy today," I said.

"I love to watch you. . . . You are so beautiful and so nice," he replied.

I smiled and tipped him the usual hundred.

He looked down and I noticed he was holding a white folder with gold writing. "This was left for you," he said, handing it to me.

"What is it?" I asked, puzzled.

"I don't know," the valet answered.

I grabbed the folder, curious as hell. When I opened it up, there was a white sheet of paper with gold writing:

LOOK ACROSS THE STREET.
SEE THE BLACK BENTLEY.
GO GET IN.

I raised my eyebrows in confusion. Nevertheless, I looked across the street. Sure enough, there was a black Bentley parked, with a driver dressed in black waiting beside it. He waved me over.

Before I went, I fumbled through the folder again. There was a set of keys, and that was it. I walked across the street, very slowly, cautiously. I was bugging out from this. I got to the car. The driver held the back door open for me.

"For you, madam," he said with a thick English accent.

Before I climbed into the car, I looked inside. The inside was filled with dozens and dozens of bloodred roses; then I noticed on the seat another card and a bottle of Cristal.

"Madam, Sir Lance has instructed me where to take you. But it is a surprise," the driver said.

Lance! It was the last client I'd gotten off. Big La La, a multiplatinum rapper from Houston. He was rich as a motherfucker, and when I got him off on charges of murder and conspiracy, he was forever grateful. I knew Big La La wanted to fuck me, but we'd never gotten the chance. On the last day of his court hearings, he'd promised me that I would see and hear from him again.

Excited, I climbed into the back of the Bentley. The driver seemed to breathe a sigh of relief and he went around to the front, got in, and began driving. I picked up the card and it read:

DON'T WORRY, THIS IS ALL FOR YOU.
I TOLD YOU THAT YOU WOULD SEE ME AGAIN.
BIG LA LA

I could hardly fit in the car, there were so many roses. I was smiling from ear to ear. No man had ever just whisked me away like this. I still had no clue where I was going, but I noticed the driver going toward the piers. I was lost in thought, not knowing what to expect. Just as I started feeling a little unsure, the car stopped.

"Madam, we have arrived," the driver said. He climbed out and opened the door. He reached in for my hand to help me out. We were at the piers, for sure. There were several large cruise ships, boats, and yachts docked. I stood up and looked around; I was still trying to figure out just what the hell was going on. Then I heard his voice. The smooth, even tones of Big La La.

"Ms. Lomax, *mmph, mmph, mmph*, my sexy-ass lawyer," he called out. I whirled around, smiling. He looked so damn good. He reminded me of Tyson Beckford, the male model. His lips were so perfect, and those damn pearly whites were too good to be true.

"Hey, what's this all about?" I said, smiling.

"This is all about you. All about how you did ya thang in that fucking courtroom with that cracker-ass judge," he replied.

I beamed.

"C'mon, let me show you," he said, motioning for me. So I walked to him and he grabbed onto my hand and led me toward a huge yacht that was docked at the pier. At first, I assumed he rented the boat to take me around the water once or twice. Shit, I was dead wrong. When I got close to the boat, I noticed the gold lettering on the boat's mast, LA LA'S LOVE. I don't know if he noticed how my mouth hung open.

"Ladies first," he said, opening his arms to welcome me onto his yacht. I could hear one of his records booming through the ship's speakers. That fucking boat was truly gorgeous. We walked up a winding staircase into the yacht's suite. The shit was fully furnished like a full house—complete with couches, plasma TVs, expensive throw rugs, and wall art. There were beautiful women and La La's entourage hanging around different spots on the ship. There was a game room, movie theater, and an indoor pool on the yacht. Now, I had been invited on a dozen beautiful yachts, but this one was the most lavish I had seen. I was really impressed.

"I can't stay. I'm not dressed for a party," I said, acting shy.

"Ms. Lomax, you are always dressed to kill. Look at you! Rocking Louboutins just to go out on a regular day— I so admire your style," he answered. "Anyway, this fucking party is for you. Without you, my ass would be doing time," he remarked, ushering me into another room.

Inside the yacht's stateroom was a long table, covered with all white centerpieces and white and gold place settings. At one end there was a large, beautifully decorated sheet cake that said: *THANK YOU!*

"See, this is yours," he said proudly.

"Oh, thank you, but you didn't have to—" I started.

"I'm sorry, but I had to. You are the fucking bomb, and I think I want to get to know you better, now that the trial is over," he said, moving close to me. I could smell his cologne and it was hypnotizing.

"Thanks, but I was just doing what you paid for," I answered, still staying modest. Just as I said that, I could swear I felt the boat moving. "Wait, did the boat move?" I asked.

"Hell yeah! I know you didn't think we were staying in Miami," he said.

"I don't even have clothes!" I said, kind of upset.

"You do now," he said, opening another door to expose a bedroom. On the bed were all kinds of dresses, jeans, bathing suits, and shoes . . . lots of shoes. "I had my personal stylist pick out a few things for you," he said.

My eyes were as wide as saucers. All of the designers— Gucci, Diane von Furstenberg, Hermès, Prada—shit, you name it, it was there.

"I don't know what to say," I remarked as I checked out all of the stuff he'd purchased. He even had a toiletry bag there for me with toothbrush, hair accessories, La Mer facial moisturizer, and everything I liked for pampering my body.

"Don't say a word, just enjoy. Go ahead and change. We are having cocktails on the third deck in about thirty minutes," he explained, walking out the door.

I flopped down on the huge bed, on top of all of the beautiful clothes, and smiled. I had to pinch myself to make sure I wasn't dreaming. Nope, I was awake. I called Ophelia to let her know I'd be away for a while and told her to let my office know.

I picked out a silk Missoni knit minidress, with a pair of aqua Jimmy Choo sandals. The dress fit me like a glove, and the shoes were my exact size. I still couldn't figure out how La La knew my sizes. I looked just like a runway model in the outfit. I chose not to wear any underwear—shit, I was doing it just like the real stars—no panties. I was all ready. I grabbed a small aqua Prada clutch and headed up to the third deck. I didn't make it three feet before La La met me.

"Mmm, shit! You look like a million fucking bucks!"

"Thanks to you," I said jokingly.

"It's all good. It's for a good cause," he remarked.

We headed up to the third deck together. From up there the view was off the chain. The sun was setting and the water was crystal clear. There were a bunch of chicks up there—dressed to kill. La La introduced me to several people, but I was too overwhelmed to even remember them.

We sat on a long white leather bench that was built into the yacht's walls. There were movable tables in front of the bench. The tables held all kinds of food—shrimp cocktail, lobster tails, beluga caviar, and all the highest-priced liquors you could name. These fucking rappers really know how to party, I thought. La La asked me what I was drinking and I ordered a Washington Apple. There was also a full wait-staff on the ship, so the waiter was back in a flash with my drink.

Everyone was vibing and having a great time. I could smell so much weed smoke, and I noticed a few people were sniffing coke. I wasn't into that shit anymore. I may have a few tokes off a blunt, but that cocaine shit wasn't for me. I had already fucked that up.

We partied into the night and the ship kept sailing. I still didn't know where we were going and for how long. That first night I slept alone. The next morning I was met with breakfast in bed. The service was complete, with white-towel service. This was the way to live—I was living like the real wealthy people.

After breakfast La La came to my room. The boat had docked and he wanted to get off and show me where we were. I got dressed in another beautiful sundress, a large sun hat, and a beautiful pair of Valentino shades. I felt like a Barbie doll. La La and I left the boat, and the first thing I noticed was the white-sand beach. The beach was absolutely breathtaking. White sand, blue water, and coral surrounded us. The sun was hot but comforting on my skin.

"Greetings," a woman dressed in a tropical getup said.

"Yes, I'm part of the Lance Wallace party," La La replied. I'd forgotten his government name was Lance Wallace—that was his client name to me. Calling him "La La" had taken some getting used to.

"Ah, yes," the woman said, snapping her fingers at someone behind her.

A man came running toward us. "Welcome to Barbados," the man sang with his accent.

I turned toward La La and smiled brightly. "How did you know I'd never been to Barbados?" I asked.

"I do my research, Ms. Lomax," he replied.

"Would you please call me Yoshi. I mean, you picked me up off the street, took me to a strange place, and laced me in luxury—the least I could do is let you call me Yoshi," I said, laughing. He laughed, too.

We were led to a waiting limousine. It was kind of old, but for a small island it was the shit. The driver kept talking to us, but La La and I were too busy enjoying each other's company. I felt like I was falling for him, and I didn't even know him outside of our professional relationship and whatever I'd heard about him in the media. He was always in the media because of his status.

The limo finally pulled up to a crowded street. "This is Bridgetown . . . our shopping center. There is the duty-free shopping center," the man instructed. La La and I got out of the limo and headed into the duty-free shopping center. I was in awe. For such a small island, that shopping center had everything: Gucci, Prada, Fendi, and Chanel, to name a few.

"Look, you don't have to take me shopping. Trust me, I have plenty," I said to La La seriously.

"Stop acting like that. Take this and do what you do," he replied, handing me his black card.

"I can't do that," I said.

"Yes, you can. It's easy as this." He took my hand and

placed his card into my palm. I smiled and didn't say another word. He didn't know me very well. I loved to spend other people's money. I hit Chanel first. I purchased the new Coco Cabas bag in two colors—denim and chocolate leather. I got two pairs of Chanel shoes, which totaled more than $2,000, and then I moved into Gucci. I was always a Gucci girl; at first, it seemed that I had all of the bags that the small island flagship store carried, but then I found one that I didn't. I purchased it, along with some new sandals and a pair of slides to wear around the boat.

La La and I went from store to store until we had too many bags to hold. It was the first time I'd gone on a real shopping spree that I didn't have to pay for myself.

After we finished shopping, the limousine driver took us to a beautiful mansion to have lunch. La La told me he owned this huge house that was right on the beach. He said it was one of his many vacation homes. Barbados was fucking beautiful, but that house with the private beach was absolutely amazing.

We didn't stay in Barbados; La La told me he had so much more planned for us. I didn't argue; I'd already decided to take it all in and have a good time—and that was just what I did. I let him take care of me and I was loving it. I loved the way he had ditched his entourage just to be with me. I couldn't ever remember a time that I'd seen him on the red carpet, record signings, or anywhere else without his crew—but for me, he had told them all to fall back and do their own thing.

When we returned to the yacht, we were both exhausted. All of the shopping, La La's treatment, his fine ass, and his cologne had me horny. But I wasn't going to make the first move. He told me to get showered and change for dinner. The boat would be sailing to our next destination. I took a long, hot shower in the beautiful frosted-glass-encased shower. I wet my hair and made it curly—exotic. I slipped into a BCBG silk slip dress and a pair of Giuseppe Zanottis. When I arrived on deck, I found him . . . alone at a candlelit table.

"Damn, girl, you always look good," he remarked as I sat down.

"La La, tell me what this is really all about. I mean, you can't possibly be that grateful that I got you off," I said, motioning for the waiter to bring me my signature drink.

"Yoshi, you have no idea how grateful I am. You saved my life and career. I heard that you were the best at what you do, and you proved yourself," he explained.

"I have received gifts from clients before, but nothing like this," I remarked.

"I'm different. I'm also very attracted to you," he said, placing his hands on mine.

I felt my heart thump and my pussy tingle. I was blushing, and I just knew it. "Well, I thank you for all that you've done. Shit, I'm gonna have to buy a new closet when I get back," I joked.

Before I could say another word, La La leaned across the table and kissed my lips. Shocked, I pulled away, but he continued with his advances. Next thing I knew, we were down on the lower deck and were ripping each other's clothes off. We kissed wildly and the heat between us was serious.

The next thing I knew, he pulled off his shirt, exposing his chest. He didn't bother taking off my dress, he just hoisted it up and buried his face in my pussy. That motherfucker ate my pussy until I was dizzy. Then he slipped on a condom, put his dick up in me, and fucked me like his mind was going bad. I returned his pumps for as long as I could and then I came all over his dick. Panting and out of breath, we lay next to each other in a daze. I didn't know what I had just done—fucking another one of my clients—but it was some good shit.

Next he got up and got a blunt. He lit it up, took a pull, and offered it to me. I was so into him, I grabbed it and took a long pull. I immediately started coughing. I also knew right away that the blunt was laced with coke. I felt good as hell. After that first puff, I stopped indulging. I couldn't go down that road again. We island-hopped for two whole days . . . ending up in St. Barts—a well-known celebrity hot spot. La La and I shopped some more, fucked even more, and enjoyed each other. I had never been treated like this by a man in my entire life—too bad. I knew as soon as I returned to Miami, I would be dropping his ass like a hot potato. I couldn't be tied to one man—it would be bad for my business and my residuals. I always received gifts and big pay from my clients. If they thought I had a man taking care of me—especially a man like La La—those clients might think twice about rewarding me.

Chasing It Hard

Ophelia was cleaning off my china cabinet when I walked into the foyer of my home. She said good morning and told me about a ton of messages I had by the telephone in my study. After I put all my things down in my bedroom, I went inside my study to see exactly who had been trying to contact me. When I picked up the notes attached to my computer, I saw that Donna and Sheldon had called. I wasn't expecting a message from Sheldon at my home—I give only clients my cell number. How in the hell did he get my unlisted home telephone number? I ran back into the foyer area of my house, where Ophelia was cleaning. She had her back turned to me, so I startled her when I unexpectedly approached her. Holding the note in my hand, I immediately asked her, "When did Sheldon call, and what exactly did he say?"

"He called yesterday, ma'am," she said, her accent rolling off her tongue.

"What did he say?" I asked once again.

"He just asked if you were home and I told him no. And when I asked him if he wanted to leave a message, he told me to tell you to call him back as soon as you got back in."

I sighed heavily. "Alright," I said, and then I stormed back into my study. When I arrived at my desk, I picked up my BlackBerry and dialed Sheldon's number. He answered after the third ring.

"I'm returning your call," I immediately said.

"I was expecting you to call me back yesterday."

"I was out of the country, so I didn't get your message until just now," I told him, my heart clocking fifty miles per hour.

"I tried calling you on your cell phone, too, but I got no answer."

"That's because I turned my phone off. I don't like to be disturbed when I leave the country," I said, biting my tongue. Because I honestly did not want to give him an explanation. I mean, who the fuck did he think he was?

"Were you working on my case while you were out of the country? I mean, I am shelling out twenty-five hundred an hour, so I would like for you to be working instead of bullshitting while my freedom is hanging in the balance."

Utterly appalled by his abrasiveness, I took a deep breath before I went off the handle and cursed his ass out. I mean, how dare this bastard try to scold me about my whereabouts and remind me what he's paying me an hour? Shit, I was his fucking attorney—not the other way around—so he needed to pump his fucking brakes before I dropped his case. I didn't need his ass for real! I was rich already and I had a lot of other clients who paid me just as well as he did. So, he needed to chill the fuck out.

Now before I lost my cool and gave him a piece of my mind, I counted to ten and thought of a better way to come back at him.

"Mr. Chisholm, I understand your frustration right now, but there is a better way we can handle this situation, so you can get whatever it is you want."

"Look, all I want is for you to be available whenever I

call you, and for you to start doing what I am paying you for so you can win my case."

"I understand all of that, but was there something you wanted to discuss with me that you felt was an urgent matter?"

"What I wanted to know was, how are things going with my case?"

"Mr. Chisholm, I am working really hard on your case, so you don't have to worry about anything. All I want you to do is get us a bottle of expensive champagne because we are about to have a celebration."

"You better hope so!" he replied sarcastically, then hung up his line.

After I put my BlackBerry on my desk, I got an instant headache and decided to leave my place and head back into the streets. I needed a hit of something to calm my nerves. I promised myself that I'd stay in control.

Venturing to the West Side to buy cocaine was a first in a long while for me. After looking around at all of the empty souls who roamed the streets on that side of town, I told myself that I was too high-class for that shit, especially after this ignorant-ass nigga walked up to my car like he was somebody really tough. His short ass reminded me of Gary Coleman from *Different Strokes,* but with cornrows, standing before me wearing all red. It was no secret that this asshole was a gang member.

"Whatcha need?" he asked, trying to sound like he was running shit.

"You got coke?" I asked.

"How much you trying to spend?" he asked.

I held out a one-hundred-dollar bill. "I want a hundred dollars' worth."

He took the money out of my hand and then he waved another guy dressed in all red to come over to where we were. As soon as the other guy approached us, Gary Coleman's look-alike threw a couple of fingers up at him and then he walked off. Two seconds later the other guy handed me a quarter-sized, clear plastic bag filled halfway with what I assumed was coke, and then he walked off.

I dropped my little package onto my lap and sped off. Once I got at least a couple of miles away from where I made my score, I pulled over on the side of the road to inspect my product. I dipped the fingernail of my pinky inside the powder and then I licked it off with the tip of my tongue. It definitely had the numbing effect, so I believed it was okay. I transferred the coke to a small glass canteen and placed it in my purse.

Traveling back in the direction I had just come from, I started thinking about how silly I was to have done what I just did. I could have easily gotten carjacked and robbed or, worse yet, gotten caught up in a drug sting. And if that would have happened, my career would have gone up in smoke right before my eyes. So, from now on, my coke would come to me from high places. This street-copping shit was not for Yoshi Lomax.

Now with coke in hand, and with Sheldon's case on my mind, I had to go do some fucking work. I figured I'd have to go into the office and at least try to prepare my motions and information for his pretrial hearing—just in case Brad tried to fuck me over. I had reached out to him three more times with no answer. I was too preoccupied with what was going on in my own life to worry too hard about Brad, but I definitely needed to stop into the office.

I sped my car into the parking garage at the job. Again, I noticed a car in my spot. "What the fuck is this now?" I cursed, pulling up to my reserved spot. I couldn't believe someone had the audacity to park in my spot—I mean, my fucking name was on the spot. There was a black BMW parked in the spot, only this time there was no ribbon or card on the car.

I quickly pulled out my phone and called Donna. She didn't answer. I drove around to an unreserved spot, threw my car into the space, and rushed to the office. I was going to get to the bottom of this shit. Nobody parks in my spot! I thought fiercely. I folded my arms across my chest and tapped my foot, impatiently waiting for the elevator.

I had the right mind to take the stairs, but my office was on the twenty-fifth floor. When the elevator doors opened, Paul and a guy I didn't know were getting off.

"Fuck," I mumbled under my breath. I didn't need to see his ass right now. Paul looked me up and down, and I did the same to him. Neither of us really wanted to be the first to speak. He plastered a wicked smile across his tanned face.

"Hey, Yoshi . . . this is Armand Schwartz, our newest associate partner," Paul introduced snidely, like he was rubbing it in my face. I decided to be bigger than him and play it off.

"Hi, Armand, I'm Yoshi Lomax. It's nice to meet you," I returned, not once looking back at Paul.

"I've heard great things about you, Yoshi," Armand commented, shaking my hand firmly. He was attractive in a Brad Pitt way, kind of short for my taste, but still handsome. I could tell right away he was not someone I would fuck—why would I? There would be nothing for me to gain, and I don't fuck for love.

"Well, believe all of it," I said to Armand, smiling and stepping onto the elevator. Before the doors could fully close, Paul stuck his foot in the way. I glared at him.

"Yoshi . . . one more thing. I've assigned your reserved

parking spot to Armand. We will discuss your parking options later," Paul said, quickly removing his foot, letting the elevator doors close before I could respond. I stood inside that elevator with my mouth open for the entire ride. I was more in shock than anything, but nothing could've prepared me for what was coming next.

As soon as I stepped off the elevator, I knew something was up. I noticed the usual office behavior when something was going down. A bunch of the lawyers who worked for Shapiro and Witherspoon were huddled around the watercooler whispering. When they saw me, all the whispering stopped and they just stared in my direction.

"Happy to see a superstar?" I beamed, smiling like nothing. They were always staring at me and I was always willing to give them a fucking show. I heard snickers as I walked to my office. "Fucking idiots," I mumbled, and kept up my confident stride toward my office. Before I could reach my suite, I ran directly into my assistant, Donna. The first things I noticed were her red-rimmed eyes and then the box she was carrying.

"Donna, we have a lot of work to do on Mr. Chisholm's case," I said demandingly, acting as if it were business as usual. I really wasn't interested in asking her why she'd been crying.

"Ms. Lomax . . . um, uh . . . I . . . ," she stammered, tears running down her face.

"Donna, what is going on with you? You have to pull yourself together, this is a workplace," I snapped. I needed to get to my office so I could snort this coke I had just picked up. I didn't have time for her bullshit.

"I've been replaced and—and . . . your off—" Donna started, but I cut her off.

"Replaced? What are you talking about, Donna? Pull

yourself together!" I roared, growing frustrated. I could barely understand her words behind her cries.

"I've been fired!" she yelled, tears and snot going everywhere.

"Fired! Who the fuck fired you? You're my assistant!" I screamed, my face turning beet red. I had been stopped dead in my tracks.

"Mr. Shapiro," Donna blurted out, followed by more racking sobs.

"No, you come to my office. This is not fucking happening right now, of all times, not right now. Come on, I will call Paul for a meeting," I instructed, grabbing her arm.

"You don't have an office in this suite anymore, Ms. Lomax. Paul had your stuff moved last night and he gave your office to a new partner, Mr. Schwartz," Donna cried, stopping me from pulling her. Her words slammed into my head like a boulder and I was kind of thrown off balance. I didn't even think I understood her correctly.

"What? What is going on?" I asked again, not sure I'd heard right.

"Yes, Mr. Shapiro informed me that I was fired and you were being moved to the small hall," Donna explained as she started to calm down.

"Oh hell, no he didn't!" I screamed even louder.

There was a huge crowd gathering, made up of all the people that hated me at the firm. They were all now spectators of my misery, watching me like I was in a gladiator arena about to be devoured by a lion. Eric Bretner had a front-row seat. His face was filled with joy, like he was watching his favorite movie. All that was missing was his tub of popcorn. He was loving the hell out of seeing me in misery, fucking bastard! I looked around at all of them. Every one of them I had probably stepped on or over to get where I was in the firm—they all were taking great pleasure in my pain.

"There is no fucking show here. Go back to losing cases, all of you fucking losers!" I yelled. The veins in my head had popped and I drew my eyes into little slits to hold back the tears that burned at the back of my eye sockets. I wasn't about to let these motherfuckers see me cry. I stormed down the hallway to survey my office, and just like Donna had explained, there was a new assistant in her old seat in front of my office, and on the door the gold name bar no longer read: YOSHI LOMAX, ESQ. It now read, ARMAND SCHWARTZ, JJD.

I rushed past the assistant toward my old door. "Excuse me, miss," the guy started. He was very effeminate, wearing eyeliner and a tight nylon shirt.

"Listen, you little punk. This is my office!" I boomed, pointing in his face. I turned the doorknob on the office, but it was locked. I tried my key, but the locks had been changed. The heat of embarrassment climbed my chest as fast as mercury in a thermometer. I didn't know what to do with myself. Then I noticed several boxes stacked outside the door. In black Magic Marker was my name. This fucking Paul had used Magic Marker to label my shit—like I was a piece of trash, like Yoshi Lomax was a fucking nobody. This was it. This shit meant war. Paul had gone too far. I guess this was his type of revenge, but he didn't know who he was fucking with.

I composed myself, tired of letting these bastards have a show at my expense. I calmly walked to the ladies' bathroom, which I'd never used because my old office suite had its own full bathroom. When I entered, there were several of my female counterparts standing around snickering, I'm guessing about my situation. I gave them all the evil eye.

"What the fuck you bitches looking at? You think this shit is funny?" I asked, my voice piercing, bouncing off the walls.

They all got quiet and I could hear them filing out of the bathroom, one by one.

"Yes, get the fuck out of here before I slap the shit out of all of you!" I screamed as they began to head out. I was beyond pissed and I was acting all outside of my usual cool character. After everyone had gone, I took a quick peek down under the doors to the other stalls. I was alone. "Finally," I said with a sigh.

I dug into my Fendi Spy Bag and found my little glass canteen of coke. I dumped a small amount onto the silver purse platform in the stall and, bare-nosed, I inhaled. All I needed was a small amount to get myself ready to deal with Paul. As the drug took effect, I felt my confidence building. I was ready. I was going to see Paul Shapiro and he wasn't going to like it. When I finally left the bathroom, I had a contrived smile on my face. I walked calmly toward Paul's office, which was situated three doors down and one door across from my old office suite. I approached, and Paul's assistant—who I knew was fucking him, too—jumped up. We hated each other and we made it known.

"Is Paul back yet?" I asked.

"Paul is not taking any visits or conducting any meetings today," she said sternly, her face in a scowl. This bitch just didn't know who she was fucking with today. I was ready to slap the shit out of her.

"I don't want to visit his ass, nor do I want to have a fucking meeting. Now get the fuck out of my way before I call your trailer-park-ass husband and tell him about how you are fucking your boss." I retaliated with vicious words.

She was left speechless and she stumbled back down into

her seat. I burst into Paul's office and he was on the phone. He looked up at the doorway in shock.

"Let me call you right back," he said to the person on the other end of the phone line. He turned his attention to me. "What can I do for you, Yoshi Lomax?" he asked sarcastically. His fake-ass smile cracked his crispy-ass face.

"What kind of fucking games are you playing, Paul?" I sneered, biting into the side of my jaw. I had promised myself that I was not going to break down in front of Paul.

"Games? I don't know what you're talking about," Paul replied, playing dumb.

"Oh, so giving my office and parking spot to a fucking newbie is not a game?" I screamed, feeling the growing fire that was my temper burning in my chest and rising quickly up my neck.

"Well, Yoshi, you are a junior partner and he was hired as an associate partner. And, besides, you really didn't need all that office space, because sooner or later the feds would have come and torn the walls off in there and ransacked everything, causing the firm thousands of dollars in repairs. And I told you, we can't have that type of nonsense going on in here—that's why we moved you to the back office. Back there, no one will even know that you're here," he answered, his words feeling like daggers stabbing me through the heart. "Speaking of which," he continued, "did you ever find out what the hell they were looking for? Because I would sure like to know."

"Fuck you, Paul, and the fucking boat you sailed to this country on!" I snapped. I had had enough of his bullshit. I had put my life and career at risk for the firm, and for what? I felt like an idiot standing in his office—an office I aspired to have one day. I wanted so badly to cry, but the hardened, cold, and vindictive person that I'd become wouldn't let a tear drop. Instead, I immediately thought of something that would get to his ass.

"Okay, Paul. You want to play that game, huh? Well, let's get ready to take a ride, because I'm about to get into the driver seat of this car and I am going to take you on a fucking whirlwind. I like revenge, just like you, and I think Mrs. Shapiro would love to hear from me," I started.

I could see the anger rising on Paul's face. But I continued; "Yeah, Paul, how about I tell your precious wife how you come in my pussy and in my ass and suck it back out. Oh wait—no, how about I tell her that her precious Paul likes it when I fuck him in the ass with my dildo and act like I'm another man!" I gritted my teeth, letting the words sink in. I just wanted him to feel like I was feeling—hurt, lost, used, and afraid. Paul's eyes darkened to a color that I don't think I've ever seen before—black, with a flash of red, and piercing. His face turned a burnt orange as blood rushed to his cheeks. In one swift motion, he leaped out of his chair and was standing so close to my face I could smell the cinnamon Altoids on his breath.

"You bitch! If you even go near my wife, I will kill you. You think you can threaten me? I know all about you. All about how you came from a peasant-whore bitch who sucked cock to feed her daughter after her husband walked out on her ass," Paul started, small drips of his spit landing on my cheeks.

But before Paul could finish talking about my mother, I slapped the shit out of him. It was a knee-jerk reaction, so he knew I was pissed. At the same beat of the drum, Paul grabbed my face roughly, like he was about to do me some serious bodily harm. Just as he was about to raise his fist, his door swung open. It was his nosy-ass assistant. She must've heard the commotion and figured we were having an afternoon fuck session.

"Mr. Shapiro . . . Mr. Witherspoon is on line one," she said, looking from me to Paul and from Paul to me. Paul let go of my face and straightened up. That poor white-trash bitch didn't know she had just saved me from whatever wrath Paul was about to unleash. I inhaled deeply, kind of relieved. I brushed myself off and stormed toward his door.

"You think you won, Paul, but as God is my witness, you will pay for every fucked-up thing you've ever done to me or anybody else."

"Get out of my office!" he yelled.

"With pleasure," I replied, and then I stormed out the door.

After I left Paul's office, I stormed by everyone's office that I couldn't stand and made loud and lewd comments about them. They all looked at me like I was crazy, but I didn't give a fuck. The way I was feeling, I could've spit in all their faces and not even give a damn about what consequences I would've faced. The way things were looking for me around here, my chances of becoming partner were slim to none. As a matter of fact, the likelihood that I was going to be working here in the next several months looked even bleaker. So I saw that I was going to have to get on the ball and get shit rolling. Shit, if these bastards around here wanted to throw shit on my lawn, then I was going to throw shit right back on theirs. And watch and see who got the last laugh. What was going to fuck their heads up even worse was when I left this place altogether and started up my own firm. I mean, hey, I had the revenue and the fucking clients to do it. So, to hell with all these motherfuckers! I was always going to remain on top. And I would die doing it.

On my way to my small-ass office, I didn't bother to look for Donna. I mean, it was clear that she'd been fired. So, why run down behind her when I was walking on thin ice myself? When I stepped inside this box, I immediately felt claustrophobic. The room was so damn small, I didn't have enough room to put all my things inside it. So, you know I was fucking furious. I mean, how could I go from a penthouse to a fucking studio apartment? That shit didn't make sense! On top of that, this room didn't have a fucking window. And if I'm not crazy, this room used to be a fucking utility room. And now they wanted to stuff my ass in here. Well, no can do! I would not tolerate this type of treatment, so something would be done about this. And I meant it. Instead of unpacking my things, I just left everything the way it was. I grabbed my car keys and my handbag and hauled ass out of there before anyone could blink their eyes.

"Leaving so soon?" Eric asked as he accompanied me on the elevator.

I stared at his ridiculous-looking ass from head to toe and said, "Mind your fucking business, please!"

He snickered to himself like I had said something humorous. It irritated the hell out of me. I knew he was doing this to ruffle my feathers, and it was definitely working. "What the fuck is so funny?" I snapped.

"It just amazes me how you will not humble yourself under no circumstances. Look at you, you still have this cocky attitude and your world is falling apart right before your very eyes," he commented.

"Oh, so you think because Paul kicked me out of my office, my world is falling apart? Well, let me be the first to tell you that it's not. That little fucking office he stuck me in has no bearing on the reputation I have as an attorney. I am very wealthy and I am nothing to fuck with, because I know the law better than you know yourself. So instead of filling your mind up with the ridiculous theory that my world is falling apart, try concentrating on your own fucked-up life. 'Cause if I can recall, you haven't won a case in the past four months. And if you don't get yourself on track, you're going to be the next one Paul shoves in one of those back offices. Better yet, he might just get rid of your ass altogether. I mean, it's not like you're a top earner around here," I replied, the venom spitting from my mouth.

"You bitch!" he uttered, his face bright red.

Right when I was about to let his ass have it, the elevator door opened, so I only called him a loser. I stepped off the elevator and then I turned all the way around and waved good-bye to him as the elevator door closed back up.

Walking away from that scene made me feel really good. Eric had always gotten under my skin. He had been hating on me since the first day I started working here, and I honestly couldn't take it anymore. Hopefully, he learned a good lesson from this, and that's not to fuck with Yoshi Lomax. I was one chick you don't need to play with.

On my way home Maria called my BlackBerry twice, but I pressed down on the ignore button and kept it moving. How dare she try to contact me after all the shit that went down? I mean, what could she want to talk about after sending her boys to ransack my fucking office? Was she snorting the same fucking drug I was? Because if she was, then she'd definitely have a good explanation for her actions.

But in all fairness, I knew Maria and I knew she had to have had her back against the wall for her to turn on me like she did. So I didn't hate her at all. The only problem I did have was that I knew she and I weren't going to be cool like we used to be. That friendship we had was now over for good—so that meant no more trade-offs of information for money, which was going to really hurt me in the long run. But I'd be okay. Trust and believe, I'd find another source in this corrupt city. All I had to do was turn over a couple of rocks and they'd come crawling out.

One Bad Bitch

That small-ass office I was forced to move into was really bothering me. My recreational cocaine use was getting a bit out of control. I found myself spending my own cash and copping my own shit, almost on a daily basis. I was in control—that was what I told myself every single day I found myself pushing the straw up my nose. Although I was getting high, I was still one bad bitch, and I still had mother-fuckers requesting me to represent them daily. I was just too embarrassed to let any of my clients see my new workspace, so I always escorted them to one of the four conference rooms that the firm had. It had been working out pretty well, if I say so myself.

Now, Paul was another story. He was trying to throw shade every which way he could. I also told myself I could handle his ass as well. I had promised myself that after my little meeting with him, I was going to send his wife an anonymous letter, just to let him know I wasn't playing with his ass.

But somehow or another I got lost in all the shit I had on my plate and I didn't even bother. For instance, the first thing that happened after my meeting with Paul was that Judge Casey was carried out of his courtroom in handcuffs by the feds on national television. The feds had him on charges of bribery and gratuities. So I am like, "What the fuck is going on here?" That was the first time, in a long time, that I was scared as hell. I was so fucking shook, hoping that Casey didn't turn me in as one of the attorneys who had paid him for favorable outcomes in the courtroom. I waited days and days after I saw the news report of his arrest and nothing happened. I'd reasoned that he wasn't stupid enough to turn me in.

Other things in my life had also spiraled out of control— I mean so fast that my head was spinning daily. I had now gone from using cocaine once daily to three to four times a day. The shit happened so fast, I couldn't remember where I'd gone wrong. I knew shit was getting bad when I contemplated selling one of my Rolexes for cash. Although I had money stashed in all kinds of accounts, I also knew a high-priced cocaine habit could make a bitch broke in no time. So instead of spending my own fucking money, I figured that there were many people with access to good coke who owed me their lives.

In short, I went back to fucking with Luis Santana and his wife, Adrianna—and, trust me, they had an endless supply of coke. That funny coke those fucking Santanas kept was the kind of shit that made me feel like dancing.

When I first called Mr. Santana, I hung up the telephone six or seven times before I got up the courage to say that I wanted to see them again.

"Come on by," he said. "Adrianna has been asking about you a lot lately," he continued.

"That's nice to know," I said, setting my sights on the pile of coke I knew they would have at their disposal.

When I arrived at their estate this night, the guard at the security gate let me right in. Damn, am I that well-known over here already? I thought. This time when I arrived was different; there were no smiling faces at the front door to greet me. This time, Luis had his maid let me in, which was strange, because I'd become accustomed to him and Adrianna greeting me.

I followed the maid inside. I walked into the massive foyer of their mansion—the mansion I had helped them keep by getting him off. I had a habit of mentally taking credit for every single thing that he had acquired. Even if Adrianna bought a new pair of drawers, I would think, It's because of me that this bitch can afford those drawers.

I was asked to wait in the huge den that sat off the front foyer. I waited there for Luis and Adrianna and their cocaine—free cocaine. The maid did kind of a little bow in front of me and left. It was a weird feeling, being at their house. It always was. I mean, it wasn't that long ago that he was my fucking client and needed me; now I fucking needed his ass. Something I would never admit to him or anyone else for that matter.

I looked around the den. I could tell that they definitely had an interior decorator—only a professional could put that ugly-ass furniture together with paint and accessories and make it look as good as it did. There were huge paintings of Luis and Adrianna hanging on all four walls, two of them together and one of each of them individually. How vain was that? I made a mental note to have my portrait painted and hang it up in my penthouse.

"Ahhh, Yoshi," Luis called to me from behind. He grabbed me around my waist, like he was my man and happy to see me. His hands were cold and I winced as he moved them up my bare back. I immediately felt uneasy. My greed for cocaine was keeping me anchored there, because my logical brain was calling me a stupid bitch for being there and risking everything I had worked so hard for.

"You look stunning as usual," he commented, referring to my tight white second-skin Cavalli jeans and my open-back drape-front BCBG MaxAzria top.

I kissed him on both cheeks, as this was now our customary greeting. Luis had on just a robe, and when I leaned in to kiss him, he let it fall open. He exposed his beautiful nine-inch dick that I was desperate for.

Seeing his dick made me have a flashback to the night of his party. Back at the hotel room, he had sprinkled cocaine on the tip of his dick and I sniffed it off; then I sucked the huge piece of meat until I gagged.

"Adrianna awaits us at the pool house," Luis said, ushering me toward a large glass door. I really couldn't care less about Luis or Adrianna—what I wanted were the good drugs they supplied. I entered the pool house and I was taken aback. There were about six extra people there. I immediately looked at Luis, confused and a little angry. He had set me up.

"Yoshi, this is our swinging group. We wanted them to meet you," Luis explained.

Swinging! I screamed in my head. Luis must have been losing his fucking mind; I thought our little thing was exclusive. My heart started racing and little sweat beads lined up like soldiers on my hairline. I took the back of my hand and swiped my forehead. I had to think. I couldn't participate in anything like this and risk being exposed. Luis had promised that our little thing was private . . . just between us. He had betrayed me!

"Luis, I can't stay," I said nervously, not wanting any of the other people to recognize me. But when I looked over at the wooden bar and saw the cocaine, all logic and thoughts of leaving went out the window. I told myself that if I stayed for only ten minutes, that would be enough time to get two lines in and get out of there. Luis didn't even have to speak the words. He already knew that I had it bad for the co-caine.

"Yoshi, don't look at it. Help yourself," he said, pointing toward what I had really come there for.

I walked over to the bar, picked up their customary metal straws, and snorted two lines. Two lines made me feel right. Adrianna knew me so well that she was right on top of me after I finished. If they came on to me immediately after I did a line, I was down for whatever. But after my drugs wore off, I was terribly embarrassed and always raced home.

"C'mere," Adrianna said seductively. She was always so high, I could never tell if she was ever sober. I followed her lead. One of Gloria Estefan's songs was playing, which was regular in their household. Adrianna took me over to a small curved chair; it was purple suede and S-shaped.

Without saying a word, she pulled down the front of my shirt, which was barely covering my titties anyway. She took a handful of cocaine and smeared the white devil pow-der all over my tits. I started giggling like a high-school bitch about to get her first piece. Adrianna smiled, looked at me wickedly, and buried her face in my chest. She snorted up the powder like her nose was a vacuum cleaner. Then she licked me from nipple to nipple, flicking her tongue roughly over my erect nipples.

The drugs sent a tingling sensation through my areolas, which made them very sensitive to her tongue. I was in ec-stasy for real. Before I could say a word, another girl, whom I did not know, came over to join us. The girl stood about five feet five inches and had jet black hair. At first glance, she looked like Kim Kardashian; I had to do a double take.

The new girl lifted Adrianna's thin see-through skirt and began eating Adrianna's pussy from the back. That drove me wild. I frantically started fidgeting with my pants buttons. I was so horny from the drugs and Adrianna that I didn't know what to do with myself.

When I got my pants down, Adrianna did the same thing with the cocaine, but on my clit. She sucked on my clit like it was a pacifier, and as swollen as it was, that is exactly what it looked like. I could feel my chest heaving with excitement. Adrianna moved from my clit, took her hands and parted my pussy lips wide open. I was dripping wet by now. She stuck her tongue in and out of my hole rapidly with no countable rhythm. I threw my head back on that little curved chair and let her work. I felt like I was in some kind of heaven . . . maybe not the one saints go to, but this certainly wasn't hell. I felt cum welling up in my loins and I was about to explode.

"Arrghhh," I moaned. I grabbed Adrianna's head forcefully and pushed her farther into my pussy. She jumped up and stopped. My eyes popped open to see what happened, and just as I opened them, I saw Luis getting on his knees with his dick in his hands. He mounted me and drove his dick so far up in me I screamed out in pleasurable pain. Luis pumped up and down on me and Adrianna came and stood over my face. She put her pussy over my mouth and I stuck out my tongue to oblige her.

Luis fucked me until he was ready to come. Right before he was about to burst, he stood up and let his cum shoot all over my face and Adrianna's pussy. The black-haired girl was right there and she came over to me and started licking Luis's cum off my chin.

I had never felt so good in my life. All my years of fucking men for money, positions, and drugs, I had never had this kind of experience or orgasm—not even with Brad. I was hooked, not only to the bomb-ass cocaine they had, but to the Santanas themselves.

That night ended like all the others. I was high to the point of delirium, and I ended up being put in my penthouse by God knows who.

I awoke to my BlackBerry ringing. I grabbed for it and read the messages. There was one from Sheldon Chisholm. I sat up in my bed, wincing at my spinning head. I placed the phone to my ear and listened.

"Ms. Lomax, I was arrested for a murder I didn't commit. You need to come see me now!" he barked into the receiver.

I almost dropped the phone. What the hell did Sheldon go and do now? He was supposed to keep his shit clean; I mean, he knew his ass was out on bail. I was barely prepared for his simple drug trial with all of the judges getting hemmed up by the feds, and now this.

I stood up on wobbly legs and walked to the bathroom. When I looked up at myself in the mirror, I was horrified. My hair was standing up on my head, and my slanted Asian eyes were almost swollen shut. My cheeks were puffy and my skin was ashen. I was immediately reminded of the old . . . not-so-fabulous me: the Yoshi who barely had two outfits in college and who wore no makeup and never had her hair professionally done.

Looking in that mirror took me back to a sad place in my life—to a time when I was fucking for money just to eat and to help my mother pay my way through school. I looked at myself again and remembered that although I had diamonds, cars, a penthouse, and every designer label imaginable, I was still a third-generation Korean-peasant piece of shit.

I held my head down over the sink and splashed water on my face. I had to do something with myself; I couldn't go back to those days and that was right where I was heading.

I was at the point that I wasn't just dabbling with cocaine; I was full out chasin' it. And it was getting out of control. So out of control that I didn't know if I was coming or going. I knew one thing, though. If I didn't get my shit back in order, I was going to fall flat on my face, and no one was going to help me get back up—not even Maria.

So I yelled for Ophelia to get me a drink from my mini-bar, while I took a hot shower. I knew I was going to need some type of alcohol in me to deal with Sheldon's bullshit this morning. Immediately after I stepped into my tub, I buried my face underneath the shower nozzle for a good five minutes until I was completely awake. Moments later I bathed myself and then I got out of the shower to get dressed. I knew time was of the essence, so it didn't take me long to throw on some attire. I ended up slipping on a pair of Chip & Pepper jeans, along with a cute little button-down Polo shirt. And since I wasn't in the mood to do anything special to my hair, I combed it back into a ponytail and headed out the door.

On my way down to the Miami-Dade County Jail, I told myself to stay calm. Sheldon needed me; it wasn't the other way around. I also told myself that I would be charging his ass another two hundred thousand for this murder case. He'd paid me to get him off on those drug charges, but a body? Nah, he was going to have to come up out of his pocket for this shit. I had already placed a call to the district attorney's office to find out who was on the case. I was told the assistant district attorney assigned to the case was Tiffany Wheatt, and she wasn't one of the ADAs on my payroll.

"Fuck me!" I cursed out loud when I found out who I was assigned. Where the fuck was Brad? He had taken my fucking money and promised me freedom for Sheldon, and up until now I hadn't heard from his fucking ass. I had a bone to pick with him.

I sat in the attorney waiting area as I waited for the CO to bring Sheldon over to me. I didn't realize it at first, but my legs were shaking back and forth nervously. I had to catch myself—this wasn't me. I was usually cool as a cucumber under pressure. But I had noticed that my nerves had been on edge since I started tooting again. So when I looked up and saw them approaching, I inhaled and thought of what I would say.

Sheldon hobbled over to the chair in front of me. He was handcuffed in the front, and his feet were shackled. His face, as usual, held no expression, except for the ugly grill he was born with.

"It's good to know you got my message," he said, frowning.

"Yes, I did," I said, and then I looked down into my folder, like I was looking over some notes.

"So, what's gonna happen now? What are my chances of getting out of here?"

"Mr. Chisholm, they are denying bail this time. You were lucky to get out on bail on those drug charges, but they are not having it this time," I said somberly. I didn't want to admit to him that I couldn't pull one fucking string that day to get him out. It was usually nothing for me to get my clients out on bail, even on fucking murder charges. I had no idea what the fuck was going on. There were new judges everywhere, and when I made some phone calls to my old connections on my way down here, I got nowhere.

It was as if all of my connections had either left abruptly or gotten into some kind of trouble. If I was paranoid, I would think someone was setting them all up just to fuck with me.

"I did not do it," Sheldon said coolly.

"I believe you, but what exactly happened?" I asked. I needed to know all of the circumstances surrounding his arrest.

"I don't know. The police came to my business in the afternoon with a warrant for my arrest. They said they had information about a body that turned up in the ocean two months ago, and that information developed that I was the killer. This fucking murder was a year old," Sheldon explained.

This encounter was the first time I'd really looked him in the eyes, and beyond his tough exterior, I saw a scared little boy. A little boy who'd been wronged by others all of his life, just like Maria had said. Maybe Sheldon and I did have something in common after all.

"Who were the detectives?" I wanted to know.

"Wilson and Maxwell."

"Why didn't you have them contact me before they brought you here?"

"They didn't let me say shit! All they were concerned with was putting me in the back of their squad car."

"Did you answer questions, or did you invoke your right to remain silent?" I shot questions at him like rapid-fire bullets.

"Fuck no, I didn't answer any questions." Sheldon answered me in the same manner.

A dangerous gangster, yes; stupid, no. Sheldon was very smart, and that was why I knew I had to be careful representing him. He had already made things clear for me.

"Listen, I apologize I didn't get here sooner. I was in court all day yesterday on another case. Plus, I've changed offices. I became partner, so I have a new office." I told lie after lie and didn't even blink. That was the telltale sign of an addict, lying without thinking or blinking.

"Well, what's the plan? I can't be in here. I have too many enemies," Sheldon complained, concern underlying his words.

"I'm going to try to get bail set again. But for murder, I'm not so sure. Your record isn't exactly squeaky-clean. I'm going to see what I can do . . . ," I said hesitantly, sending him a clue that I meant I needed more money.

"How much is this new case going to set me back?" Sheldon asked, catching on quickly.

"My retainer and billable hours are each one hundred thousand more than the drug case," I informed him, looking around, to ensure our privacy.

"Call my brother Karumbo, and he will give you your money. Now I want you to remember that I am still paying for my freedom, so don't bullshit me on this one," Sheldon said in a low, harsh whisper, threatening me. He tapped the table, signaling the CO to come get him. I sat there and watched them carry him away.

Believe me, my mind was racing a mile a minute, so I had to think quickly. Since Brad hadn't made the federal case go away yet, now I had to deal with the fucking state case. Although I had connections in the Dade County District Attorney's Office, I didn't know the bitch who was assigned to Sheldon's case. I still needed to find out from Brad what he could do. The feds always had the option to step in and take over a state case. That was exactly what Brad better do.

As I walked to my car, I dialed his number. The first time I dialed it, I got a disconnected message. I thought I had the wrong number, so I redialed it. The same message played, so my blood started boiling.

"This motherfucker disconnected his phone number? What kind of shit is this?" I questioned. And since I knew I would get the answer only from him, I headed right over to his place, going at the speed of one hundred miles per hour. Unfortunately for me, though, when I finally got there, I realized that the bastard wasn't home. How fucking convenient. But it was okay, because I knew where the fuck he worked. So he would be seeing me sooner than he realized.

New Problems

I left Brad's place, drove around the block a few times, and then I turned back around and went right back up to his doorstep. I banged and banged on his door, but still there was no answer.

"Brad, open this door. I know you can see me on those fucking cameras," I called out. I stood there for a good ten minutes; no light was shining from under the door. I pressed my ear to it and no sound came from behind it, either. This was weird. I hadn't given him enough money to say that he had run off with my loot and left me hanging, so I really needed to find out what the hell was going on.

After standing on his front doorstep for an additional five minutes, I decided to leave. Just as I left, I got a call from Maria. I wasn't going to answer it because of our beef with one another, but I really needed some questions answered. I picked up the call. "Hello," I said.

"You finally answered," she commented in a sarcastic manner.

"That's because I feel like talking to you now," I responded.

"So, how have you been?"

"I've been fine, but cut the bullshit and tell me what you

want." I got straight to the point. I mean, there wasn't any reason to beat around the bush. I wanted to know why the hell she was calling.

"I called to see if you were ready to confess."

"Confess about what?" I barked.

"Come on now, Yoshi. You and I both know you had something to do with the disappearance of my agents' informant."

"Are you still on that same bullshit, Maria?"

"Just answer the question."

"Whatcha playing—detective now?"

She sighed. "Yoshi, kill all of that and come straight with me, please. You know I know your ass like a book, and you'd do anything for a fucking dollar, so tell me what went down."

I laughed right in the receiver of the phone. "What is this, a fucking joke? You have got to be kidding me, right?"

"No, Yoshi, this is a serious matter."

"Well, if it's that fucking serious, then you need to go out into the field and start your investigation, because you aren't going to get anywhere on this end. I had absolutely no connection with Juan Alvarez's case blowing up in your guys' faces, and I had no connection with the disappearance of your informant. I am an attorney. And like I've said many times over, I get paid to represent my clients in a courtroom. I don't run around town sabotaging criminal investigations. That's just not what I do. So I suggest you turn off the recorder and get off the phone with me and start investigating your own agents, because that's where the deception lies."

"Yoshi, I'm not recording this conversation. What kind of person do you think I am?"

"The same one who had her agents bust into my office and search it from top to bottom for some bullshit that wasn't there."

"I'm sorry that had to happen. It was out of my control."

"Bullshit, Maria! You know you made that call."

"Seriously, Yoshi, I didn't."

"Well, who dropped the ball then?"

"I can't get into that."

"Well, there's nothing else for us to discuss then."

"Well, okay, that's fine. But let me give you a word of advice, and this is off the record," she said; then she paused.

I let out an irritated sigh. "I'm waiting," I murmured.

She hesitated for a moment and then she said, "Yoshi, it is going to be in your best interest to give up Sheldon Chisholm's case."

Right away I felt that what she was saying was utter bullshit. "Are you fucking nuts? I've got my head buried so far in this fucking case, it's insane, so I can't drop it like that!"

"Yoshi, it's a lot of shit going on, and I think the best thing for you to do is to walk away right now."

"Are you out of your mind? I can't give that case up," I replied, indignantly taken aback by her candor in telling me which case to take and which case to let go of. Who the fuck did she think she was?

"I'm telling you that case reeks of a setup. My agents weren't even notified about the body Sheldon was charged with until this morning. And there are rumors circulating that someone very important wants Sheldon out of the picture and would do anything to do it. I'm telling you, Yoshi, that case stinks, and you better get out while you're ahead," she informed me and warned me, all at the same time.

"Alright, is that it?" I asked, sounding a bit agitated. At this point I wanted nothing else but to get off the phone with her. She was beginning to freak me out, and I wasn't liking it one bit.

"Okay, don't say I didn't warn you. You got caught in the cross fire once. These drug wars involve a lot of unsavory shit, and the bodies start piling up fast . . . lawyers too," she warned again.

She was starting to piss me off, so I ended the call. "Alright, I've heard enough. Talk to you some other time," I said, and disconnected the line.

After Maria's little lecture I pretty much rode home in silence. I realized that things between her and me would never be the same. Even though she gave me leads, she was on one side of the law, and I was indeed on the other. For me, there was no going back. All I could do was wish her the best, because I was going to be fine with that extra five million I had sitting in my account. Too bad Maria didn't have enough sense to get in on the scheme of things. She could've been sitting pretty with a cashier's check, too. But no! She wanted to play all diplomatic, like she had always upheld the law. Well, I had news for her; times had changed and I had turned over a new leaf. I was always going to look out for Yoshi, and there were no ifs or ands or buts about it.

As I drove in the direction of my penthouse, my hands began to shake because I wanted to get high off some of that coke I had in the bottom of my handbag. I knew I had only about four blocks left, but my mind was telling me that was too long a drive. So I reached inside my bag and fumbled around for my drugs, but I couldn't get to it. "Shit!" I cursed. I needed it bad. Finally I stopped at a red light and dug around in the bag a little deeper. "Yes! Found it!" I mumbled.

Now I was going to sniff a quick pinky-nail-full right there in my car. Just a quick toot before I pulled up to my building. But just as I was about to stick my finger into the plastic bag, the red light changed, so I pulled my foot back from the brake. I pressed down on the accelerator really hard, because at this point I was frustrated. I was this close to feeling the potency of that magic dust, but the fucking light changed before I could blink my damn eye. When I sped off, I lost control of my wheel, trying desperately not to drop a speck of my shit. And right about the time I was trying to regain control of my car, flashing red lights broke up my party as quickly as it was about to start. Startled to death, I looked into my rearview mirror and noticed that an unmarked police car was dead on my ass. It seemed like they just popped out of nowhere.

"What the fuck are they pulling me over for?" I screamed, banging my hands on the steering wheel. My nose was dripping snot and my mouth was watering, waiting for a hit of that snow.

I pulled over and put my hazards on. When I peered through the back windshield, I saw a plainclothes officer step out of his car. I was dazed and confused. I threw my coke under my seat. I was so heated. This was a major inconvenience, and I would bet every dime in all my accounts that this bastard knew who I was. Shit, everybody at the Miami-Dade Police Department knew who I was. My license plate spelled out the very letters of my name. I wasn't worried about him giving me a ticket. I wasn't even worried about the cocaine. I was a damn lawyer, I knew my damn rights, and I knew he couldn't search my car without my consent, an arrest, or a search warrant—all of which were distant thoughts in my mind.

"What's the problem, Officer?" I asked as soon as he approached my car.

"Ma'am, I'm stopping you because I witnessed you swerve your vehicle over the yellow line," the cop said as he stood before my window.

"Swerving? That's crazy! I wasn't swerving," I tried to

lie, hoping he'd buy into my lie and give me a warning. Shit, I had only two blocks to go before I reached home. So I knew it would not have been much for him to let me go without any more hassling.

"Ma'am, can I have your license and registration, please?"

"For what? I wasn't swerving, I told you," I began to protest.

"Have you been drinking, ma'am?" he asked.

"No, I haven't." I lied, knowing damn well I had a drink right before I left my house hours ago. I was hoping the shots of Patrón had worn off by now.

"Can you turn off the ignition and step out of the car?" the officer asked. He did not wear a name badge, and he spoke with a really horrible Cuban accent.

"Are you arresting me? If not, I am not stepping out of my car." I both asked *and* told him at the same time.

I watched as he spoke into a small shoulder microphone strapped to his right shoulder. Before I knew it, there were about five cop cars, marked and unmarked, surrounding me like I was a mass murderer. Finally I relented and got out of the car. I failed the Breathalyzer, which, of course, placed me under arrest. In turn, it gave those fucking pigs probable cause to search my car. It was known as a search incident to arrest. This was something I'd helped numerous clients get out of. Cops are so fucking crooked, I thought.

"Bingo!" I heard one cop yell as they all rifled through my shit like they were digging for buried treasure.

I knew right then they'd found my cocaine, so I was definitely going to jail. Not only that, I would be on the other side of the fence with criminals like the ones I defended every day . . . or, worse, with poor criminals who couldn't afford a lawyer of my caliber. I wasn't going down without a fight. I kicked, screamed, and called those cops every name in the book. I acted like a straight fool. I flailed my arms and legs and screamed my name out.

"Y'all don't know who the fuck ya messing with!" I kept screaming. "I'm Yoshi Lomax! The most wealthy and powerful attorney around here! I know your fucking superiors, so I will have your badges and you will be in the fucking unemployment line before you can blink your eyes!"

Those officers were not fazed at all by ranting and raving; they couldn't care less who I was—I was losing my touch. There wasn't one face on the scene that I recognized from my contacts in the police department, and nobody there was on my fucking payroll. With no other recourse in a desperate time, I started name-dropping, hoping to help my situation. I even dropped the name of the Miami-Dade chief of police; that just made shit worse. The cops seemed to grow angry at my egotistic move. They were looking at me with contempt, as if to say, "Who does this bitch think she is?" I was fucked, and I knew it. One Black cop looked at me and grumbled to a Hispanic officer, saying, "This is the bitch that got all those detectives hemmed up in that corruption investigation."

"Oh yeah, she was the one who was documenting the bribes and shit," the Hispanic officer replied.

I had no idea what the fuck he was talking about. An investigation? I had no clue what was going on, but I planned on finding out as soon as I got out of this mess.

On the way down to the precinct, I started praying to God that the arresting officers took me in front of my magistrate friend Karen Studds. But if they didn't, I also prayed that she'd be somewhere in the vicinity. All my worries would be over because she and I went back a long way. We'd been friends for a few years, so I knew this little problem of mine would go away like magic. Especially after all the shit I'd done for her. Shit, I'd represented her husband on several charges. Not to mention the fact that I charged her way below my normal fees. So I knew I had a favor coming from her. Besides, it was only a little coke and a DUI charge. Anybody with some damn sense, and knowing who I was, would look at my charges, laugh, and let me go immediately. That was what I needed right now, and that was what I expected to get when I set foot inside that jail.

Rock Bottom

Sitting in jail made me think of some things my mother had said to me as a child. Anytime she wasn't pleased with me, she would say, "Yoshi, you are going to be a drug addict and an alcoholic and end up in prison just like your father," her shrill voice cracking in Korean. From what I could gather, my mother hated my father's guts after he left. She spoke of him only when the situations around the house got really bad. Like when we didn't have food, or when a man would leave her bedroom and leave her crying. It was my father's fault, all of it. When she made me smile for the men and wear sexy lingerie for them, if I ever complained, she would blame my father. But I dismissed it and thought how crazy her ass was.

I believed to this day that if he had never left New York, or if we had followed my father down to Virginia, my life would've been a lot better. I wouldn't be so bitter and hard toward men. But, hey, what can I say? Wishful thinking. So I don't dwell on that.

I still do have three pictures of him, and from what I observed, I'm the spitting image of him. Granted, he was a Black man, but he was a fine Black man with prominent features. His head was covered with tight curls, like he was mixed with some other race—maybe half white or Spanish. Believe me when I say my father was gorgeous. I believed that if he was still alive, he would probably look the same.

Unfortunately for me, when he passed away, not more than six years after he left New York, I was unable to attend his funeral. My mother told me that the next time I saw my father would be when I met my Maker. And she was serious as hell, too. Because when it was all said and done, I was still in New York while the funeral service was going on. I remember crying like a baby when she denied me from going down South. And what was really crazy was that she didn't have to pay for my travel. My father's mother, Grandma Anna, and my aunt Priscilla told my mother that they would drive the six and a half hours it took to get to New York to come and get me. But that didn't matter to her. She stuck to her guns and kept my ass right in New York. I knew she did it to get back at my father, but she didn't realize that it didn't affect him, it affected me. And to this day, I was still being affected by it. I just hoped that one day I'd be able to get over it and forgive my mother for keeping me away from him.

Watching all of the prostitutes and crack addicts move like zombies around the crowded holding cell, I thought about what my mother would say if she could see me right now—probably something very demeaning, as usual. This shit was definitely beneath me. Here I was, decked out in designer clothes, sitting in a fucking jail cell with all of my shit confiscated. I sat still on the hard bench inside the jail like a mannequin on display. If another cop or detective or even a clerk had come to the cell to peek at me, I was going to scream. Apparently, word had gotten around that I was locked up. Was I the famous, or the infamous, Yoshi Lomax? At this point I couldn't even say myself. I put my head in my hands and tried to think about my next move.

There weren't many options, because as soon as I was

processed, they took me straight in front of the magistrate. It wasn't my girl Karen, so you know I was pissed. They took me in front of this idiot, Timothy Hawthorne. He was a fucking redneck, and I'd never liked him. So it didn't surprise me when he denied my bail. "Bail denied!" he said sharply.

I looked at the tobacco-chewing son of a bitch like he was crazy and said, "What kind of shit is this? You are acting like I killed some damn body! I am an officer of the courts!" I protested.

He laughed. "You call yourself an officer of the courts?"

"You damn right I do! It's evident! Check out my fucking stats and turn on the television sometimes. I'm on damn near every fucking channel." I got cocky in my response to him.

"You are a disgrace, is what you are," he commented. "You are out of line. Return to your seat or I will have you removed," he barked, looking directly at the deputy who stood beside me.

Steaming, I damn near spat in that motherfucker's face. I said, "You're a piece of shit! You tobacco-eating fucking redneck! I got people like you cleaning my fucking toilets at home, so you could never be like me. You jealous bastard! I bet you want to fuck me, that's why you carrying me like this. As a matter of fact, all of you underpaid motherfuckers want to fuck me, but it'll never happen! I'm too high-class for you! You'd never be on my level! Never!" I screamed at the top of my voice.

By the time I uttered the very last word, the deputy had dragged me back to the holding cell. Everyone who was standing around, including my other criminal counterparts, looked at me like I was fucking crazy, but I didn't give a damn. I was mad. I was mad to the point that I'd swing at the next person who said something smart to me. At this point I couldn't care less what would happen next. I figured the worst has already happened; I was in fucking jail and these bastards were acting like they didn't want me to leave. But fuck that! They were going to let me out, one way or another. I could guarantee you that.

Twelve hours passed and it was time for me to go in front of the judge. I just prayed that it was one that I knew. Other than that, my options were going to be very limited.

A few hours earlier they gave me the green light to make my one phone call, but I elected not to use it. I figured, what would be the use? I had no one to call. Everyone at my law firm hated my fucking guts, so this would be the opportune time to laugh right in my damn face. It was also of no use to call my housekeeper, because it was not like she could've come and bailed me out. And I couldn't call Maria, and deal with more of her wrath. If I called Brad, he would be too embarrassed about his precious reputation to come down and rescue me—there was no way he'd be associated with something like this in public. I couldn't call Paul, because my arrest would be the kind of news that would make his day. He would liken my downfall to the fact that I wasn't fucking him anymore. Not only would I get fired, but he'd also have a field day with my reputation.

My mind then went immediately to Luis and Adrianna; I knew they'd pick me up and pass no judgments on me. Plus, they'd have some of that blazing-ass coke waiting for me. But then, at the last minute, I decided against it. I figured, I might as well wait and see what happened when I went before the judge. Taking a chance on my own destiny was what I'd been doing my entire life, this situation was no different.

"Lomax!" the officer called, startling me out of my thoughts. There were about twenty officers outside the cell staring at me. If looks could kill, I would've dropped dead. I got up from the bench and walked to the cage door. The tall, lanky officer opened the cell and placed me in hand-cuffs. I was led out for court and my legs felt like mush. Not only did I need a sniff to get me over the anxiety that was bubbling in my stomach, but my nerves were like prickly needles that stood on end. The slightest noise, movement, or touch made me feel like screaming. My mouth was cotton-ball dry and I could feel sweat descending my spine like a leaky pipe—one drop at a time. I just knew my bowel would release at any time.

When the officer ushered me through the solid oak doors at the side of the empty jury bench, I looked out into the crowded room. I was astonished at how many people were there. I'd never paid attention to how much despair riddled the faces of the loved ones of the defendants. Right now, that was exactly what I was—a defendant, one who had no-body in the courtroom and no one to call on for advice. Even though I could afford a lawyer, I was too embarrassed to contact any well-known ones for fear they'd ridicule me—their peer. I began to wish I had somebody, anybody, to call. It was then that I realized what Maria had been drilling into my head for years: "Yoshi, you can play big and bad, but everybody needs somebody."

Walking into the courtroom as the defendant, and not the defense attorney, was the most humiliating thing I'd en-countered since the day my mother beat me with a broom-stick in front of my friends. I wanted the ordeal to be over quickly, and I prayed all the way to the front of the defen-dant's bench that I did not run into any attorneys from Shapiro and Witherspoon. I looked up and noticed the judge. *Whew!* I breathed a short sigh of relief; it was a judge I knew.

The judge looked just as surprised to see me there as I

was to see her. We exchanged telling glances, but neither of us said a word. When I stood before Judge Rita Marshall, I knew I was going to be set free.

I had so much dirt on that bitch, she knew better than to play around. I'd had her on a trial once and she was just doing me in, never letting any of my objections be sustained and always cutting me off midsentence with "Counsel, let's move on." So I fixed that bitch. I'd heard that she swung both ways, but I also knew she was married to the deputy mayor, who wanted to run for mayor someday.

First, I hired a private detective to get some dirt on a few of the jurors. Then I had him follow Ms. Rita for a while. Sure enough, jackpot! The private detective provided me pictures of the judge inside a lesbian hot spot at the southern tip of Miami—and oh yes, she was tonguing down a chick. During my next court session, I threw the envelope with the pictures in it right onto her bench, after one of her "Counsel, let's move on." Judge Rita Marshall almost turned invisible, that's how white she was with shock. Needless to say, court was adjourned early that day and I won my case hands down.

Now here we were, in another face-off of sorts.

"Judge, we propose that the defendant be remanded without bail until the preliminary hearing," the prosecutor said as she stood up. It was the same bitch, Tiffany Wheatt, who was assigned to the Chisholm murder case. My heart sank when I heard her name. That was all I needed, for Sheldon to find out his high-priced lawyer was a jailbird cokehead.

"This is the defendant's first offense, Your Honor. She is not a flight risk, nor did she have enough drugs to qualify for distribution charges. I would think release on her own recognizance, with a date to return for service order, is enough," said Lucy Green, my little court-appointed lawyer. I remained silent, waiting for the decision.

I wondered if Judge Marshall was going to try to fuck me royally, like I'd done her. I decided to play it tough-ass. Maybe if she thought I still had those pictures, then her husband, who was now the mayor, would be humiliated, so I winked at her. In turn, she grunted and turned a sick-looking shade of pink. It was as if someone had thrown pink paint blotches on her face from a distance.

"Ahem"—she cleared her throat—"defendant will be released on her own recognizance for return in thirty days for service plan," she said begrudgingly. I looked at Rita, as if to say, "You better had, you lesbian bitch!"

After I was processed out of this roach-infested jail, which took another two hours, I ran out of the courthouse. I was mentally and physically exhausted. A few weeks ago, I was a superstar with everyone, including Paul and Maria, in my corner. Now it seemed like nothing else could go wrong and I was all alone. My experience with getting arrested, and almost not having any options, taught me that everybody needed somebody. I just wanted to go home, take a nice, long, hot shower, and get my mind right.

Wake-up Call

When I became a free woman again, I had nothing. They'd kept my car and all of the belongings I had with me. I was given a voucher and told I could pick up my shit on the next business day. Were they fucking kidding me? I needed money. How the fuck was I supposed to get home? After thinking about it for a minute, I reluctantly decided to walk to the firm. The courthouse was closer to my office than to my house, and I had a small amount of cash and cocaine in the bottom locked drawer of my desk. I needed both right now—the cocaine to get me through the rest of the day and my cash to get home. I knew I had a little ways to go and I needed to make it to the office, so I kicked off my Gucci sandals and got to walking. I could not believe this shit. I—the great Yoshi Lomax—had to fucking walk the streets. As I passed the regular working-class people, with their slumping shoulders and heavy loads, and the homeless people, with faces of hunger and despair, I realized that all the stuff that I had could be gone in a flash. I guess I wasn't immune to failure after all. I looked at a homeless woman slumped up against an office building. She looked half dead, and I wondered if she was ever as great as me and had let drugs be her downfall.

My mind was heavy as I continued toward the office. I

realized that I was slowly losing it all, and as much as I thought I was in control of shit, I could see that maybe I wasn't as strong and disciplined as I always thought I was. If I believed in voodoo—as fast as shit was going bad for me—I would've believed that someone had put a curse on me.

By the time I reached my office building, I was beat the fuck up and haggard out. My feet felt numb, and the aches I felt for a hit of coke had me almost running into the building. I knew I looked like pure shit, but I couldn't care less what the motherfuckers at Shapiro and Witherspoon thought about me right now. Since I'd been put out of my office suite, I knew I could make it to my new tiny hole-in-the-wall without running into Paul. When I had about fifty feet left to get to the building, I slid my sandals back on, held my head up high, and walked through the front doors of the firm like my shit didn't stink. I sped past all of the nosy-ass lawyers that I called my coworkers and burst into the safety of my office.

I closed my door, put my back up against it, and slid down to the floor. If I was the crying type, I would've broken down. Instead, I sighed and shook my head from side to side. "What are you doing, Yoshi? What has become of you?" I asked myself under my breath. I couldn't even answer my own questions, but I knew that I really needed to pull myself together. As much as I thought about losing my job, my home, and my good name, none of that could stop my urge to get high. I looked over at my locked desk and scrambled up off the floor. My cocaine was waiting for me—calling out to me. I got down on my knees and searched under my chair for the spare key to my desk.

"Got it!" I said, growing excited. With my hands unsteady, I fumbled with the lock. I felt like a real fiend. It was sad, but I kept going, and when the drawer finally slid open, there it was. My girl . . . snow white! I sprinkled the beautiful powder out on my desk, and just as I put my head down to snort, there was a loud knock on my door. I almost jumped out of my skin. I couldn't just leave that beautiful white dust there, it was calling to me.

"Fuck!" I grumbled. I sniffed half the pile of coke, and swiped the rest back into the canteen. The knocking grew louder and louder, so I became paranoid and I was pissed at the same time. "Who is it?" I yelled, but I got no answer.

I got another knock, though. "Who is it?" I screamed again as I got to my feet. On my way to the door, I smoothed my clothes out as best I could. Then I grabbed a hold of the doorknob and flung it open as hard as I could. And standing right before my eyes was Paul's worrisome ass. Someone either told him I was in the building or he smelled me.

"You are skating on thin ice, Yoshi," he threatened, pushing his way into my office.

My heart thumped. Oh, my God, did he know about my arrest or about the cocaine in my desk? I could never confess to it. He would hang my ass out to dry. But what if he had cameras put in my office after our little disagreement, I thought as he bullied his way around me. Ultimately he invited himself in and closed the door behind him.

"What are you talking about now, Paul?" I asked, sniffling. I was hoping there was no coke residue on my nose.

"You sent my wife a letter, you bitch," he growled, whispering and accusing me.

"I did what—" I started, but Paul jumped into my personal space.

"Don't play dumb with me, Yoshi! You know what the fuck I am talking about!"

"Look, I don't have time—" I began to say, but yet again he cut me off in midsentence.

"Bitch, you better have time!" he spat back. "You are so lucky Witherspoon and the firm's board don't want to fire your sleazy ass! But I will tell you this, you are going down," he threatened, storming out just as fast as he'd come in.

He hadn't let me get a word in edgewise. I had no fucking idea what note he was referring to. I hadn't told his wife anything. Although I kept saying I was going to send her an anonymous letter telling her stuff about Paul, I never had the time, between fucking the Santanas and chasing my high. I giggled to myself. Paul was all bark and no bite, I reasoned. He wasn't going to do a damn thing to me. Like he said, no matter what, I was protected by Mr. Witherspoon and the board. Those motherfuckers knew I was still the firm's top biller, so they'd be a fool to let me go. Besides that, I was the only attorney they had who would take on some of the most dangerous clients. Those corny-ass lawyers in this entire firm wouldn't even take the cases of rappers. I didn't know if they were afraid or just straight prejudiced. Whatever the reason, I was fine with it. They just left all the big-paying clients to me and I loved it.

As soon as Paul left, I locked the door behind him and picked up where I'd left off. I snorted up the entire canteen of coke. I felt really lifted and better about my situation. No one would ever find out I'd been arrested and humiliated. The drugs had me feeling confident and powerful again, like the old Yoshi Lomax. I picked up the black drawer insert in the center drawer of my desk and took out the small stack of cash I had stashed there. It was my emergency fund, just in case I ever got a client who needed to be impressed. I flicked through the money. There was enough there for me to get more coke and to get home in a taxi.

I decided to check my messages before I left. I lifted my phone and punched in my code for my office voice mail. There was a message from Maria. She was telling me how angry she was at me for not heeding her warnings. I didn't even listen to the entire message; I deleted it.

Next, there was a message from Sheldon. As usual, he wanted to speak with me and it was urgent. Every fucking thing with him was urgent. I would go and see him tomorrow. Which reminded me, I needed to start working on his murder case, and I definitely needed to get in touch with Brad. That bastard had changed his phone number. Brad owed me the acquittal for Sheldon's drug charge, and he was going to come through or else. Sheldon's pretrial hearing would be in another week. If I was late or missed that, he was liable to send someone after me.

There were two messages from Luis Santana. He wanted to invite mc to another private party. I erased the messages, with a sick feeling in the pit of my stomach. He had gotten too comfortable with inviting me to his little parties.

"Well, I got what I came here for. Now I need to get home and wash my ass," I mumbled to myself. I felt dirty as hell. I looked around my office one last time. That small-ass office was a reminder of just how badly shit was going for me . . . down-fucking-hill.

As soon as I opened my door to leave, I was startled by two men; they were standing directly in front of my door, like they were waiting for me.

"Shit! You fucking scared me!" I said, placing my hand over my heart. I had no idea who the two huge men were, but after a few seconds, I kind of had an idea. Neither of them said a word. "Can I help you?" I asked.

Then one stepped forward and began walking toward me, backing me up into the office. They both came in as I walked backward to my desk.

"Who are you?" I asked nervously.

"Mr. Chisholm has been trying to reach you," a very tall,

bald black guy growled. He was standing so close to me, I could see the enlarged pores on his face.

"I just saw him, not even twenty-four hours ago. What could he want now?" I asked.

"He wants to have another meeting with you. So he wants you to come back down to the jail so you two can talk," the same guy said.

"I have court in the morning, so that's going to be kind of hard," I replied.

"Well, Mr. Chisholm needs you down at the jail, so I'm sure you'll do the right thing."

"I do have other clients," I snapped back.

"I'm sure, but Mr. Chisholm will take precedence right now," he threatened, simultaneously sweeping his hand over his waistband to make sure I saw his gun. The fucking nerve of him! I was Sheldon's lawyer, not his fucking slave or his fucking wife. I was enraged, but I held it back.

"Tell Mr. Chisholm I will come see him right after court, which will probably be no later than noon." I had to play tough. They had me pissed the fuck off, invading me like this.

"No. You will go tomorrow morning, first visit," the same man said. His Haitian accent was very prominent. He looked similar to Sheldon; I wondered if it was his brother or some other relative of his.

"Alright, I will be there," I relented. It didn't make sense to say I wasn't going to go, because either they'd kill me right there in the office, or we would be there all day going back and forth. And I wasn't in the mood for that bullshit! I wanted to get home and take a fucking shower. I felt like shit. If one more fucking strange thing happened, I was liable to have a nervous fucking breakdown. I was paranoid now, between the shit with Paul and then Sheldon sending his henchmen. I didn't know what the fuck was coming next.

After Sheldon's men left, I walked downstairs and caught a taxi to my house. But before I walked out of the building, I had a dozen eyes staring at me. They were all wondering why I was looking the way I was looking. But they weren't that bold to ask.

And what was even funnier was when I stepped to the curb to hop into a nearby taxi, all the valet drivers stood there in disbelief. I imagined they were wondering where the hell my car was. And why was I dressed down in a pair of jeans with my hair thrown back in a ponytail?

I had never come to work like this, so I knew that they were assuming something was really wrong with me. At this juncture I didn't care how they looked at me. I was on a mission, and until everything came to a head, they might see me like this a few more times.

Drama and More Drama

With the police department seizing my Aston Martin, I was forced to use an alternate method of transportation to get home. That was some bullshit, but it was procedure for Miami PD. If a defendant was busted for drugs, they had to await the outcome of their case before the car was returned to them. As the taxi driver drove away from the firm, I sighed and sank down into the cracked leather seats. I sat in the back, leaned my head back, and prayed for my bed.

When I reached my building, I'd never been so happy to see the smiling face of my doorman. For the first time since I'd moved into the swank high-rise, I didn't have enough cash to offer him a tip for opening the car door for me. I could've given him what I had left of my cocaine money, but my brain was telling me that no one else deserved to spend my fucking money, but me.

I started to apologize, but then decided he'd gotten plenty from me in the past. "Fuck him," I mumbled under my breath. The doorman looked at me strangely; it was like he pitied me. I saw his entire demeanor change through my peripheral vision as I walked away. I turned around to give him a brief stare, just to catch him off guard, but my whole mission was thrown off when I looked back and saw an unmarked car posted on the other side of my street facing my building.

Inside were two detectives in plain clothes. Both of them were Caucasian men with crew cuts, like they were straight out of the military. But what spooked me about them was that they weren't trying to hide themselves. They sat in their car with their front windows rolled down, like they wanted me to see them.

At that moment I became angry, because not only did they invade my office, but now they were bringing that shit to my home. I couldn't have that. I knew I couldn't walk over to them and tell them to carry their asses away, because they were on public domain. But I could give those bastards my ass to kiss and then take myself up to my penthouse apartment. That would make me feel real good. But then I figured, what good would that do?

Instead of giving those clowns any of my time, I walked back up to the doorman and asked how long those detectives had been parked there.

"Oh, they've been parked there for about an hour now," he replied.

"Have they been into the building?" I wanted to know.

"No, they haven't gotten out of the car," he continued, and then he said, "But I'm sure they're staking out someone who lives in this building."

"I'm sure they are, too," I responded. The words he had uttered pierced my mind and gave me an instant stomach-ache. I had to get away, so I walked off without saying another word. It was obvious that this clown had no idea what was going on. If he knew that those detectives were there watching my every move, he'd probably shit bricks and tell everyone inside the entire building. I couldn't have that. That would be too much drama for me.

I held the keys to my penthouse in my hand during the

elevator ride and all I could think about were those idiots who were parked outside. I knew they were from Maria's office, so I was tempted to call her to see why they were posted outside my damn building. Hadn't they had enough of invading my privacy? This shit was getting out of control, and I wasn't going to take too much more of their bullshit! When I reached my door, I noticed a package in front.

"Now, why hasn't Ophelia picked this up?" I grumbled. I lifted the small paper-bag-colored box. It was addressed to me, with no return address. I hoisted it under my arm and continued inside. My first thought was that Maria's people must've left it there to set me up. But then I remembered my doorman telling me that they hadn't come into the building, so it would've been impossible for them to set this package here.

Immediately after I entered my home, I inhaled deeply and exhaled slowly, once I passed the threshold of my own door.

"Phew, what the fuck is that smell?" I complained aloud. Now, I knew Ophelia could not have been here, because if she had, she damn sure had some fucking explaining to do. There was a stench emanating throughout my entire penthouse. It smelled like rotting garbage coming from my kitchen, and I wasn't about to go clean or take out any fucking garbage. That is what I paid Ophelia to do.

I threw the box onto the small occasional table that sat in my foyer and headed straight for my bedroom. I needed a hot shower and my own bed. Everything in the house was just as I'd left it thirty-six hours ago. It looked like Ophelia had never come in to clean or do any of her regular work.

Although I hadn't ventured to the front of my penthouse, where the kitchen was, I could still tell that Ophelia hadn't done anything at all in the house, and that fucking smell was killing me. Not only that, Ophelia not showing up for work struck me as strange. She had been so loyal to me over the years, so something had to be wrong. Maybe she had a family emergency and couldn't contact me because I was locked up. Yeah, that probably was it. And since I had too much shit on my mind to dwell on it, I went about my merry way.

I peeled off the dirty-ass clothes I had on the entire time I had been detained. If my outfit hadn't cost two grand, calculating the top, the bottom, and the shoes, I would've burned that shit. I left the dirty clothes right where I stepped out of them. That was my usual way. Ophelia would get them, and so I wasn't worried about it.

After I turned on the shower, I hopped inside the tub and let the steaming hot water rain down on my body like it was coming from heaven itself. I picked up my Origins coconut shampoo and washed my hair, over and over again. I wanted to wash away the dirt from that jail cell and, if possible, the demons that were haunting my brain.

When I stepped out of my glass-encased shower, I immediately clicked on the TV that hung over the tub. It was a force of habit. The weather was on the news; I'd missed all the headlines, so I just clicked through the channels. "Nothing on TV as usual," I complained into the air. I walked back out into my bedroom and flopped down on my soft pillow-top bed. "Ahh, home sweet home."

I looked around my room and realized that I really had it going on. I lived in the lap of luxury, and I wasn't going to lose my shit at no cost. Since my personal belongings, including my BlackBerry, were with the police, I flipped open my laptop to retrieve my messages. I was sure there'd be a bunch. I assumed there would be a lot of new client requests, and more messages from Maria.

I really didn't want to hear from anyone. It was bad enough the fucking DEA was parked outside my building. I couldn't tell you what they were doing, because I'm not a mind reader. However, if they thought they were going to catch me speaking to Juan Alvarez, they had another thing coming. My business with that man was over. That chapter of my life was closed. So they had better move along and investigate someone else.

I was able to pick up my BlackBerry messages through my computer and there was a message from an address that I didn't recognize: **OPEN YOUR PACKAGE**. I looked at the e-mail address and could not place it. I sent a message back, but got nothing in return.

I noticed that the e-mail address was a phone number, like it had been sent from a cell phone. I reached over and grabbed my house landline and dialed the number. It just rang, and when the voice mail picked up, there was no one's voice on the other end, just the standard computer-generated greeting.

I'd actually forgotten someone had left me a package, until I read that message. I immediately wondered if it was another gift from Luis and Adrianna, or maybe Mr. Choo. Then again, it could have been Mr. Heimlich, another rich bastard whose life I'd saved. I put on my plush white terry cloth robe and walked back into the foyer to retrieve the package.

When I lifted the box, I took a mental note that things inside the box were shifting around. There weren't too many people loving me right now . . . so curiosity had me ripping at the box like a maniac. When I finally got the box opened, the first thing I saw shining at me was a badge. I picked up the small gold badge with blue writing and read it. *DEA*. Then I read the badge number: *7757*. "Maria's badge?" I mumbled. A pang of panic struck me in the gut and I frantically began pulling things out of the box.

I found Maria's DEA credentials, with her picture and

her gun holster. I dropped the items back into the box, shaking my head back and forth. I was confused. My hands were suddenly shaking uncontrollably. This shit was strange and didn't seem right. I raced into my bedroom, tripping over my own feet. I dived onto the bed to reach my phone. I hit the speed dial for Maria's number. Her voice mail came straight on. Her phone was off. I scrolled through my contacts and dialed Hanna, Maria's sister. No answer.

"What the fuck is going on!" I screamed. Although our last conversation wasn't all that pleasant, Maria's belongings being mailed to me just didn't sit right with me. Wouldn't she need them for work every day? I contemplated calling the police. She could be hurt and whoever had her had sent her things to me, to send me a message. Then I decided against it. What if this was a false alarm? But then I figured that it couldn't be. People don't play games like this.

While I was trying to make sense of what was going on, I hadn't even realized I was walking around my floor in circles. Then a couple minutes later, six or seven loud knocks hit my front door. The shit startled the hell out of me. And before I could make my way to see who it was, the knocks got louder and became more frequent. The knocks sounded more like loud bangs.

When I approached the foyer that led to the front door, I stared down the hallway. I couldn't believe it, I was scared to go near the door. I had no idea what the fuck was going on. The knocks grew louder and louder, and whoever it was who was knocking was not going to give up easily. Finally I grabbed Maria's things and stuffed them back into the box. I hurriedly put the box in my hallway closet before I approached the door.

"Who is it?" I screamed from my side of the door.

"DEA!" a man's voice called out from the other side. I didn't trust that shit. Not right now. Not with Paul sneaking up on me and Sheldon's goons threatening me. It could've been anyone behind that door. But then again, I figured that it would be the idiots who were posted outside my building. So I immediately thought, what did they want with me? To search my house for evidence that could link me to Juan Alvarez? Nah, that couldn't be it. And if it was, it was definitely a lost cause for them.

"What can I do for you?" I asked, my face pressed close to the door.

"We need to talk to you about Maria Hernandez," the man stated. He had me when he said Maria's name. I pulled back the door to find the same two men who had been sitting outside in their unmarked car. They wore the usual black suits, wingtip shoes, and low buzz-cut hair. Both men immediately rushed into my penthouse foyer before I could say a word.

"I need to see some ID," I demanded. Both men pulled out credentials at the same time.

"What is going on?" I asked.

"Ms. Lomax, we are here to investigate the disappearance of Maria Hernandez. From what we understand, you may have been the last person to have spoken with her," the taller agent Patterson, stated.

"Where is she?" I asked; the question just rolled off my tongue unconsciously. My nerves completely took over my actions and I could not recant what I had just said, even though I wanted to do it badly. All I could think about was the package with Maria's things in it, and now this. . . . The total picture wasn't looking so good. And it appeared that I was smack-dab in the middle of this shit. At the very moment my stomach knotted up, I wanted to vomit.

"That's what we need to find out," the other agent interjected.

"Well, we would normally have lunch a couple of times

a week. But lately my schedule has been so hectic, I hadn't been able to commit."

"Cut the crap! We know you two haven't been on good terms since our investigation with Juan Alvarez went bust!" the taller agent insisted.

"Well, if you know everything, then why are you here asking me questions?" I snapped.

"Let us ask the questions, please," the other agent spoke up.

I stood there with disgust written all over my face. I wanted to tell these crackers to get out of my damn house, but I wasn't trying to ruffle their feathers. I figured the best tactic to use would be to be nice and to cooperate so they could carry their asses away. "Look, I spoke with her less than forty-eight hours ago. We talked very briefly, and then that was it. I haven't spoken with her since," I explained.

My mind was racing with thoughts. I didn't know if I should tell them that someone mailed me Maria's things. The way things were looking, they weren't too happy with me because of Juan Alvarez. So I knew if I told them about the package, they wouldn't believe me. They'd probably handcuff me on the spot and haul my ass down to their headquarters. They went strictly by the "arrest now, talk later" policy, and I wasn't up for that one. I had just gotten out of jail, so I couldn't stand for another overnight stay. And the way things were looking with this, there was no telling how long I'd be there with them.

"Did Maria say where she was, when you last spoke with her?" the shorter agent asked. I thought about it for a minute and reflected back on our conversation.

"No, as a matter of fact, she didn't," I said flatly.

"Where have you been for the past thirty-six hours?" the taller agent asked.

Shit! I thought. If I tell them I was locked up on other charges, it was bound to get back to Paul and the other attorneys. I would be a laughingstock, and these bastards right here would tell it all. So I hesitated for a second, trying to think of a good lie, but then I decided against it. Who was I kidding? These motherfuckers were going to check my alibi as soon as they walked out my front door. And when they found out that I was lying, they were going to really be down my ass then, and I couldn't have that, especially when I hadn't done shit. So, what was I to do? I definitely couldn't tell them I had been arrested for possession of cocaine. After all, they were the DEA—so their next question would be, where did I get my drugs from? Now that was some heat I did not need.

"You guys know that I am a defense attorney, so I've been back and forth to court, and I spent days at my office preparing for my upcoming trial," I lied.

It seemed like they were suspicious of me for some reason. They looked from me to each other, and then around my foyer. Both of them kept putting their arms over their noses; I guess they were smelling the same shit I smelled when I first came it. I had grown immune to it after being in the house for a while. But that fucking garbage was stinking. I was embarrassed as hell, but I just played it off. Ophelia was really going to get cursed out by me.

I knew they wanted to ask if they could look around, but they didn't. If they thought that I was some regular old lawyer, fresh out of law school, they probably would have coerced me into searching my house. But since they knew who they were dealing with, they didn't try me. Not only that, I was very vague with them, answering only the direct questions that they asked. I was not volunteering anything. I definitely wasn't going to tell them about Maria's stuff until I could speak to her family. I avoided direct eye contact with them. I was always taught that lies shined through a person's eyes.

"Okay, Ms. Lomax, if you should hear from Maria, or think of anything or anyone that would help us, please call me," the taller agent said as he handed me a business card. The other agent let his eyes rove around my foyer and down my hallway toward the kitchen. He didn't look too comfortable with my answers, but he remained quiet and didn't say another word.

"I will definitely do that," I assured them. "May I ask you a couple of questions before you leave?"

"Sure, go ahead," the taller one insisted.

"When did you realize Maria had gone missing?"

"Sometime after she had spoken to you," he replied without hesitation.

"But how?" I wondered aloud.

"We aren't sure."

"Have you spoken with her sister?"

"No, we haven't spoken with her, as of yet. But we have a few more agents parked outside her residence, even as we speak. So we'll get her as soon as she arrives home."

"Kind of the same way you got me, huh?"

"You can say that."

"Well, do you know where she could have gone missing?"

"I'm sorry, but we don't have the answers to those questions. I wish we did, but something will surface," he said with assurance.

Listening to the confidence level in his tone got me even sicker. I hadn't put a shred of food in my stomach, but it sure felt like I had. My nerves were tearing me apart, and I definitely needed a hit of coke now. There were too many things being thrown at me at once and I couldn't handle it.

"Alright, gentlemen, will you please excuse me?" I insinuated that it was time for them to leave. I couldn't take the pressure any longer.

They both took heed and stepped toward the front door. "Don't forget to call me if you hear anything," the shorter one reminded me.

"I won't," I told him, and then I let them out.

By the time the DEA agents left, my entire body was drenched in sweat and I felt sick inside. If something had really happened to Maria, I wouldn't be any good. She was basically the only friend I had, until this mess came about, and I would take all the blame. I just wished she would not have told me about Juan Alvarez and then we would still be cool. And who knows—we'd probably be somewhere having lunch and a few cocktails.

When they left, I watched through the peephole as they got onto the elevator. When I was sure they were gone, I grabbed the box out of the closet. I poured out the contents and sifted through the items for a second time. That was when I noticed the silver rewritable DVD inside. I lifted it up and there were black words written in horrible handwriting, *Play Me*. I almost dropped the DVD.

This shit had become scary now. Someone was sending me these things for a reason, and I knew that I wouldn't find out what they were until I stuck the disc inside my DVD player and pressed play. It took me about three minutes to get up the gumption to do just that. When I raced into my living room and slipped the DVD into the player, I caught an instant headache. I grabbed both sides of my head, like I was about to pull my hair out at the roots.

"Arrggh, what the fuck is going on!" I screamed, thinking about the huge possibility that I would find out what happened with Maria on this very DVD. And then a thought flashed before my eyes. What if she needed my help? I had to make sure she was okay. I finally decided to press play. My heart was racing at the speed of light and my palms immediately got sweaty. I tried to focus on the screen, but the picture was blurry. It wasn't my flat screen that was off, it was the poor quality of the video itself.

I took a seat on my sofa and waited for whoever filmed this crap to focus their camera lens. The first thing I saw was a note that the person with the video camera zoomed in on. The note was written on a crumpled piece of yellow legal pad paper, like the legal pads I used every day to take client notes. The note read:

This recording has already been sent to the police and the DEA. Good luck defending yourself out of this one, Ms. Lomax, famous defense attorney.

"What!" I reacted out loud, my eyes wide. That note made me fast-forward the video. I stopped when I saw what looked like the inside of my apartment being videotaped. As the camera moved from room to room, and as I watched more and more of the DVD, I realized it *was* the inside of my apartment! There was video of my bedroom, just as I'd left it, my bathrooms, my kitchen . . . and that was when I noticed her.

I pushed back onto my couch at the sight of her. My mouth hung open and goose bumps came up all over my skin. It was Maria! "No!" I screamed. Tears immediately invaded the surface of my eyeballs.

Maria was tied to a chair in my kitchen. My heart thumped so hard, I couldn't breathe. I started coughing. I kept my eyes glued to the screen; I couldn't move. I was stuck. I watched as a tall female, with long black hair that looked just like mine, walked over to Maria and slapped the shit out of Maria's face.

"Mmmm," Maria groaned under the duct tape that covered her mouth. I could see tears in Maria's eyes. I watched the female as she moved. She really looked like me from behind, even down to her height, her walk, and her shape. The impersonator was wearing my red Chanel suit, the one I'd worn the day I was shot in front of the courthouse—what I'd saved as my "bad luck" suit. I was astonished. I had to do a double take myself.

The impersonator on the tape slapped Maria again. Maria's head bobbled like it would break off from her neck. Maria struggled and wriggled against the thick nautical rope. I had to watch closely, because the female even had on my shoes and jewelry. The unknown female walked over to Maria and said something to her . . . but I couldn't hear it. I fumbled with my TV remote, trying to turn up the volume. Finally I turned it all the way up, but I still couldn't hear anything. Then Maria's voice resounded through my apartment. "No, Yoshi, don't do this to me!" she screamed ferociously.

I hurried to turn the TV back down. I could never tell who might be in my hallway listening. I was panting for breath now. I felt light-headed and sick to my stomach. By now, on the DVD, Maria continued screaming as the woman on the tape walked toward her. The impersonator covered the screen with the back of her; then the camera zoomed in on Maria's face.

I could see the fear in her eyes as tears crowded up in her eyes and fought to fall down her face. The female was back, her face obscured from the screen, just her body showing. She grabbed Maria's hair roughly and wrenched Maria's head back. "Mmmmm!" More muffled screams came from Maria from behind the thick wads of tape covering her mouth. Her head lurched back again, and next a sickening gush occurred. Then blood splattered all over the camera, and the television screen suddenly went black.

"Nooooo!" I screamed. I couldn't take it and I leaned forward and threw up all over my carpet. I couldn't breathe and the room was spinning. I couldn't think. Maria had been murdered right in my house by someone dressed as me! I'd watched as she begged for mercy with her eyes. She had been my friend since college days and now was gone. The only person who understood me had been killed right in my fucking house!

Weak and wobbly, I held on to the walls and hesitantly walked down the long hallway inside the penthouse toward the kitchen. I was afraid of what I might find, but I had to know. As I reached the threshold of the kitchen doorway, the smell hit me like a boulder, knocking the wind out of my chest. Again I lurched over, and I threw up. I was weak, but some force beyond me propelled me forward. I peeped into the kitchen and that's when I saw it. Blood everywhere—all over the walls, the floor, and the counters.

"Aggggh!" I screamed. My world was spinning and my vision became blurred; the next thing I knew, I passed out.

I wasn't aware of how long I was out, but when I came to, I opened my eyes to the sunlight. It was the next day. I scrambled to my feet and thought about calling those DEA agents who had come to my house. But what if they already had the DVD? I had to weigh my options very quickly. What chance did I stand to defend myself? I was damned if I did or damned if I didn't.

If I ran, I would look guilty. If I stayed, I would be charged with murder—there was no doubt. I was the last person she'd spoken with. I was sure her phone records proved that, and the DEA already believed that. And what was even worse was that her fucking murder took place in my house. I had no fucking chance in hell. I had to get the fuck outta Dodge. Shit was really falling apart.

At first, I thought I should clean up the kitchen. At least, when the police or the DEA agents came back, they wouldn't find the evidence right there. But then I thought about it. How would I get that amount of thick arterial blood up from ceramic tiles? The blood was sure to be soaked through the grout by now. I was fucked! I decided that I wasn't going to try to clean up the massive amount of blood; that would've taken all day. I just had to go—go and never come back.

Then I thought about Ophelia. What if she reported to work and decided to call the police when she saw all of that blood? I couldn't let that happen, either. I had to call her and tell her I was leaving and not to come by. My entire body was shaking. I didn't even know how I was still standing.

I rushed into the bedroom, grabbed my phone, and dialed Ophelia's home number. The phone barely rang once and someone answered it.

"Ophelia?" I called out when the line was picked up.

"My mother is not here," her daughter answered.

"Is she on her way to work?" I asked.

"Is this a cruel joke?" her daughter sneered.

"What do you mean?" I asked, confused at her reaction.

"The homicide detectives haven't contacted you?"

"For what?"

"My mother was found dead two days ago! She left home earlier in the morning to catch the bus so she could get to work, but she never made it!" Ophelia's daughter began to sob uncontrollably.

"Oh, my God, how could this be?" I said, tears beginning to stream my face.

"She's gone, Ms. Lomax! She's gone!" her daughter screamed louder.

I couldn't take all the crying and the emotions behind it, so I hung up the phone. Not only that, I really didn't know what else to say to the girl. Ophelia was dead? What the fuck? That can't be right! I questioned it over and over as I stood with the phone in my hand in a daze. People were dropping dead around me, so I was beginning to feel like I was in the middle of a horror film.

At the same time I was still in utter shock about Maria. Was I like a disease? Maybe whoever killed Maria also killed Ophelia. Oh shit, maybe that is how the killers got my key to get inside my house. They'd killed Ophelia to get into my house! The poor woman had died because someone was trying to frame me—so there was no way I could stay here. I took a deep breath and said a silent prayer. Then I grabbed a bag and began throwing some clothes together.

I dumped Maria's stuff into the bag that I was taking. I wasn't going to leave it behind; that would just make things worse. I couldn't afford for the police to find that shit in my house. It was bad enough that it looked like I murdered her right in here. I started moving through the house like a lightning bolt. My nerves had fucked me up.

I didn't have a concrete plan on what I would do, but I had a stash at a bank in West Palm Beach. All I had to do was make it there, get my money, and go. Where I would go was still a mystery, but West Palm Beach was only a couple of hours away. All I had to do was hop a car service to the bus or the train. I didn't want to take my car and leave it parked at the station where it would certainly get stolen or vandalized. I frantically grabbed as much as I could. I definitely couldn't go anywhere without some of my fly shit. My closet was too massive to even try to take a third of the clothes and shoes I owned, but I needed some. So I took several of my newest pairs.

Just as I began to walk out of my closet, I remembered Sheldon Chisholm and the serious looks on the faces of his henchmen who had visited me earlier. They'd warned me sternly that I needed to go see Sheldon, but at this juncture I couldn't. I had too much shit going on right now. My career and my life were at stake, so I needed to get away so I could think of a way to regain control. I had to get away so I could figure out some shit. I needed to know who was trying to destroy me. Most important, who was behind these murders?

I knew I had taken Sheldon's money, but it would truly be impossible right now for me to show my face in court to represent him. Maria's agents surely would arrest me. I could see them having a fucking field day, handcuffing me in the middle of one of my trials. News reporters would be all over that story and I would be the talk of the town. How would I be able to get myself out of that one? Paul and the rest of the attorneys at the firm would turn their backs on me. It seemed like they needed the smallest reason to do so, and this would be the icing on the cake. So to shield myself from any embarrassment right now, I was gonna have to bail out of town.

I couldn't tell you where I was going after West Palm Beach, but I could tell you that I would be heading north. Perhaps I needed to hide out at one of my relatives' houses on my father's side. Virginia would be the last place anyone would look. No one knew about them but Maria, and now she was dead. My mother wouldn't be able to speak about them, either, because she wasn't in her right mind. That was a blessing in disguise.

"I'll leave before anyone has a chance to realize I am gone," I told myself out loud. I was leaving and I was never coming back. I'd have to leave my lavish lifestyle behind.

But I was fine with it, because I figured with the money I had stashed away, I could build another one. Perhaps get my face reconstructed if shit got really hectic. All I wanted to do was stay alive and keep my freedom. I didn't care how much it cost or what means I had to go through to do it. I had to think about me and only me. And that's exactly what I intended to do.

The Setup

I stood in front of my elevator, literally ready to piss on myself. I was that nervous. Here I was running from a crime I didn't even commit, with no fucking way to prove that I didn't do it. I mean, who would murder the only friend they had in the world? That shit made no sense. I didn't even have time to mourn for Maria—although my heart was in pieces over her murder. It was my fault, too.

From the DVD I could tell whoever murdered Maria wanted revenge on me—this shit was the setup. She had been used as a pawn in a game to take me down—but why? I knew people were jealous of me, but this was taking it too far.

Although I had everything I could dream of, and I stepped on people's backs occasionally to get where I needed to be, I would never have expected that someone hated me so much that they'd frame me for murder. And it wasn't just any murder—the murder of my best fucking friend in the world. I didn't even have time to grieve right now. If I would have stayed around crying and feeling sorry for myself and for Maria, I would have been going up the river without a paddle.

Now, while I was standing inside the elevator, listening to the classical music playing, sweat was dropping off me

like pellets. I was literally about to have a nervous breakdown, watching as every number of the floors I was passing
by lit up on my way down to the lobby. And just when my
ride was almost over, the fucking elevator slowed down and
stopped at the tenth floor, and the door opened. I was evil
as hell, but I held my composure. I held my head down to
prevent me from speaking or giving eye contact to the person who was about to join me. But, of course, that didn't
work.

Stopping at the tenth floor, I should've known that I would
have run into Mrs. Mitchell. She was the gossip queen of
our building. She had to be every bit of eighty years old, but
she had a lot of spunk. And she had gobs of money. Word
had it, her little old Caucasian ass had been married three
times, and every last one of her husbands had been millionaires. When they died or divorced her, she got every stick of
their money. Lucky her!

So, when she came aboard the elevator, she made it her
business to strike up a conversation with me. Dressed down
in a tan Polo jacket, a pair of khaki Polo shorts, and the sun
visor to match, Mrs. Mitchell greeted me with her pet
Pomeranian in arm. She looked like she was about to take
him or her out for a stroll.

"What a pleasant surprise!" she said cheerfully.

"Good afternoon, Mrs. Mitchell."

"It's Ms. Now. You know my last husband left me for a
younger woman." She gritted her teeth. I guess the statement she made took her back down memory lane.

"I'm sure he paid for it," I commented.

Her face lit back up. "Oh yes, my dear! He definitely did
that."

I didn't respond to her comment. I wasn't in the mood to
speak to her from the very beginning, so I pressed down on

the button to close the elevator doors. I was ready to get the hell out of there.

"I see you're all packed up and ready to go."

"Yes, ma'am," I said, hoping she'd leave me and my business alone.

"So, where are you off to?" she pressed on.

"I'm representing a client in another state and his trial starts in a couple of days," I lied.

"My goodness, how long are you going to be gone?"

"One week. Maybe more. Depending on how long the trial lasts," I continued.

"You really know your stuff. I remember that last high-profile case you were on, and you were on television every single day."

"All that comes with the territory," I said modestly.

"Do you ever represent anybody other than those drug-dealing thugs?"

"Mrs. Mitchell, not all of them are drug-dealing thugs. Most of them are well-respected business owners and real estate tycoons."

"That's not what the prosecutors or the news reporters are saying."

I sighed heavily because I was truly sick of having this conversation with this woman. And besides, she didn't know what the hell she was talking about. "It's their job to paint the ugly picture," I finally said.

"Well, I know you're being paid very well, living on the top floor and all. Mrs. Draper, who lives on the fifth floor, told me you're driving a brand-new Aston Martin."

"Yes, ma'am, that's true."

"So, have you ever thought about settling down? I've never seen you bring a man home."

"I'm sorry, but that's not in the cards for me right now."

"That's a shame! You are such a beautiful woman."

"Thank you very much."

"Take my advice. Please don't let time slip by. Before you know it, you're too old to have children. I regret all the chances I had to have children. I probably would have saved my first marriage if I would have given my first husband a baby."

"I'm sorry to hear that, Mrs. Mitchell."

"Don't be sorry for me. Just take my advice."

"I will," I said, just to appease her.

Finally we were on the first floor and I was relieved. I reached down and grabbed the luggage that was placed by my feet, and when I took the first step off the elevator, the two DEA agents who had come to my apartment earlier stood in the entryway before me. This time, though, they had a whole troop of agents with them. My heart immediately fell into the pit of my stomach. I didn't know what to say. I was speechless as hell. They must have gotten to a federal judge and gotten a search warrant after they visited me.

"Going somewhere?" the taller agent asked.

"I don't think that's any of your concern," I responded sarcastically.

"I'm sorry, but it is. We have a warrant to search your premises," he continued as he flashed the warrant in my face.

I didn't have to turn around to see Mrs. Mitchell's mouth, because I heard her gasp for air like she just got the shock of her life. I remained cool, though. I was not going to let anyone around me see me break down. "What are you looking for this time?" I inquired in a calm manner.

"We'll let you know," he said flatly.

Seconds later all the agents walked onto the elevator with me. They let Mrs. Mitchell off in the process. Before the elevator door closed, she turned around and looked directly in my face. I couldn't tell you if she wanted to say something to me, but I did see the look in her eyes. It was a look of disappointment, like I failed her or something. It was really weird, so I brushed it off because I had a far worse problem to deal with at the moment.

All the agents stood quietly, with their guns in hand, the entire ride back up to my penthouse, but I knew their minds were racing at the same speed as mine. The one thing I couldn't stop thinking about was what the hell they were looking for. I knew one thing—if I were a magician, I would make myself disappear right now. The thought of me going back to jail had become too unbearable to imagine. This time it would be for murder, so I knew the world would have to come to an end before I was released.

When we finally made it back up to my floor, all the agents walked either beside me or behind me until we arrived back at my place. A short Hispanic-looking agent took my bags out of my hands, while another agent escorted me to my living-room sofa.

"Can someone tell me what this is about?" I sighed. "I do have somewhere to be." I continued talking as my legs trembled. I knew it would be a matter of time before they went into my luggage and found Maria's things and her blood spattered all over my kitchen. All I could do was hold my head down and wait for the inevitable.

"Hey, Patterson, you've got to come in here and see this," yelled another agent. It sounded like he was yelling from the kitchen. And as soon as the tall agent ran in that direction, my suspicions were indeed correct. My heart started pounding uncontrollably. I wanted to make a run for my front door, but there were two more agents camped out around the foyer. I knew my chances of regaining my freedom were slim to none. If only I'd left about ten minutes earlier, I'd probably be about five miles up the road and on my way to West Palm Beach.

Damn! What was I going to do now? I couldn't do anything else but sit back and watch all the movement around me. It was so quiet throughout my entire house, I could hear a pin drop. It seemed like everybody was going in slow motion. But as soon as I realized that the Hispanic agent who had taken my bags from me had gone into my luggage and had retrieved Maria's things, it seemed like everything started spinning out of control.

Every agent in my entire place ran toward the Hispanic agent to see the objects that belonged to Maria. The next thing I knew, I was being interrogated smack-dab in the middle of my living room. Agent Patterson towered over me like I was a quarterback and he was a linebacker. And for the very first time, I felt wholly defenseless.

"What are you doing with Maria's badge and gun holster?"

"Someone left them at my front door," I managed to say, despite the lump I had lodged in my throat.

"That's bullshit! Where is our agent, Yoshi?"

"I don't know!" I screamed.

"You wanna play games with me?" he snarled.

"I am not playing games!" I began to cry. "I told you, someone left a package with her things at my front door."

Out of frustration Agent Patterson stormed away from me; then several seconds later he turned back around and came walking back toward me. "If you don't tell me where my agent is right now, I am going to haul your ass downtown and have you charged with murder!" he roared.

"I told you, I don't know." I screamed even louder, my face turning flaming red. I began to cry, to the point I caught an instant headache. It didn't faze even one of these bastards, though. They all thought I was a fucking joke. They really thought I was lying.

"Ms. Lomax, you are under arrest," he told me, and then he snatched me up from my sofa and handcuffed me. He roughed me up a little bit while he read me my rights, but I didn't fight back. Why should I? Things would only have gotten worse if I had retaliated. As a matter of fact, I didn't utter another word. I guess I was in total shock.

After they bagged up all the evidence they felt they had on me, they escorted me out of my apartment. I was pushed into the elevator and roughly carted out of my building to a waiting black Suburban. Although I held my head down, I could still see the surprised looks on the faces of my valet, security guard, and some of my high-class neighbors. It was like a scene out of a movie or from the eleven o'clock news.

I also knew what this meant to my future—no matter what. This was the end. It was the ultimate setup, and I had no wins. I had all the fucking incriminating evidence right inside my bag, and they found it. I was sure that they'd seen the DVD of the murder by now. And if they hadn't, they would when they got back to their headquarters.

While we were in transit, all I could think was, why couldn't they see that this whole thing was a setup? Why would I murder my best friend right in my own house? Nevertheless, whether they thought logically about it or not, I was fucked . . . royally fucked. And even though I knew I was in a terrible situation, I knew it wouldn't be wise for me to answer any questions without a lawyer. I knew how the system worked, and as soon as a person invoked their right to an attorney, all questions must stop.

No one in the car spoke a word, but I could feel the stares burning holes in my back and into the side of my face. For the entire ride I could tell that everyone around me was furious with my ass. I couldn't blame them, either. One of their own had been murdered, and shit like that hit home for law enforcement officers. On top of that, Maria wasn't just an agent; she was the director of the Miami DEA field office, and her brutal murder was big news. I could tell by the agents' body language they wanted a piece of me. All they knew about me was that I'd killed their supervisor, a fellow officer. I knew the kinds of shit law enforcement officers did to cop murderers, but I also knew that these DEA agents were smart enough to know that they couldn't touch me because of who I was.

After we arrived at the DEA building, I was manhandled out of the Suburban, and although those agents didn't fuck me up like they wanted, they did place me in a typical dirty, dim, and dank five-by-five interrogation room. I'd seen hundreds of these kinds of rooms when I'd gone down to rescue my high-flying clients from interrogations. This room down at the DEA headquarters was no different than the ones at the local police stations—plain, drab walls, hard-ass chairs, a long table, and the famous double-sided mirror. I knew they were watching me through that fucking mirror, so I was trying to be as calm as I could be.

My body was calling for a hit of coke; I needed something to get me through this. My nerves were literally jumping; I felt my eyes flickering and my hands shaking. I placed my hands underneath my thighs—no need to let them see my shit shaking like I was guilty. Finally, after a couple of excruciating hours of waiting, a tall White man I recognized as the deputy director of the Miami office entered the room, with Agent Patterson in tow. They both wore serious faces, and they had somber eyes. They'd clearly been crying for days over what had happened to Maria. They also both wore black suits, with their badges hanging around their necks from silver-beaded chains. The badges were covered with a small black band across the DEA emblem, which meant they were mourning a fallen officer. All of these things didn't make my case any easier. I was wishing I had one of those black bands to put around my entire body, considering how hurt I was over Maria's murder.

"Ms. Lomax, I'm Frank Sinetti, deputy director—" he started.

"I know who you are. Maria was my best friend. She talked about you all the time," I cut him off.

Those words seemed to anger him. He furrowed his eyebrows and pulled his chair very close to me. "Don't tell me she was your best friend, you fucking murderer! Tell me where her fucking body is!" he growled. His face turned crimson and his eyes hooded over.

Frustrated, I screamed back, "I don't know where her body is! I didn't kill her! So you bastards need to go out and find the real killer!"

That was all I was going to say, I promised myself. These agents knew what buttons to push to get you to talk without a lawyer.

"Where were you on—" Agent Patterson started to ask.

"I'm sorry, but this little interrogation of yours is over. I will not answer another one of your questions until I have an attorney present," I said, using my lawyer tactics to buy some time. I didn't want them to know I had been in jail for the cocaine possession.

"I thought you were an attorney," he spat out, a look of disgust on his face.

"Look, I know my rights, and I'm not answering any questions without my lawyer," I said.

"A lawyer can't help you, Ms. Lomax! You better hope God comes down from heaven and acts as your lawyer, as much evidence as we have against you," Patterson said furiously.

Instead of commenting, I buried my entire face in the

palm of my hands. I couldn't stand being accused of something I had not done. Especially something that could destroy everything I'd worked so hard to achieve. And despite my request to have my attorney present while they questioned me about Maria's murder, they continued to harass me.

"Maria was your best friend, huh? I guess that is why she wrote this," Patterson continued, sliding a diary in front of me. I looked down at the page and read Maria's handwriting:

March 11

Today wasn't such a good day. I called Yoshi and I confronted her about the Juan Alvarez case. She denied blowing the investigation, but deep down inside, I knew she had something to do with it. She's a money-hungry individual, so I knew she cooked up something to get that information to Mr. Alvarez. What's even worse is that I have no evidence to prove her disloyalty. Right now, I am facing a possible reprimand or maybe even a dismissal for leaking information about the investigation to Yoshi. Hopefully, with everything I've done around my unit, my deputy director will weigh in my favor and give me a slap on the wrist.

Aside from that, I've noticed that Yoshi's behavior has changed. She hasn't admitted it, but I know she is getting high again. I saw it in her body language the other morning when she appeared at Sheldon Chisholm's preliminary hearing. She tried to play it off by telling me that she hadn't had much rest, but I knew what time it was. Knowing her as well as I do, she's going to take this secret of hers to her grave, unless it gets out of control beforehand. When I spoke with her just the other day and told her that she needed to drop Sheldon Chisholm's case, she almost blew up on me.

It's like she won't listen to anything anyone tells her and I truly believe she is headed for disaster. I can't say how much she charged Mr. Chisholm for his case, but it wouldn't surprise me if she taxed him for at least two hundred and fifty grand. And with the new murder case he just picked up, she's bound to hit him up for at least four hundred thousand more.

I went to visit her mother, again, the other day and she still asks for Yoshi. The doctors told me her condition is getting worse and that she might not be around much longer. She begged me to convince Yoshi to come see her. I told her I'd try, but if Yoshi knew I was visiting her mother, she would forever be upset with me. Yes, she's a drama queen! Always has been and probably will be until the day she dies, so what can I say?

Later that evening when I got off the phone with Yoshi, I got a phone call from one of my contacts at the federal building saying that a few state and federal judges, along with a couple of narcotics detectives, three United States Attorneys, including Brad Carlton, had been arrested because of bribery schemes cooked up by Yoshi. According to my source, she was documenting her bribes inside a notebook file of her Black-Berry and somehow Paul Shapiro got ahold of that information and leaked it to the investigators. Surprisingly enough, she didn't have my name written down in her ledger. I must admit that I would've been devastated if she had. I would have been arrested right along with everyone else and my career here as an agent would have been over before I could blink. But what's more terrifying is the fact that Paul was the one who turned her in. They were fucking, for God's sake! Why the switch-up now? I mean, what in the hell is he going to get out of all this? A lot of people's lives are going to be turned upside down because of him, so I hope it's going to be well worth it.

Now, as far as Yoshi is concerned, I've been battling with my heart about whether or not I should inform her about the bribery investigation. My heart is forcing me to tell her, but my mind is saying something different. So I guess it would be wise to go with my mind, being as she fucked me with that Juan Alvarez case. Sooner than later, she will find out what's coming to her. And, believe me, I am not going to be anywhere around. I've got my own shit going at the administration to deal with. Trying to keep my ass from being reprimanded or fired is at the top of my list right now, so Yoshi is going to be on her own. I wish her the best because she is going to need it.

Those were the last words that Maria had written. The words were staring back at me from the paper, like they were taunting me—each line cut deep. I sat with my mouth hanging open after I read Maria's diary entry. She already knew I was getting high again and she had been visiting my mother, which I hadn't done in over a year. Why didn't she just tell me? I thought. Maybe it was because Maria knew me so well. She knew how fucking self-centered and selfish I was. Maria always chose her words carefully when it came to me; she was more of a friend than I could ever be. I realized then that I was the kind of bitch who was only out for herself; it was all about Yoshi Lomax and my climb to the top. It didn't matter who I stepped on getting to the top, but now it looked like I would have to get through all of those people on my fall back down. What had I done? I finally let go of my tough-girl role and the tears began to stream.

Both Sinetti and Patterson just stared at me with contempt and hatred showing on their faces. I could hardly breathe, I was crying so hard. Maria had only been trying to help me; she was trying to warn me on all scales. So, who would kill her to get back at me and for what reason? I had to convince the DEA that they had the wrong person so that the real killer could be caught, but where would I start? I couldn't call Paul, he had turned in all my contacts . . . and no wonder I couldn't get Brad on the damn phone to discuss Sheldon Chisholm's case. He was locked the fuck up.

Just thinking about Sheldon Chisholm suddenly gave me a chill. I was supposed to visit him today, as per the instructions of his henchmen. I guess if I was locked up for murder, there would be no way for him to get to me. Although if I ever got out of this bullshit mess I was in, I'd have an entirely different set of problems to deal with—trying to convince Sheldon that I was held against my will is something I'm sure he wouldn't care to hear.

Playing Them
at Their Game

Once the DEA realized that I wasn't stupid enough to answer any more of their questions, they allowed me to make a phone call, which in the federal world is not just one phone call. I knew that the Feds rule was they'd let you place as many calls as you needed to procure an attorney. When I was left alone with the telephone, I immediately dialed Donna, my former assistant. She was the only person I had left who I trusted enough to tell my situation. At first, Donna was apprehensive about helping me, but with the cash I offered her, she couldn't refuse. Donna knew the kind of money I brought in with my clients. I quickly explained the situation to her and she agreed to help me. Donna had gone to work for a rival law firm—Tuttle, Watts, and Hoffman—after Paul fired her. The law firm Donna worked for now had tried several times to steal me from Shapiro and Witherspoon. When they had been trying to offer me everything under the sun, I already had everything I could dream of.

I didn't get into great details with Donna, but I told her enough to let her know my situation was serious.

"What do you need me to do?" she asked.

"Which attorney do you work side by side with?" I wondered aloud.

She told me that the defense attorney she worked for was a man named Scott Maxwell, and she believed that she could get him to help me. Hearing those words made me a very happy woman. I knew Scott Maxwell very well; in fact, we had been rivals in law school. Both Scott and I were at the top of our law school graduating class, which was no easy feat for a half-Asian woman and a Black man. Throughout my years in school, I was glad to have Scott around; he made me step up my game as a lawyer. And to look at me now—with all my skills, I'd taken the easy way out, bribing and paying off judges and police officers. Now that I look back on it, it just wasn't fucking worth it.

After Donna told me that she was working for Scott, I became a little apprehensive about getting him to represent me. To have him look me dead in my face because of everything I've gotten myself into would make me feel so ashamed. But then I figured to hell with all of that! I needed someone good to rip this case apart and Scott would definitely be the man to do it. Where I used bribes and blackmail to get my clients off, Scott used pure courtroom skills.

I remember thinking that if I ever were to settle down and get married in the very distant future, I would've wanted a man like Scott. He was handsome as hell. His skin complexion was perfect. He had a little facial hair, which comprised his mustache and goatee. Aside from that, his face was clean and free of blemishes. He was tall and his physique was medium build. He put me in mind of P. Diddy. I'm speaking of his dress style and his swagger.

I recalled a couple of years back when he asked me to go out with him. But, of course, I turned him down. I felt like I needed to be around men who could further my career, and he was definitely not on that list. It had been at least a couple of months since I last ran into him, so it would be really good to see an old face. I just hoped he didn't get cold feet on me and run like the rest of them. We would see, though. Shit, I could use any help right about now.

When Scott arrived at the federal lockup, where I was being held, I don't think I'd ever been that happy to see anyone in my entire life. He flashed his perfect smile when he saw me; as usual, he was dressed nice. He wore a classic tailored navy blue Brooks Brothers suit, with a beautiful Gucci tie and Gucci loafers. I knew designer clothes so well, I didn't even have to look twice at his stuff to know the designer. His hair was cut low and lined up perfectly. His almond skin was smooth and clean-cut, as always. And his eyes were just as I remembered them—sleepy, but not shut, dreamy, and filled with spunk.

"Hey, Yoshi." Scott beamed as he gave me a quick hug.

"Hey, Scott. Thank you for coming," I said somberly. At this point I couldn't smile if I wanted.

He took a seat at the table in front of me and pulled out a legal pad and a pen. I sat firmly with my back against the chair, handcuffed to the table before us. I looked like a criminal for real, but I didn't let that deter me from getting down to business. "So, what did Donna tell you?"

He sighed. "Well, first off, she told me that you were in some pretty heavy shit! But what I need to know from you is, did you do what they are charging you with?"

"No, I didn't, Scott. I was locked up on other charges when the murder took place. I was set up, plain and simple."

"What other charges were you locked up for?"

"I was stopped by one of the local cops on a traffic violation. One thing led to another and I was given a Breathalyzer. When my alcohol level exceeded the limit, they searched my car and found about thirty bucks' worth of cocaine in my car. So they arrested me and charged me with cocaine possession—end of story."

Scott's eyeballs nearly jumped out of his head. He was obviously surprised that I admitted to having cocaine. But, hey, I had to tell him because he was going to find out anyway.

"Was the cocaine they found, yours?" he asked, even though I'm sure he already knew the answer. But in our legal profession, you could never assume, so it was always best to ask.

"I'm ashamed to say it, but, yes, it was."

He shook his head like he was disappointed, but he didn't make any comments about it. "How long were you detained on those charges?" he continued.

"At least twenty-four hours or more. They still have my car down at the pound."

"Well, if all that checks out, then all we have to do is put you at the jail during the time Maria was allegedly murdered."

"You know, all that sounds good, but Maria was killed in my house. So, how do we explain that?" I questioned him.

"That's a good question, and I'm sure that after we put our heads together, we'll come up with something," he said, and then he looked down at his pad and scribbled something.

Our entire conversation lasted for about a good hour. I sat there and told him about my relationship with Maria and how long we'd know each other. I even spilled my guts about my cocaine addiction, my trysts with the Santanas, and the affair I had with Paul. I wanted to be perfectly honest with Scott. So I did something that I had not done in years—told the truth. Scott took copious notes, which he kept reviewing, and he'd put his pen up to his mouth while he pondered over the notes, just like he had done in law school. His brain was working hard to process the information I had loaded on him, and then he had a thought.

"Did all of this start happening to you after you took on Sheldon Chisholm's case?" He looked at me, puzzled.

"Well, kind of, sort of . . . ," I said; then I paused to gather my thoughts. "Okay, things started happening to me right after I told Paul I wasn't sleeping with him anymore, and then shit started getting really crazy after I took the Chisholm case. And these two events happened in a two-day span," I explained.

Scott shook his head in disbelief. "What were you thinking?" he asked.

Puzzled by his question, I said, "What are you talking about?"

"You don't see it?"

"See what?" I asked, looking at him strangely.

"Well, first you represented Luis Santana, and then you turned around and took on Mr. Chisholm."

"And . . . ," I said, waiting for Scott to lay his theory out.

"And . . . Santana and Chisholm are rival drug kingpins, and have been for years."

"Oh, my God! I didn't know that."

"How could you not know this?"

"I never asked any of my clients who they had beefs with. All I do is express interest in representing them, they show me the cash, and the deal is made. Anything other than that, I don't get into it."

"I understand where you're coming from, but this is a very critical situation you're in. And I am not one hundred percent sure, but if my theory is right, I would bet you that Santana wants to eliminate Sheldon once and for all. And this incident with you would be a perfect way of doing it without getting his hands dirty and bringing the heat on himself," Scott explained.

All of a sudden it seemed like lightbulbs started going off in my head. I just stared into space.

"Yoshi, you okay?" Scott asked.

"Oh, my God, Scott! Do you think Santana had something to do with Maria's murder? I mean, it would all make sense to have me set up so that I wouldn't be able to represent Chisholm. Right before she got murdered, Maria tried to convince me to drop his case, but I flat out told her I couldn't. Damn! I should've listened to her!" I screamed, banging my fists on the hard plastic table, the handcuffs scratching up the surface.

"Yoshi, I am going to need you to calm down. And you know if you don't, the agents are going to come in here and take you back into lockup."

Listening to Scott reason with me calmed me down, but my tears began to run down my face like an endless waterfall. He reached into his jacket pocket and handed me his handkerchief. I wiped my eyes and said, "I am fucked all the way around the board, Scott. The cocaine charge is going to ruin my career, and this shit with Santana and Chisholm is going to have me sinking in sand. I can't tell you how I am going to get my way out of this one."

Scott grabbed both of my hands and held them very firm. "We are going to get you out of this. Don't you worry."

"I can't help it, Scott. I trusted Mr. Santana, and all the time he was setting me up while he was baiting me in with the drugs, the sex, and all the expensive-ass gifts!" I cried out.

"Hey, wait a minute. Do you think Paul may be in on this?" Scott asked. That was a damn good question and I couldn't say for sure.

"The Santana referral did come from Paul. So he does

know Mr. Santana," I told Scott. It seemed like the more we spoke, the more pieces to the puzzle came together.

"Well, your preliminary hearing is in a few days. So now we just have to figure out how to undo this mess," Scott said seriously, looking like he was thinking hard.

"What about Chisholm? If I get out, he is surely going to be looking for me," I explained. My heart started racing as I thought about how dangerous Sheldon was.

"We have to get you out of here first," Scott said. I knew he meant what he said, too.

"Please don't worry about money. That's the one thing I did manage to do right. I have money put aside, enough to pay you and live comfortably for a while," I assured him.

"Money is not an issue, Yoshi. Like you, I have plenty. This thing right here is going to take a little bit more than money," he said. And he was right. I've always had the mentality that money can get you out of a lot of things. That is exactly what I had been taught all my life—to use what you got to get what you want! But, now, reality had kicked in my back door and I was gonna have to face it. Thankfully enough, I had Scott on my team to go through this whole ordeal with. Regardless of the outcome, he and I were going to fight this thing to the very end. So, believe me, somebody was going down with me.

Right before Scott left, he told me that I'd have to give him some information in exchange for his help. I was in no position to ask questions, so I told him I'd give him whatever information he needed. Scott assured me that he was going to be on top of my case and urged me not to worry about a thing. He knew that would be very hard for me to do, but I said okay anyway. On his way out, he kissed me on the cheek and told me that I owed him a dinner date after all of this was over. I gave him a half smile and said, "You got it!"

* * *

I sat in the holding cell for about six hours until these bastards figured out that they needed to process me and send my ass off to federal lockup. I believed they took their sweet time because they wanted to piss me off. But it was too late—I was already pissed off when they charged me with that bullshit-ass charge. It was okay, though, because whether they believed it or not, my time was coming. And I was going to shine on all of them.

Trying to Figure Shit Out

The CO came into the jail and screamed out my name. I was groggy from sleep and thought I was dreaming. "Lomax!" she screamed again. I finally stood up in my cell and walked to the bars. "Get ya shit!" the fat CO screamed at me. I didn't know what was going on, but I did as I was told. I had been in jail almost a week now, and I frankly thought I'd never get out. When I had my stuff, the CO yelled for the guard to open the gates. I stood and let the gate open, with the entire tier of hard-looking women watching me. I stepped out onto the tier and followed the CO down the long corridor.

"What's going on?" I asked.

"What else would be going on? Do you think I'm taking you out on a date or something?" the sarcastic-ass CO spat.

When we approached the release office area, my heart jumped. I wasn't going to ask any questions, it was clear that Scott had found a way to get me released on bail. My bail was set at $3 million during my preliminary hearing a couple of days ago. I was processed out through the system like a cow being herded through a cattle call. When the gray gates of the jail opened up and I saw the Miami sun, tears streamed down my face.

"Yoshi!" I heard my name. I placed my hand up to my eyes to shield them from the sun and noticed Scott.

"Hey, Scott," I called out, walking in his direction.

"Feels good to be out, huh?" he asked. I was finally standing next to him. I didn't know whether to hug or kiss his ass.

"How did you pull this one off?" I asked.

"Magic," Scott answered. I climbed into his BMW 750 and we sped off. It felt so good to be in a luxury car again. I knew I looked like shit, but Scott still complimented me.

As we rode through Miami, I suddenly realized I had no where to fucking go. My condo was a crime scene and I just knew that the feds had probably taken everything, so I sat in the passenger seat with the dumbest expression I could muster. I asked him where we were going, so he smiled at me and said, "Listen, don't worry about a place to stay. You can bunk with me."

"Are you sure that would be a good idea? I mean, I would hate to be an intrusion, because it would be nothing for me to stay at a hotel," I assured.

"No, you can stay with me. So let's not discuss that anymore," he said.

"No problem," I said, smiling. And from there we rode in silence until a thought popped up in his head. The things he told me changed everything. He told me that his investigators had spotted Paul and Mr. Santana hanging out and playing golf together a few times since my arrest. He also told me that he had a recorded conversation between the two about the plot to bring me down. To think that I had been fucking both of those slimeballs—I really got sick to my stomach. They had been playing me all along, which brought me back to the conversation Mr. Santana and I had at the club one night about me representing Sheldon. He had kept asking me, was I sure about representing this guy, and I had told him yes.

Damn, why hadn't I seen through that? I was now sitting on the forefront of a huge fucking murder scandal. But what I really wanted to know was, whose idea was it to get me jammed up like this? It wouldn't surprise me if it was Paul. I was on his shit list because I wasn't fucking him anymore and he was afraid that I would blow the lid on the firm's shady practices.

Scott then told me that Eric Bretner—my fucking archenemy—was really a lawyer who worked for Scott's firm. He had been sent over to Shapiro and Witherspoon to infiltrate and find out all of the firm's secrets so that the rival firm could destroy Shapiro and Witherspoon. I sat with my mouth hanging open. Eric Bretner was a fake, and he was always up Paul's ass.

Scott told me that Mr. Santana had agreed with Paul to get me back on drugs so I would fail at representing Chisholm. That would send Chisholm away for life, which, in turn, would have Chisholm's people after me—to the point where I'd have to leave town or I'd be dead. Both Paul and Mr. Santana would get their way. Scott also told me that Paul had put in anonymous calls to the feds letting them know that judges, DAs, and police officers were taking bribes from me. Paul's calls had brought down at least four judges and about twenty narcotics detectives in all. No wonder everywhere I went, people were wanting to kill my ass. They thought I was snitching!

I grew angrier by the minute as Scott unfolded Paul and Mr. Santana's schemes to bring me down. I was overwhelmed. Two men wanted to fuck me over. They were both using me! I was feeling sicker every time Scott uttered a word, and you know I wanted nothing else but revenge.

The one thing Scott couldn't tell me was who had killed Maria, and why. Scott did not know where she came into play in all of this drama, and neither did I. But I was bound to find out. And I also knew that it wouldn't be long before I did.

Arriving at Scott's house, I was tired and my brain was throbbing from all of the information I had just received. Scott showed me around his Tudor-style home, and I thought it was fabulous. He lived like I was used to living . . . in the lap of luxury.

"Yoshi, make yourself at home," Scott welcomed me in. Although I wanted to jump and take his invitation, I really didn't trust anyone at this point. I had to ask myself, why was Scott helping me so much? He gave me my own room. It was beautiful, decorated in lilac, dark brown, and white. It smelled like lilacs, too.

When Scott left, I jumped onto the bed and hugged the pillows. After sleeping on a small hard-ass jail cell bed, I thought this bed felt like heaven. The room had its own bathroom. I walked into the marble-tiled bathroom, and when I looked into the mirror, I almost broke down. I looked like a mess. Not only did I need makeup, I needed some moisturizer. The prison soap had dried me the fuck out. I took the longest shower I could stand. The water felt so good all over my body. I kept thinking about my situation and wondering what fucking clues I was missing.

After my shower Scott cooked dinner. I hadn't had pasta in weeks. To see and smell real food was so damn good. Scott was a pure gentleman. Over dinner we started talking about my case strategy. Scott planned to get an expert to review the murder video to refute the fact that the impersonator on the tape was me. He also planned to present all that he knew about Paul and Mr. Santana setting me up and trying to destroy me.

I was so angry with Paul, I told Scott all of his business. I told him all about Paul's deals with the IRS and all of his bribes of judges. It was Paul who showed me the ropes with bribing, and then he turned on me to make *me* look like the fucking bad guy. Scott was very interested in everything I had to say about Paul. I also told Scott about Paul's sexual interludes with other men. Paul didn't think I knew, but I'd mistakenly come across a video of Paul and a guy that he'd stashed in his safe at the job. Paul also didn't know I knew where he hid his safe key, and because he was so predictable, I also knew his combination.

"Scott, you put a lot of information on me tonight. Can I ask you why you're helping me like this?" I finally asked. The question was burning inside me for so long.

"Well, Yoshi, it's basically like this. My firm agreed to help you with the agreement that you help us take down your former boss and his firm," Scott answered honestly.

"I knew there had to be a catch," I said, lowering my head.

"There's no catch. We are not charging you for your murder trial or your bail. All we want is every piece of dirt you have on Shapiro and Witherspoon," Scott said.

At first, I didn't think I was going to do it. But after thinking about how Paul was trying to completely destroy me, I opened my mouth and paid the price for my freedom. I was setting Paul up the way he had done me, and I was going to make sure he went down. Now all I had to do was think of how I was going to get revenge on Luis Santana. I was the one who had gotten him off, so it was going to be hard to get any law enforcement interested in chasing him for fear they'd lose. Then again, if I was willing to tell them everything I knew about Santana—all the things that Santana had shared with me under attorney-client privilege—his ass would go down, too. In turn, I would probably lose my license to practice law anymore. But then I figured, why care? If Miami prosecutors got a conviction from my cocaine possession charge, then I was bound to lose my license anyway. So fuck it! If I went down, so did everyone else.

After more thought, I agreed to help Scott destroy Paul and everyone connected to him—that included Luis. I knew he was a very powerful man, and I might have to go into witness protection behind his ass, but, hey, that was the chance I was going to have to take. Hopefully, when all this was over, Scott and I would be able to prove that I had not murdered Maria.

Not only that, I also need to make a special visit to Ophelia's house and pay my condolences and help out any way I could. I mean, that's the least I could do. I was the reason she was murdered. I just couldn't reveal that information to her family. They would probably hate me for the rest of my life, and that was too much drama for me to have to deal with at this point.

Getting My Shit Off

After I agreed to give Scott all the dirt I knew on Paul, he went straight to work. I told Eric Bretner how to get into Paul's safe to get his IRS records and that sex tape. We sent anonymous letters to every law enforcement agency in Miami, detailing Paul's bribes and his connections to the drug game. I sent a nice long letter to his wife, I told her all about Paul's deviant sexual behavior, and I made sure to mention his four tattoos, his birthmarks, and his missing toenail. I wanted her to know that I'd seen Paul without his clothes on. I placed an anonymous call to the IRS detailing how Paul laundered his money through his brother's wine vineyard in California and through offshore bank accounts. That was just the first day.

After Eric returned with the tape, Scott made still photos from it and sent them to the local newspapers. Scott also made several copies of the tapes and sent them out to the news media. I couldn't front—all of this revenge was making me feel more sinister by the minute. I felt like I had been stepped on and I was finally going to get mine.

Scott didn't want anything to do with bringing Mr. Santana down. I knew he wasn't going to get down with me on that one, but I wasn't going to let that shit go. I called the DEA, Miami-Dade Police, ICE, and any agency I could think of. I detailed the insides of Santana's house, where he had drugs and how often he threw parties and catered a half kilo for personal use. I told them about the body of one of his soldiers, which Mr. Santana had confided in me. He'd told me that he murdered the guy in front of the guy's kids because the guy had had sex with a very young girl who'd turned out to be Mr. Santana's niece. He told me that he had the body chopped and burned. I knew Mr. Santana was a ruthless motherfucker. He said his logic for killing the guy in front of his own kids was because he wanted the guy's kids to suffer for life, like his niece would.

I also made a blocked call to Mr. Chisholm's partner and let him know that Mr. Santana was trying to set up Sheldon to do a bid so he would be out of the picture, and out of the game. I knew that call alone would start an all-out drug war, and I couldn't care less. I could see Mr. Santana running from the feds and Haitian Mafia. How sweet that would be! That motherfucker would be dead within a week, I was sure of it.

And as far as Paul was concerned, he was going to be brought to his knees, too. All the shit that came out about him would surely bring that fucking firm down, and humiliation would plague his face. Come to think about it, he might jump off a bridge after we got finished with his ass.

I got pure satisfaction out of everything I did, and I didn't feel one bit of remorse. Fuck Paul and Mr. Santana! I thought about how easily I had almost lost everything. I'd let my greed for more and more money almost destroy me. In the process I lost my best friend and almost lost a fortune.

Three days had passed and things were still quiet. I hadn't heard anything from all of the calls and shit I'd made. Damn, what's going on? I was starting to think. Then Scott rushed into the room where I was staying.

"Yoshi, you gotta come see this shit!" Scott screamed, excited, grabbing my arms up off the bed where I lay.

"What! What happened?" I asked, confused. I rushed into the living room with Scott. He flicked on his fifty-one-inch flat screen. The news flashed across it:

In breaking news, high-profile attorney and part owner of the prestigious law firm of Shapiro and Wither-spoon caught on tape with a male prostitute. Mr. Paul Shapiro was found on tape having sexual relations with a male prostitute. When confronted, Mr. Shapiro had no comment.

"Aaaahhh," I started screaming and laughing. The shit had hit the fan now. I knew Paul was somewhere about to shit himself.

"After this hit the news, our firm's phones were ringing off the hook with clients from Shapiro and Witherspoon that wanted to hire us instead," Scott said, smiling brightly.

"Wow, business is going to be booming for you," I said somberly. I missed getting those big retainers and big paydays.

"Yes! Thanks to you, Yoshi. Now, do you see why we are not sweating you for representation fees? We were going to get paid anyway, using you and having you as a client," Scott returned.

When he said the words, my heart sank. He had used me just like everyone else. Although I was happy to be free for now, shit was just getting crazier by the moment. He jumped up and down at the mere thought of how his career was about to take off to the next level. I sat there stoically, pure disgust written all over my face.

Several minutes later he popped a bottle of Moët to celebrate, but I was still not in the mood. I returned to the room

I was staying in and promised myself that the next day I'd get a hotel room and just wait for my trial. While I was in the room, I pulled out my checkbook and wrote out a check in the amount of the bail Scott's legal partners had put up for me. Sick to my stomach, I pondered ways to get away from all this havoc after I was exonerated from all my charges.

Scott and everyone else probably thought that I was going to come on board with their firm, but they had another thing coming. I was getting the hell out of here. I had made my mind up that I was packing my bags and I was moving north, never to come back to this godforsaken place. I knew my family on my father's side would welcome me with open arms. And who knew, perhaps I might be able to open up a small practice there in Virginia. Where they lived was a small, urbanlike city, so they might need my expertise.

I knew one thing, if I decided to open up a practice in that state, I was going to have to keep it low-key. I couldn't dare let anyone from around here find out where I was, especially Sheldon's and Santana's people. After what was about to go down, my best bet would be to stay behind the scenes, at least for a couple of years. Maybe longer, who knew?

Fucking Shit Up

As soon as Scott left for work the next day, I scribbled a note and left. I didn't want to make him angry, because I still needed him for my trial, so I just let him know that with everything that had happened, I needed some time alone. I pinned my hair up and put on a huge-brimmed sun hat that I'd purchased after my release. I covered my eyes with a large pair of black Valentino shades and threw a silk scarf around my neck. I took a taxi from Scott's place to the South Beach Ritz-Carlton on Lincoln Road and checked in under my mother's maiden name. I still carried all of the credit cards I had opened in her name when I was in college, ones she never knew about.

"Would you be needing turndown service, Ms. Aoki?" the Korean concierge asked me.

"No thank you," I said, in the best Korean I could muster.

Inside, the room was gorgeous, just like I knew it would be. I'd had several fuck-and-go sessions with judges in this very hotel. I felt some kind of sick connection to the Ritz, and besides that, it made me feel like Yoshi Lomax again. Once inside the room I did all of the things I was hesitant to do at Scott's house, like masturbate myself into orgasm. Shit, I needed to come because I was backed up for miles.

After I was done, just out of curiosity, I dialed Paul's office. When a man answered, I asked for Paul. "He's no longer with this firm" was the man's response. Then I decided to call my old office line and retrieve my messages. There were more than twenty-five messages—the maximum the system could hold—and they were all from Sheldon Chisholm or one of his men.

In the last message, Sheldon said, "Ms. Lomax, I just want to let you know that I've been keeping up with what's been going on with you. Too bad, you done fucked around and got a murder beef like me." He let out a sinister laugh. "I guess now you see what it feels like to be behind bars. And now that I know you're released on bail, I want you to either make arrangements to have my money refunded or find me a lawyer. Shit is getting really critical right now. So . . . if me or my family doesn't hear back from you in the next twenty-four hours, something drastic is going to happen." His chilling words sent a shiver up my spine. Between my murder charges and Sheldon's threats, it seemed like leaving Miami was the best solution I could have ever envisioned.

After I heard the rest of my messages, I flopped down on the king-sized hotel bed and stared at the ceiling. I knew people said running from your problems was the cowardly thing to do . . . but in my case, what fucking choice did I have? It seemed like everyone who admired me was now my enemy. And the ones who envied me were waiting patiently for my downfall, and I couldn't let them have the last laugh. My pride wasn't gonna let it go down like that. While I was thinking back on my past mistakes, my train of thought was broken by the hotel telephone.

Shocked, I sat up and stared at it, contemplating whether or not to answer it. "Who the fuck could that be? No one knows I'm here," I reasoned, and snatched up the receiver.

"Ms. Aoki, this is the front desk. Would you like in-room meals? We forgot to ask you during check-in," the pleasant voice on the other end said.

I took a deep breath . . . a sigh of relief and answered yes.

After two days I had become a master at disguises. I'd tried several different ones before I was comfortable going outside. So far, I learned that Paul was forced to resign from the firm. In addition to that, he lost his stake in the firm, and was under investigation by the IRS, DEA, and the local police. Every day his name appeared in the newspaper, right alongside the reports of the dead bodies of Mr. Santana's people and Sheldon's people. There was definitely a war raging between the two.

I was feeling bold and confident in my disguises and decided I would head out once more. I got dressed, again, with a different wig, dark shades, flat heels—something I never wore—and blended in with the Miami crowd. I rented a simple little sedan, and first I visited all of my banks. I had to get my stashes together; I knew I'd need the money to live off. I wasn't planning on sticking around much longer.

After I visited every bank and my safe-deposit boxes, I started to head back to the hotel, but something was drawing me toward Paul's neighborhood. It was like some force beyond me was pushing me—I wanted to see that bastard's face in misery, I hoped. It was a fairly long drive and all the way there I pictured myself walking up to Paul's house, ringing his bell, and slapping the shit out of his face. I knew I couldn't do that, so I planned to settle for just watching outside of his house and waiting to see that bastard. He probably looked old and fucked-up right now, I said to myself, knowing that his stress level was probably through the roof with all the shit that Scott and I had made happen in his life.

Before I knew it, I was outside Paul's estate. I parked my car almost five huge houses away and still had a great view of his place; that was how big it was. For the first twenty minutes, there was no sign of him or his wife and kids. I watched his neighbors walking their little dogs, taking their kids to school, and power walking or jogging through their quiet neighborhood. I stared at Paul's house, wondering how my life would've been had I chosen to have a family. Me as a mother? Shit, I knew I was too self-centered for that. Sure, having a rich husband would not have hurt anything, but who the fuck wanted to be tied down?

Lost in my own thoughts, I finally saw something or someone stirring in one of his front windows. I pulled my dark shades down so that they were just resting on the tip of my nose—I did this so I could see better. It was Paul, and I had a perfect view of the window to his office. He walked past the window again, this time with something in his hands—it looked like the telephone. He was moving back and forth so fast, I sensed that he was pacing. That kind of made me feel good because it sent a clear message to me that he was pacing because he couldn't rest easy, which was exactly what I fucking intended. I was so busy watching him move back and forth, I didn't immediately notice his wife coming out of their front door. There were two people with her, a man dressed in all white and a woman dressed in black and white—her hired help, I assumed. The man tugged a large suitcase out the front door and then several more. The woman was helping the children out the door, fussing over them and seemingly preparing them for a long trip. Paul's wife didn't seem to be speaking much, just hustling in and out of the house. I looked back to the room where he was, and now he was standing in the window as he watched his wife and kids. It wasn't hard to tell what was going on.

"She's finally leaving his ass," I whispered. It had taken a few weeks, but it was finally happening. I had come just in the fucking nick of time to see it go down. My insides were hot with excitement; this was good for Paul's ass. I gritted my teeth so hard, I was taking pleasure in watching this. Paul's silhouette in the window was very still and his arms were by his sides. I could see that the kids were visibly upset, probably crying. White kids have always thought divorce was the equivalent to the end of the world, so this was probably tearing them up. I didn't feel bad at all—shit, I grew up without a father, they would live. The male servant came out of the house with the last set of bags and he bent down to tell the children something. It seemed like a long good-bye because, one by one, the children threw their arms around the servant's long neck and gave him a hug. He closed his eyes and gave each of the children a long squeeze. The female servant just stood aside with a tissue and blotted her eyes.

I assumed that she was probably their nanny, and this was probably extra hard for her. It was clear that wherever Mrs. Shapiro and the children were going . . . they were not coming back. As all of the long good-byes were being exchanged, I watched Paul, standing, watching his life walk out the door, leaving him alone with his troubles. Suddenly a black Mercedes G-wagon pulled up to the house, and Mrs. Shapiro, the children, and the hired help all turned toward the vehicle. The process of loading up the G wagon started, just like it had for taking the bags out of the house. One by one, piece by piece, slow and methodical, their lives—Paul's life—were packed away in the back of a luxury SUV.

"Good for you, bastard. She should've left your ass a long time ago, fucking dirty piece of shit," I mumbled, loving the fact that I had a front-row seat to Paul's misery. I wished I could be up close to see his pain firsthand. After what he'd done to me, I wanted him to feel just how I felt, to go through just as much bullshit as I had to go through. I wished I could force-feed his ass a mountain of cocaine, just so he knew what being addicted felt like. I gripped the steering wheel in the rental car until my knuckles turned white. I didn't even notice my rapid breathing, I was so furious.

I looked at Paul in the window and noticed he was holding something next to his head. "What the fuck is he doing? Oh, my God! Is that a gun?" I whispered aloud, secretly hoping it was. I couldn't see very clearly, and I so wanted to get out of the car for a better view. But I couldn't chance him noticing and recognizing me. So I stared at him and for one minute I averted my eyes back to his wife and kids. They'd finally gotten all but one of the bags into the G-wagon.

When I looked back up to the window, I realized Paul had suddenly disappeared. *Bang, bang, bang!* And then I saw that shattered glass from the window where Paul had been standing, not even a minute ago, was now lying on the lawn outside the home. My heart dropped to the pit of my stomach. Startled by the same sound, Mrs. Shapiro, the children, and the servants had all looked up toward the window where the sound had come from. And the next thing I knew, Mrs. Shapiro and the children started screaming. They all ran back into the house and left their door wide open. I could see straight into Paul's foyer, but there was no sign of anyone. Then suddenly someone raced past the doorway, running frantically. I couldn't tell exactly what had happened. Maybe it was a gun that Paul had held. Could it be that he had blown his own brains out right there in his house?

As I speculated, I noticed it—a large, wet, red spot on the top pane of the window. "Oh shit, that motherfucker did shoot himself!" I said loudly to myself, covering my mouth at the same time. I couldn't believe it! His shit-talking ass took the coward's way out and he didn't even wait until his wife had left with the children. He blew his own brains out with his kids only a few feet away. That was some sick-ass shit, if you asked me.

It was crazy, because I saw White people doing that type of shit all the time. I mean, it could not have been that bad! Or could it? Shit, I knew that if my life was fucked-up, like his was, then I probably would have just gone into hiding. Fuck killing myself. There was not enough shit going on in the world that would have me wanting to commit suicide. That's just not what I was made of. I had too much to live for, in spite of the fact that I had a ton of enemies.

Aside from that, I didn't know what to feel, because the evil side of me felt vindicated, but a small part of me felt sorry for the kids. It was only a matter of seconds before the wail of ambulance and police sirens came crying down Paul's street. It really felt strange how I was around when he killed himself. The shit was really bugging me out! I mean, how coincidental was that? But what was even stranger was the fact that I wasn't satisfied. I wanted to see that mother-fucker squirm on his stomach. I wanted him to get a taste of what it felt like to be behind bars, too. Everything I went through was because of him, and I wanted him to get a taste of his own medicine. But I now saw that was not going to happen. So I was going to have to take what I could get and keep it moving.

Realizing that the block was being flooded with the para-medics' vehicles, the coroner, and at least a dozen cop cars, I decided it was time for me to get the hell out of Dodge. With this much action one of the local newscasters was bound to be out here in the next several minutes, and I could not afford to let them see me. I could see me now, face plastered all over the front page, with the headlines saying that I was the cause of his suicide. That was the kind of press I was going to stay away from. And the sooner I got off this street, the better my chances were that I wouldn't have to face them or the police.

Also, I wasn't even supposed to be anywhere near Paul or anyone else associated with Shapiro and Witherspoon, per the conditions of my release. As a matter of fact, the other conditions of my release were that Scott had to keep me under strict supervision and make sure I made it to all my court dates, since they figured I was a flight risk. In addition to that, I had to turn over my passport. I was mad as hell about that shit, too, but then I figured that that was a very minor request—considering I was getting my freedom.

Finally, after maneuvering around a few cars that were already in the neighborhood, I was able to make my escape without being seen. And when I got back to the main freeway, I raced back to the Ritz-Carlton. I was a little shaken-up. After watching Paul, I decided that I wasn't ready to face the music of my situation. I was getting the fuck out of Miami, because either I was going to jail for murder one or I was going to be murdered by Sheldon Chisholm—neither of which were choices I had envisioned for my life. Back at the Ritz, in full disguise, I raced past the front desk.

"Hi, Ms. Aoki," the concierge said.

I never answered her. I didn't have time to talk or be nice today. I was now on a mission to get gone. The only reason I had even returned to the hotel was because I decided that I needed to get my real identification so I could go to my overseas stash account and retrieve the remainder of my money. I knew leaving the country would mean leaving Scott high and dry, and the strings he had pulled to get me out on bail were surely going to get him in trouble . . . but I had no choice. There was no fucking way I was going to deal with the trial and Sheldon Chisholm without losing my mind. I was already tired of disguising myself; if I had to do this for another day or so, I knew I would be on the brink of having a nervous breakdown. And I couldn't have that, because how many people that you knew ever came back to their full capacity after that? I didn't know any. So my best bet would be to keep my mind on target and to keep the drama to a minimum.

As I waited in front of the bank of elevators, I paced back and forth. Although the lobby was crowded with people coming and going, I didn't notice anything strange, and I never made eye contact with anyone. Back in my room I dug through the little bit of things I had there and got my stuff together. My identification was the most important thing I'd come back for.

As I made my way around the room, I noticed a manila envelope on the bed. *Ms. Lomax,* it said on the front. My fucking heart immediately went still; I had to remind myself to breathe. No one at the hotel knew me as Ms. Lomax; in fact, only my clients referred to me as Ms. Lomax. Who the fuck knew I was there? Panic struck me like a hammer, crashing into my plans. I thought I'd done a great job keeping a low profile, but obviously someone had figured out my little game.

I looked around the room, feeling like I was not alone. Hands shaking, I slowly picked up the envelope and unwound the little red floss that held it closed. Inside were pictures, several pictures. I stared at the first of the stack; it was a picture of Mr. Santana. I furrowed my eyebrows as I stared at the picture. Mr. Santanta was strapped to a chair, naked and bleeding all over his face. Blood covered his entire chest. There was so much blood, I couldn't tell if he was dead or alive. One thing was for sure, I knew he wasn't going to be alive after they finished with him.

"Oh shit!" I gasped, because deep down inside I knew that this had to be the work of Sheldon's people. So to know that they had finally gotten to Santana before the police could, that gave me a bittersweet feeling. And then I started thinking about how in the hell they were able to get ahold of Luis. I mean, this guy always had at least ten bodyguards around him at all times. So I figured that this had to be the work of an inside job.

The next picture was of Adrianna and it was clear that she was already dead because of the way her eyes were rolled up into her head. All of her fingers were gone, her throat slit, and her body posed in a sexual position. The way I saw it, they wanted to humiliate her, even in death. The whole thing made me sick, and I began to gag.

As bad as I thought I was, and as much as I wanted revenge, this shit was crazy. What had I done? I was the cause of these people getting murdered—the solution I thought was the right one for what they'd done to my life. And although I didn't want to see any more, something beyond me forced me to keep looking. So I continued flipping through the pictures, and the next one shocked the shit out of me.

It was a picture of Brad in a jail cell, and he'd clearly been beaten senseless. He had been hog-tied, his feet were blue, and he had what looked like a broomstick rammed up his ass. I held my chest in disbelief. What the fuck was going on? How did Sheldon find out that I even dealt with Brad? Now this shit was getting scarier by the second. Brad was dead. But why? I never saw anything in the media about his death or even about him missing.

Tears came to the front of my eyes but did not fall. Not until I looked at the next picture. It was a picture of my mother—feeble, skinny, and sick—sitting in her wheelchair and looking dazed and confused. She had not been harmed; I could tell that. Nonetheless, that picture was the thing that finally caused the tears to stream out of my eyes. These ruthless motherfuckers had gone and found my mother.

There was no doubt in my mind that he was threatening me with these pictures, basically sending me a message—telling me that he was capable of killing her if he wanted. But would they really hurt her to get back at me? I asked myself, although I already knew the answer.

I frantically moved on to the next picture. My hands were shaking so badly, I could barely hold on to the stack. The next picture answered my question. It was a picture of Scott Maxwell, my fucking lawyer, the only person I had left in the world to help me. He was still alive, his mouth duct-taped, and he was also strapped to a chair with a sign on his chest: *PLEASE HELP ME, YOSHI.* At the sight of Scott in bondage, my knees buckled. I looked around the room, scared as hell.

Suddenly the phone began to ring. My heart raced inside my chest so hard, it threatened to jump out. I got nauseous as hell because I knew Sheldon's people could be anywhere. I mean, they had to be somewhere nearby to know that I was at the Ritz-Carlton. Not only that, they could've just come in and killed me right on the spot. But there was a reason why they hadn't. It wasn't about money with Sheldon, I knew that. He had plenty of money.

The phone continued to ring, but I was too afraid to answer it. Finally I said fuck it. But by the time I reached for it, it stopped ringing. So I stood still for a few seconds, not knowing what to do. But then after two whole minutes passed, I decided that the best thing for me to do would be to get out.

Just when I was about to walk away from the phone, it rang again. It startled the hell out of me. My heart started pounding, even harder this time. I waited for it to ring four times before I answered; then I nervously snatched the phone up.

"Hello," I said in an audible tone.

"You have until midnight to bring Sheldon Chisholm's money to the West Side," a man's voice threatened. Just the sound of him gave me the fucking chills. I was scared to death. But what was even scarier was that I had been gone from Scott's house for only a couple of days and they'd already found me. So instead of responding, I slammed the receiver back down and fell to my knees; the sobs came in waves, huge waves big enough to crush a city. I cried and cried, feeling hopeless and trapped, until a knock at my hotel room door startled me out of my misery. I looked over at the door and felt like all of the blood had rushed out of my body. There it went again, a soft knock.

"Housekeeping," a soft Hispanic woman's voice sang from the other side. I didn't trust a soul and I didn't answer. I knew if it was really the housekeeper, she would be coming in with her card key, once she didn't get an answer. I waited . . . but nothing. My hands became sweaty and my eyes darted around the room. I just knew any minute Sheldon's men would come rushing in the door with machine guns blazing . . . but still nothing. I got up off the floor and crept until I was standing behind the door, listening. I could hear the housekeepers speaking Spanish to one another in the hallway. Then I heard someone put a key into my door; then there was a beep and a click. I ran inside the bathroom, but it was too late to close the door behind me. I stood still behind the door and waited to see what was about to happen next. My heart was beating uncontrollably as the door began to open wide. And then the housekeeper entered my room. I heaved a sigh of relief when I saw the little Hispanic woman roll her cleaning cart into the room. I stepped from behind the door.

"*Ayi!*" she screamed. "You scared me," she said with her thick accent.

"I'm so sorry, but you scared the hell out of me, too," I apologized.

"Is it okay for me to clean your room?" she asked.

"Yes, you can go ahead," I said, and then right after I gave her the okay, an idea popped into my head. "What's your name?" I asked as I moved closer to her.

"Blanca," she said.

I walked toward her and extended my arm around her shoulder. "Blanca, would you like to earn some extra money?"

She looked at me, really puzzled. "What will I have to do?" she wondered.

"Come over here and I'll show you," I insisted.

Now, I honestly didn't know if she'd go forward with the plan I had just come up with, but when it was all said and done, I was going to make her an offer she would not be able to refuse.

Playing for Keeps

My hands trembled as I used these dull-ass-bladed scissors to hack off the last long lock of my beautiful hair and let it drop into the bathroom sink. The sight of wads of my hair lying in that sink made me feel horrible. I'd always taken pride in my hair, keeping it long as a sign of beauty. But I now had to chop it off in order to save my own life. I felt like throwing those scissors and breaking the glass as I stared at my reflection in the huge vanity mirror; I was definitely a different person—inside and out. The new short, butchered haircut made me look gaunt in the face and it made my slanted eyes look even more prominent. "Damn!" I mumbled.

I officially looked like shit, but it was either look like shit for a little while or die at the hands of those psycho-ass Haitians. Now when Blanca had agreed to help me, I became elated as hell. I sent her on an errand to purchase me a bottle of Clairol fire red hair dye and a pair of almost an inch-long fake eyelashes. She also got me some press-on nails and a housekeeping uniform in my size.

When I first offered Blanca the $10,000 for her uniform, the little Hispanic lady started disrobing that second. As it turned out, though, I was too tall and too slim to fit her uniform. Wanting the money badly, she had told me to wait and she would get me a uniform from one of the younger, more slender housekeepers. Just like she agreed, she came through for me with the uniform.

When I offered her five thousand more, she ran to the store to purchase a few more things I figured I would need to complete this mission. When I was done changing myself into the new me, I came out of the bathroom to show Blanca what person I had turned into.

"Different, *mami* . . . you look very different. You don't look like the same person at all, *señora,*" she told me.

When I looked at myself in the mirror, I thought "different" was an understatement. I looked like a pack of crayons had exploded on my head. Well, let me just say, I felt like I was going to a Halloween costume party. How those housekeepers wore that cheap polyester up against their skin every day was beyond me.

After I was all done changing, Blanca showed me the staff entrance and exit to the hotel. There was no way I would be able to go out the front entrance, even in disguise. I was sure that these monsters probably had all of the exits covered. I also assumed that they would have the service exits covered as well, so Blanca assured me she knew a way to get me out of the hotel safely without alerting anyone.

I felt bad after I said this, but I lied and told her that I was running from an abusive ex-husband, a story I knew she would likely sympathize with. And I was right, because her face turned beet red and she immediately started flying off the handle about how she hated when men put their hands on women. I let her vent about her experiences as she escorted me through the back quarters of the hotel. By the time she finished with her story, she had taken me to where I needed to be. The only other thing I needed at this point was a ride out of here. So I asked her if she'd call me a taxi.

That's when she said, "Oh no, I call my boyfriend for you. He drives taxi."

"Okay, great! Call him," I insisted.

She pulled out her prepaid Boost Mobile phone and got her boyfriend on the line. I heard her tell him to get down to her job right now because she needed him. And when he told her that he'd be there in the next twenty minutes, she hung up. We stood around at the back entrance of the laundry chute and waited patiently.

Meanwhile, as I was standing there, I noticed how hard these women worked. Sweat was pouring from their foreheads and I had not heard one of them complain the entire time. And through it all, I couldn't help but think about my old housekeeper, Ophelia. She was a good woman and she was a hard worker. Never complained one day and I loved that about her. It was funny how you learned to appreciate someone after they're gone. Boy, I was going to miss her.

Finally, after waiting for approximately ten minutes, Blanca's boyfriend rang her cellular phone to tell her that he was outside. She pushed open the door and grabbed ahold of my hand so we could walk out together. Before I took the first step, I took a deep breath and exhaled. I wanted to tell Blanca that I was really on the run for my life, but I was afraid that if I told her I was running from one of the most dangerous drug dealers in Miami, she would have left me high and dry and told her man to get out of here before he got caught in the middle of it. I knew I was putting them both in harm's way, but, hey, what was I going to do? I needed them. And when you needed someone so desperately, then you would resort to anything.

Blanca's boyfriend was waiting outside, near the laundry drop-off area. He was waiting patiently for my arrival. When I approached his car, he got out and opened the door for me. "Thank you," I said.

He was definitely your average Hispanic. To me, all Mexicans look the same; he definitely fit the bill with his height and features. He had to be every bit of five-four. Yes, he was a very short man, stocky too. But he carried his weight well, I might add.

"*Señorita,* where you want to go?" he asked.

"I have a few places I need to go, but right now all I need you to do is get me out of here," I told him, and hopped in the backseat.

"Okay, I take you anywhere you want to go," he replied.

I liked the sound of that, but he had absolutely no idea how far I needed him to go. Although I knew I wouldn't use her boyfriend to get out of Miami, I could sure use him to get halfway where I needed to go. Blanca knew I had money and was willing to pay just to make it out of that hotel alive. Before he and I pulled off, he reached over and gave her a kiss. I kind of looked the other way to give them some privacy. And right before he got into the driver's seat, she whispered something into his ear. He looked down at her pocket, where I believed she stashed the money I had given her, and smiled.

I knew right then she had told him that I paid her a nice piece of change, which was probably a clear indicator to him that I was about to do the same for him. I didn't let on that I read right through their little whispers and eye movements, because to me, it was harmless.

"Ready to go?" he asked the moment he closed the door and looked into his rearview mirror.

I sighed. "I was born ready," I told him.

At that very moment he stepped on the accelerator and bailed the hell out of the service area. I looked out the back window and Blanca was there waving us good-bye. She looked like a guardian angel to me at that point. Somebody up high had been looking out for me; maybe it was Maria.

Now her boyfriend angled the cab down the back streets, just like I had instructed him, and I remained crouched down in the seat until we hit the highway. "What is your name?" I asked.

"Pedro," he replied.

"Thanks so much for your help, Pedro, but do you have a telephone?" I wanted to know.

"*Sí,* I have one," he told me, and reached into his ashtray and handed me his cellular phone.

I grabbed the phone out of his hand and then I dug down into my bra to get the card I had written the number on. It had taken some maneuvering to get the fucking number, since I didn't have my BlackBerry and had no idea where to find it. Maybe the cops had it. My hands shook as I fumbled with the card and the phone. Finally, with shaky hands, I dialed the numbers. I placed the phone to my ear and said a silent prayer that someone picked up. It was ringing, and with each unanswered ring, my heart sank deeper and deeper.

"C'mon . . . c'mon," I wished out loud, swinging my legs back and forth nervously. Finally he picked up the line. "Hello?" he said into the receiver.

Whew! I exhaled a sigh of relief and cleared my throat. I was never so happy to hear a man's voice in my life; his words sounded like sweet music to my ears.

"Hi, Lance, it's Yoshi," I said, my voice cracking despite my efforts to sound sexy.

"Damn, I thought I'd never hear from you, Ms. Big Shot. . . . What's good, ma?" Lance exclaimed at hearing my voice. I'd spoken to him only a few times since our little trip, and, truthfully, I expected him to curse me out and hang up, but he didn't. He was still a perfect gentleman.

"Listen, I need you to meet me at the piers. Remember you said if I ever needed you, I could call on you? Well, I need you right now." I huffed out my words, closing my eyes and waiting for his reaction.

"Shit. I'm at the studio right now, ma . . . everything alright?" Lance asked, changing his tone to serious.

"No, Lance, everything is not alright. I know you've seen the news," I said, growing tired of his little act.

"Hell yeah, sounded like you need a lawyer yourself. What the fuck is up with you?" he answered, not holding back.

"No, I don't need a lawyer right now. What I need is for you to meet me at the piers. I need you like never before, Lance. It's a matter of life and death, and this time I need you to save me," I pleaded. I didn't let my pride get in the way this time.

"A'ight, just for you. I'll be there in twenty minutes," he agreed. He was really a fucking ride-or-die type of dude. He didn't ask any more questions and didn't seem to care what kind of trouble I was in. When he had told me that he would be forever grateful to me for getting him off and saving him from a life sentence, he meant it. I was glad that I'd thought to call on him. Lance Wallace—drug dealer turned platinum rapper, former client—was my only fucking hope right now.

I looked out the window at the cab's location on the highway. Twenty minutes would be perfect, as I estimated it. Lance and I should make it to the pier at the same time. I returned the phone to Pedro, who was looking at me strangely . . . almost like he knew me from somewhere.

He kept looking at me through the rearview mirror until he had made me so uneasy, I had to address it.

"Is there a *problemo*?" I asked him, frustrated.

"No, *mami*," he answered, turning his eyes back to the road. He was fucking making me uneasy, staring like he didn't have any sense. I told him to take me to the piers and

I leaned my head back on the seat and prayed that Lance would agree to help me get away.

When we pulled into the pier, it was crowded as usual. There were people boarding cruise ships and party boats, and the rich people were boarding their yachts. I scanned the crowds with my eyes, trying to see if I recognized any of Sheldon's henchmen. They would have lots of places to hide at the crowded-ass pier. I had to be very careful, and I knew it. I wasn't in the clear just yet. As far as I could tell, the Haitians were nowhere around, but you could never know for sure. I didn't see anyone acting suspicious in the crowds. That was a good sign.

Maybe they were still looking for me in the streets of Miami? They were probably shocked that I wasn't in the hotel room, since their men never saw me leave out the front. They probably had the Ritz-Carlton on lockdown right now as they searched for me, which was good. It would buy me some time.

I lay low inside the cab, waiting to see if I saw Lance. I had noticed Lance's yacht docked and anchored in the same spot it had been the night we went on our trip.

"There . . . that white-and-green yacht, with the gold writing, pull up to it," I said to Pedro.

"Green and white?" he asked, trying to understand me.

"Yes! That boat there . . . the green-and-white one!" I yelled. I was so nervous, my frustration was shining through.

"Okay . . . okay," he replied.

"I'm sorry, I'm just in a rush," I apologized, although I knew he couldn't really understand me. He finally got what I was saying and pulled up behind *La La's Love*. We sat in the car for what seemed like an eternity, and then I saw Lance. Flashy and fine as ever, he bopped down the pier with all of his sex appeal. Of course Lance was flanked by his entourage and was talking and laughing very loud. I wished he would've come alone. I noticed him looking up and down, as if he were trying to find me.

I was so happy inside that he came at all, so I couldn't be picky about him having people with him. It was a first step. Now I just had to convince him to help me get the fuck out of Miami, and fast.

"Thank you so much," I said to Blanca's boyfriend, handing him a thousand, just as I had agreed. He immediately flipped through the money and smiled at me.

"*Gracias,*" he returned.

I slid on my dark shades and my huge sun hat and stepped out of the cab. I walked slowly toward Lance; I knew he wouldn't recognize me. He was laughing and talking with his homeboys when I approached them.

"It sure feels good to see you after all this time," I said in a low whisper, touching his chest.

He looked at me strangely; it was good that he didn't recognize me. I guess he was approached by so many women every day, his bodyguard stepped between us.

"It's me," I said softly as I tilted my glasses slightly away from my eyes; the only thing I couldn't change was my eyes.

"Yo! I didn't recognize your ass with the new look. What's up, Yoshi?" he yelled, grabbing me for a greeting hug.

"*Shhhh,*" I said, instinctively placing my pointer finger over his mouth. I couldn't take a chance on someone hearing my name. "Can we get on the boat? Can we go somewhere and talk? For a sail?" I asked, desperate to get off the streets.

"That's not a problem, c'mon, just me and you," he said. He could tell by my urgency that something was going on.

He signaled to his friends that we were boarding the yacht. At this point I didn't mind having extra people around. Lance and I walked toward his yacht in silence, taking quick steps. I knew he'd have a lot of questions and I was ready to answer them.

La La's Love seemed so inviting. I don't know if it was because I wanted to get on that fucking yacht and sail and sail until I was at the tip of the earth, or if it was because it was the last hope I had for saving my own life. He pulled up on the lever to hoist the anchor and I climbed the steps onto the yacht first. He was right on my heels and his body-guards right on his.

I started to feel good inside. We had made it onto the yacht and in a few minutes we'd be on the sea . . . free. I knew Lance owned property all over the world; I just wanted to choose a place that I could be safe.

I had made it onto the boat first; therefore, I had a bird's-eye view of the entire pier. I squinted my eyes to make sure I was seeing correctly. I swallowed hard as I watched. I watched harder and then panic hit me again.

"Oh shit," I screamed as the figures moved closer. I was in disbelief, but I was also sure of what I was seeing. There was a small commotion on the pier as three guys with long dreadlocks ran straight toward the yacht. I was frozen with fear and then I noticed their guns. Time seemed to stop ticking, and I grabbed onto Lance's arm and screamed.

"Lance! Get down!" Lance had made it onto the yacht and he was confused as I screamed frantically. "Get down!" I screamed again at the top of my lungs. Lance dived onto the floor just as the shots rang out. *Tat, tat, tat, tat, tat, tat . . .* the rapid fire of a submachine gun filtered through the air, sending everyone on the pier scrambling and screaming. The dread guys were blasting shots with no regard for the innocent bystanders around them. I saw one man fall to the ground; he was hit somewhere on his body.

The shots kept coming . . . *tat, tat, tat, tat, tat, tat, tat.*

From the sound you could clearly tell the gun was some kind of machine gun—maybe an Uzi. Lance grabbed onto me and ran down into the main cabin of the yacht. My heart was beating off the chain, I felt like I was having a massive heart attack. As we got our bearings, Lance noticed that one of his bodyguards was hit—the big three-hundred-pound bodyguard lay crying on the yacht's main floor.

"Stay down!" Lance instructed me. He was panicking just as much as me now. I was sobbing uncontrollably.

"I'm sorry," I cried.

"Yo, don't fuckin' worry about it. What the fuck is going on?" he asked as he revved the yacht's engine and got the boat moving. He usually had a captain who drove his yacht, but he'd learned how to drive it himself, he had told me. It was a good thing that he had, or else we would have been sitting ducks. The shots continued, until we made it out into the middle of the ocean. "Stay here, I need to check on my boys," Lance instructed after he put the boat into cruise control. I lay down on the floor in a fetal position and hugged myself. If anyone else was dead, it was my fault. I didn't even want to know if Lance's boy had gotten killed.

"You a'ight, Yoshi?" he asked, breathing hard as he returned.

"I'm so sorry for getting you involved. I thought we could get out of there before they came." I cried as he hugged me.

"Calm down, it's cool! Everybody is okay," he assured me. "Now tell me what the fuck is up," he said, looking into my face.

I leaned on Lance and told him everything. I told him about the Santanas, Sheldon, Paul, the drug use, Maria's murder, the setup. I poured my heart out and he was a willing receptacle. Lance was concerned and he listened to me intently. I told him that I had no plan for my life and that I just needed to get out of Miami. I told him that I didn't need his money because I had some of my own. Lance also understood when I told him why I called him, because I couldn't take a plane, since I'd jumped bail. I cried and cried when I told Lance about how I'd left Scott to be killed after Scott had helped me.

"You ain't have no choice. It's not your fault," Lance comforted. There were so many dead bodies because of me. "I got someplace you can lay up, Yoshi. . . . Don't you fuckin' worry. Those Haitians are fucking punks!" Lance spat. He had my back and it felt so good. Lance helped his injured bodyguard by placing some towels and gauze over his wound. Lucky for the guy, it was more of a graze wound than an actual shot. All of those shots and no one had gotten killed. Once again, I felt like someone was watching over me. The other guys on the yacht didn't have much to say to me. It seemed like they were pissed that I had gotten Lance caught up in some shit—especially after Lance had survived being shot twelve times when he was a street dealer. The first night Lance and I had fucked on our last trip, I had kissed his healed gunshot wounds.

"Those fucking Haitians don't know what they started," Lance barked, pacing up and down the floor. He was angry and now he was involved.

"Please just let it go, Lance. It was me they were after," I replied, trying to calm him down.

"I don't give a fuck! You don't roll up on me like that. This shit is not over," he yelled. His boys were backing him up. I had started another war. It was best for everyone that I just fucking disappear. It took hours before Lance finally calmed down enough to talk. He had so many more questions for me, but the one that struck me the most was "How did you go from high-class, high-paid superstar attorney to being on the run for murder, with people out to murder you?" That was a good question, and I was not able to answer it.

Lance and I stayed up for hours talking. Neither one of us was able to sleep. After about six hours of sailing, we finally docked in the Bahamas.

"Yoshi, you stay on with the other dudes. It's too dangerous for you to get off," Lance instructed. He said I'd be safer on the yacht and that he'd bring back everything we needed to get where we were going, which I still didn't know where. He went on land to get food and supplies. Although I wanted to go with him, he explained that he didn't want me to chance coming off in the Bahamas, since it was so close to Florida. It would be the logical place for the Haitians to look for me. He was being so good to me when he really could have told me to fuck off. When he returned to the boat, he had spared no expense. He'd purchased champagne, seafood, and caviar. I didn't have an appetite for any of that stuff.

After leaving the Bahamas, we got settled in for the night. He told me I could take the same room I had the last time, but I refused. I asked him if I could sleep with him. I didn't want to be alone. He welcomed me into his bed with open arms. The way he treated me started to seem unreal; I had never had anyone treat me so well. He and I cuddled in the master bedroom of the ship, and this time I made the first move. I grabbed him around his waist and hugged him into my body tight.

"What's that for?" he asked.

I didn't say a word. I looked up into his face and just made a half smile. I grabbed onto his shirt and pulled it up over his head, exposing his muscular chest. I kissed his chest and ran my tongue over his nipples. I moved my way down and unbuckled his pants. I wanted to taste him. I wanted him. I wanted to feel connected to something or someone. Lance had saved my life and he deserved what I was about to give him.

"You don't have to do this, Yoshi," he whispered.

"I want to," I said in return, taking his dick deep into my mouth. I wet his dick with my spit and ran my mouth up and down the thick shaft. I could feel his vein pulsing up against my tongue. My pussy was soaking wet, and my body yearned for Lance to enter me. Lance moaned softly and suddenly pulled away from me. He must have been feeling just like me, ready. He grabbed me and threw me onto the bed. My legs were shaking as he gently pulled my panties off. I wanted that dick so bad, I could already feel it. He grabbed his throbbing dick and pushed it into me deep. I winced and grabbed handfuls of the skin on his neck, his back, and his shoulders. I moved my hands frantically all over his body as he drove his dick farther and farther inside me.

Lance and I fucked to a rhythm all our own as the ship went over the ocean's waves. I climaxed first and then he did, letting every bit of his juices burst into my pussy. I didn't even care. He had saved my life, given me a new beginning. After we were done tossing each other all around the bed, and making each other come over and over again, we lay together, our legs tangled into each other. I cried softly into the skin on his chest and he stroked my head. We didn't speak any words, because we both knew the deal. Lance had his life and now I had what was left of mine—but for that moment we were with each other, as one.

After hours of no words being spoken, he finally broke the silence. "You know after I take you to a safe place, I gotta go back to the States, right?" he asked me, still stroking my head lightly.

"Why? You might not be safe now," I said, concerned. I

had gotten him involved with the Chisholm mess, and now I was worried about his safety.

"Yoshi, I got a career to think about. I gotta stack my dough some more before I can retire. I'm trying to be like the rest of these cats 'round here. I want my empire to be worth a billion before I decide to retire and settle down," he explained. His words cut through me like a knife, because I wanted nothing more than for him to ride off with me into the sunset and never turn back.

"I understand," I said softly. I really did understand where he was coming from. It was unfair for me to expect him to just drop his life for me. I was more than grateful for what he was doing for me already.

"Maybe one day, when I'm ready, I'll be back for you," he said as he continued to stroke my chopped-up hair.

"I hope so," I said, closing my eyes, letting the tears fall down my face. I was physically and mentally exhausted, and after days I finally let sleep take over me.

Stay Down

Lance and I sailed for an entire week. I had gotten used to his company and had finally started to feel at ease with the fact that I'd made it out of Miami alive. We made love over and over again, and each time I felt closer to him. The reality that he was going to leave me was still looming in my mind. He finally docked the yacht in Barbados—our favorite place in the Caribbean. He showed me to his mansion on the beach; the same one we had stayed in the first time we were there. In his neighborhood Rihanna had a house, and so did a few other celebrities. I would be living amongst the stars, in luxury once again.

"Yoshi, this is yours now. You stay here for as long as you need and you'll be safe," Lance had said, placing his keys in my hand. He had made me feel so good.

"I wish you could stay with me," I said sadly. I had left everything I knew back in Miami, and when Lance left, I knew I'd be alone.

"I'll be back to check on you, ma. Don't stress it," he said.

"Thank you for everything," I said, grabbing him and hugging him tightly.

"It's all good," he said, kissing me on my forehead. For the first time in my life, I felt like I wanted one man in my life. At that moment I would have given up everything I had left to have Lance all to myself.

Lance left and returned to the States, which was the hardest thing for me to accept. After spending more time with him, I was wishing he could be there every minute. Once he was gone, I tried to make myself comfortable in my new surroundings. He had given me his vacation home to use. The house was absolutely gorgeous. There were six huge bedrooms, and six bathrooms as well. A beach house was attached and a bathhouse, with an outdoor shower. The house sat on its own half-mile-long portion of the most beautiful white-sand beach. He had told me that he owned just a small swallow of the ocean, and now I believed him. I guess I could get used to living like an island girl.

Each day I found something new to do. Of course I had already hit Bridgetown again. I shopped and purchased an entire set of David Yurman jewelry, twelve pairs of high-end designer shoes, three pairs of shades, and six bags—including a Hermès Birkin bag. I had to replace the things I'd left behind in Miami. Indulging in the finer things again made me feel almost whole, but not being able to practice law still had me missing my old life.

Every day I thought about Lance. He'd called a few times after he left, but he was on tour now, so his time was limited. I occupied myself with other things in Barbados, too. I strolled the beach, sunbathed, learned to ride a Jet Ski, read books, and even made a few new Bajan friends. Nothing, however, beat the hustle and bustle of my career and Miami.

It had been a month since the last time I saw Lance face-to-face, but like clockwork he would call me every morning to check on me. He always wanted to know if I was alright. And after I would assure him more than a dozen times, he'd blow me a couple of kisses through the phone and then we would hang up.

This morning I woke up to the early morning sunrise, got me a cup of hot tea, took a seat on the patio recliner, and watched the waves coming in on the shore. I looked at my watch at least fives times, because I knew that at any moment Lance would be calling me to check in. I turned when I heard Lana, his housekeeper, approach me.

"Excuse me, ma'am, there's a call for you," she said and handed me the cordless phone.

Shocked that I would be getting a call on the house line, I asked her who it was before I took the phone out of her hand.

"It's Mr. Wallace's manager," she told me, then she walked away to give me some privacy.

I put the phone to my ear and said, "Hello."

"Yoshi. This is Mike."

"What's up, Mike?"

"I don't know how to tell you this, but . . ."

"Tell me what?" I interjected.

"Lance was shot last night while we where leaving the night club . . ."

My heart fell down in the pit of my stomach and I screamed. "He was what? Where is he?" I cut him off.

"Yoshi, he was rushed to the hospital right after the shooting, but he didn't make it out of the surgery."

I screamed even louder. "No, he can't be dead! Not Lance."

"Yoshi, I am sorry. The doctors tried everything," Mike said. He continued on, telling me that Lance had had a heated argument inside the club with some cats so the bouncers escorted them out of there. Lance thought everything was all good until he exited the club and bullets started flying. Everybody ran for cover, but Lance wasn't so lucky because the first couple of bullets hit him directly in the chest and the other ones hit him in the shoulder and the leg. While I was listening to Mike paint the picture of Lance's murder, I sat on the patio chair in shock. My ear was plastered to the phone while the tears fell from my eyes. It seemed like everyone I held dear was being taken away from me.

"Does anyone know who shot him?" I said, wiping the tears from my eyes.

"No, we don't. But we're assuming that it was the guys he had beef with inside the club."

"Did anyone give the police that information?"

"Yes, we did. As a matter of fact, me, Calvin, and Alonzo are on our way down to the Miami-Dade police department to give a statement and look at some mug shots."

Realizing he'd just said that he was on his way down to the Miami-Dade police department gave me the fucking chills. At that point I wanted to sever all ties for fear that my name would pop up. I was sure that Mike and the rest of his crew knew that I was on the run from the Feds and that the Haitians had a bounty on my head, so I knew I couldn't take any chances at getting caught up behind somebody's greed. From what I've heard the Feds were offering a half million dollars for any information about my whereabouts. In addition to that, Sheldon put out a $250 thousand dollar bounty on my head. Since Lance was no longer alive to keep those chumps on the payroll, they could turn on me at the drop of the hat and I wasn't about to give them a chance to do it.

I said a few more words to Mike and then I got off the phone. I was too weak to get up from my chair, so I called Lana to help me. She sprinted back out to where I was and immediately helped me get back to my room. After I sat down on the bed, an eerie calm came over me. When I looked up at her, Lana asked me what was wrong. I wanted to answer her, but my mouth wouldn't move. I must've been in shock because my mind went completely blank and I couldn't get a word to come out of my mouth. I heard her talking to me, but it was like she was talking in slow motion. Lana grabbed my arm and started shaking me until I snapped out of it. My skin felt hot and my legs felt numb. My heart began to race and it seemed like everything was spinning.

"He's dead, Lana," I finally said.

She panicked. "Ms. Aoki, what are you talking about? Who's dead?"

"Lance is dead!"

Lana's mouth hung open, but she didn't say one word. I started crying hysterically. "Oh my God, I can't believe he's gone! What am I going to do now?"

I searched Lana's eyes for an answer of my own.

She took a seat on the edge of the bed beside me. "I don't know," she finally said, her voice barely audible.

I needed to clear my head and think of how I was going to make my next move, so I decided to take a walk. I told Lana I would be right back, then I tried to stand up, but my legs wouldn't cooperate. The next I knew, I'd fainted.

I could hear voices around me, but I couldn't seem to open my eyes. They were murmuring about me, and every now and then I felt someone touch me. When I came to, I was in my bed, Lance's bed. Lana had placed a cold compress on my head and I awoke to the doctor taking my vital signs. "What happened?" I asked, my voice crackly.

"You passed out, Ms. Aoki. I called Dr. Leonard because I was scared," Lana explained, concern riddling her face.

"Hi, Ms. Aoki. I'm Dr. Leonard. I came right over when Ms. Lana called me. You looked pretty sick," the doctor stated. I just stared at him blankly.

I tried to sit up, but I still felt light-headed. Finding out about Lance's death was too much for me to handle. I knew right then I needed to get the hell out of this country before anyone realized that I had been hiding out here. After the doctor talked with me for a few minutes, he packed up his things and left. I lay in the bed for another ten minutes and then thought about what I was going to do. I knew leaving would be the best thing for me, since this house didn't belong to me. Everything around here was in Lance's name, so whoever was the executor of his estate would be coming out here soon enough to collect and in the process they would kick my ass out.

Slowly, I began to pull my plans together. After leaving that check with Scott to cover my bail, and spending like crazy down here in Barbados, I had a couple hundred thousand left in my account. I knew that wasn't going to take me very far, being as I was on the run. Everyone, including Sheldon, the DEA, and all of Miami-Dade police, were looking for me. It wouldn't surprise me if I was on *America's Most Wanted,* and if that was the case, then my chances of moving around without being seen were slim to none. Unless I went to Virginia like I had planned to do a while back. No one out there knew me except for my family, so I should be fine. The only thing I needed to worry about was how in the hell I was going to get from here to there.

Meanwhile, I got Lana to help me pack. I stuffed everything of value into five large pieces of Louis Vuitton luggage, and everything else I left behind. I figured those things could be replaced at a later date, so I'd be alright.

I waited for the taxi downstairs in the foyer of the house, and while I was waiting, Lana stood next to me, begging me not to leave.

"I'm sorry, but I've got to go," I told her. "Lance is not coming back, so I have to move on."

"Why don't you wait until his family comes first?"

"No, Lana. That won't be a good idea."

"But I'm sure they would want to meet you."

"Maybe some other time," I said. And before she was able to weigh me down about staying, my taxi pulled up. I got her to help the driver with my bags, and after everything was loaded into the car, I got into the backseat and waved her off. "Take me to the airport," I instructed the driver.

"Okay, no problem," he told me, and then he took off.

When we arrived at the airport, I was kind of leery to approach the counter to purchase a ticket, for fear that someone might recognize me. But then I figured, how in the hell else was I going to get out of here? I had to take my chances. I pushed my sunglasses back and went for what I knew. And as soon as the woman asked me for a picture ID, I handed her my passport that said Yoshi Aoki. My nerves were running me ragged while I waited for her to process me into the system.

"Where to?" she wanted to know, while she was keying my information in.

My lips were numb. I honestly didn't know what to tell the lady. But then the words "Houston, Texas," spewed from my mouth without me even realizing it. I believed Lance and Maria were subconsciously telling me I needed to take a detour to get to Virginia. So that's exactly what I intended to do. After the airport attendant printed out my baggage labels, she attached them to my bags and handed me my ticket. Once those tickets were in my hand, I let out a sigh of relief and walked off toward the gates.

But I wasn't in the clear yet. I still had to go through security in order to get on the plane, so that was the next hurdle I had to jump. The airport was really crowded. Everyone was busy trying to get everything situated so they could board their flight. I watched how security handled each and every person who had to go through their checkpoint. When it was my turn to go through, I damn near had a panic attack. But somehow or another I managed to hold myself together. When one of the airport security officers asked me for my passport and boarding ticket, I handed them both to him and smiled. He looked down at them and then back up at me. "Houston, huh?" he commented.

Barely audible, I said, "Yes."

"You have family there?" he pressed on.

"Yes, I do," I lied.

He smiled. "Have a safe flight," he told me, then handed me my passport and boarding pass.

It felt like I was holding my breath, waiting for someone to notice me. As soon as I walked aboard the plane, I let out a sigh of relief. I was almost home free.

What's Next?

My plane landed safely and my arrival to Houston's airport was not as scary as I thought it would be. My main concern was getting back on United States soil without getting caught, and so far I had managed to do that. Swiftly, I walked into the baggage claim area and retrieved my things without anyone breathing down my neck. Then I hobbled over to the rental car area of the airport with my luggage in tow and waited in line for the next available representative. The process of getting a car took less time than expected—I was out of the airport and in my vehicle in about fifteen minutes.

As I drove down highway 76, I knew I was home free. I turned on the radio and tuned in to an old joint, "Where I'm From" by Jay Z. I was bopping my head, feeling the hell out of this jam. I mean, hey, I was on the freeway heading right to VA where my family was. No one was on my heels keeping me from getting there, so I was happy as hell. I didn't know what to expect when I got there, but I guess I'd have to cross that bridge when I got there. As far as the DEA and Miami-Dade police detectives were concerned, I was on the run. But the way I looked at it, I was running for my life. I hadn't done any of the shit they had penned on me. The only thing I was guilty of was having a fucking coke habit, and that shit went out the window a while ago. It was time to start a new life, but at the same time I had to play low-key and get on the level of the people in Virginia or else I would stick out like a sore thumb. I couldn't have that. My freedom was too valuable. I just hoped my family wasn't as shiesty as the motherfuckers I left back in Miami, because if they were, I was going to be fucked up all over again. I guess I would find out soon.

PLAYING DIRTY

Kiki Swinson

ABOUT THIS GUIDE

The following questions are intended to
enhance your group's reading of
PLAYING DIRTY.

Discussion Questions

1. How did you feel about the main character, Yoshi Lomax?

2. Were the methods she used to win her cases necessary?

3. If you could change one thing about Yoshi, what would it be?

4. Because of what Yoshi brought to the table, did you feel like she should have made partner at the firm?

5. It wasn't guaranteed that Mr. Alvarez would have sought out Yoshi as his counsel after the DEA busted him. Do you think Yoshi was wrong for going behind Maria's back to tell Mr. Alvarez that he had an informant in his midst just so she could gain a big paycheck?

6. Maria did not have any proof that Yoshi blew her agents' investigation. Was she wrong for turning her back on Yoshi?

7. Do you think Yoshi was going in over her head when she took Sheldon's case and promised him an acquittal?

8. What do you think was Yoshi's downfall?

9. When Yoshi found out that Paul and Mr. Santana had plotted to turn her life upside down, do you think her actions in getting revenge were justified?

10. After everything that happened to Yoshi, do you think she learned her lesson?

Want to know what happens to Yoshi Lomax?
Don't miss the sequel to *Playing Dirty*

Notorious

Available in September 2009 wherever books are sold.
Until then, enjoy the following excerpt. . . .

Life in VA

I crossed a lot of state lines to get to my father's hometown, but I made it.

When I stepped foot into the state of Texas, I saw my picture plastered across the cover of several newspapers. Believe me when I tell you, I got the hell out of there really quick. I rented a Toyota Highlander from Enterprise, stuffed all my things into the back of it, and drove the rest of the way to Virginia. It took me approximately twenty-two hours to get to my destination. Along the way, I prayed that my father's people hadn't heard about my brush with the law and the reward that they were offering. It had been a long time since we had been together, so I was like a stranger to them, which would make it easy for any one of them to turn me in. I had to keep my eyes and ears open, and the first time I sensed that something wasn't right, I was going to haul ass without even looking back.

I had to admit that I was tired as hell when I arrived in Norfolk, so I stopped by the Marriott hotel downtown near Waterside Drive to get some rest. It was around three in the afternoon, so I was able to wear my sunshades in front of the hotel clerk without looking awkward. After I paid for my room with cash, I headed up to the fifth floor to unwind. I started to call my cousin Carmine right after I un-packed, but then decided to wait until I got me a nap.

When I woke up, it was a little after seven, so I got up from the bed and decided to make the call to my family. The only number I had was the number to my father's mother house. My grandmother had had that number for as long as I could remember, and it had never been disconnected. So I figured that when I called her I could get Carmine's number and make some arrangements to hook up.

The phone rang about four times before someone picked it up. I wasn't too familiar with the woman's voice, so I said hello and asked to speak with my grandmother.

"Can I ask who's calling?" the woman asked.

"This is her grandaughter, Yoshi," I replied.

"Wait a minute. Now I know this ain't my cousin Yoshi from New York."

"Yes . . . is this Carmine?"

"Oh my God! I can't believe it's you."

"How you been?"

"I've been doing okay. What about yourself?"

"Nothing has changed. I'm still a lawyer, trying to make a name for myself."

"Wow! When we were kids I remember how we used to talk about when we grew up that we were going to be law-yers. But you were the only one who stuck with it. Damn, that's so good."

"Trust me, Carmine, life as an attorney isn't a bowl of fucking cherries. Girl, you've got to constantly stay on the grind and stay away from the psycho-ass clients. They will try to kill you," I replied, reflecting on the shit I went through back in Miami with Haitian drug lord Sheldon Chisholm. He was part of the reason I was on the run from the law.

"Ahh, it can't be that bad. Shit, I would love to have your life any day."

"You can't be doing that bad."

"Yoshi, I am over thirty and working as a fucking waitress at the I-Hop on 21st Street. I live with Grandma and I don't have a car. Now tell me I'm not in a fucked-up situation?"

I thought about it and the answer was clear. She was in a fucked-up situation. Not as fucked-up as mine, but she was on my tail. I never would have pictured Carmine's life like this. Back when we were kids, she was always the smarter one. She was prettier, too. All the boys wanted to be her boyfriend before they ever considered looking at me. There was no doubt that I was an attractive little girl growing up, but the boys couldn't get over my chinky eyes and the fact that I was boney as hell. Those little neighborhood bastards chose Carmine over me every single time because of her almond-shaped eyes and big butt. I dealt with their bullshit the entire time I was in Virginia visiting my dad. I wondered where those boys are now? Probably in jail on drug charges or deployed over in Iraq. Whatever their status was right now, it sure wasn't helping Carmine out, because the way she just laid out everything, shit was really messed up for her. I just hoped she didn't try to come at me with her hand out because I had only enough money to last me until I could make my next power move. Now, don't get me wrong, I'd help her as much as I could, but I would not purchase her a car. Instead of making any comments about her situation, I just told her that she was going to be alright.

"Easy for you to say. You're the big-time lawyer."

I sighed heavily. "That's what you think."

"So what's going on? Last time I heard, you moved on down to Florida."

"Yes, that was true. But I just took some time off and now I'm not too far from you."

"What do you mean, you're not too far from me? Where are you?" Carmine got excited.

"I'm in Norfolk at the downtown Marriott."

"Oh my God! Are you serious?"

"Yes, I'm serious. So let's get together in about another hour so we can continue to catch up."

"Are you driving?"

"Yes, I have a rental."

"Okay, well, you can come by the house and pick me up. That way you can see Grandma and the rest of the family."

"Does Grandma still live in the same house from when we were kids?"

"Yep, she sure does. Ain't nothing changed but our ages."

The thought of my grandmother still living in that old house made me cringe. I honestly couldn't imagine anyone living in a house for as long as she has. I thought back to when I used to visit her and how the floor used to crackle because the hardwood flooring was old and had never been maintained. I also remembered her having wooden paneling on her walls, space heaters in every room of the house during the winter season, and one big air conditioner in the living room during the summer months. Everybody used to pile up in that small-ass room when it was hot. That was the only way to stay cool. I just hoped conditions for them had gotten a little bit better.

After I told Carmine to get ready and that I would be out there to get her in about an hour, she said okay and then we hung up. It took me only thirty minutes to hop in the shower and get dressed. Even though I was a fugitive, I didn't need to look sloppy, so I slid on a pair of dark blue Chip & Pepper jeans, a black wool Ellen Tracy turtleneck sweater, and a black pair of Fendi riding boots. It was kind of nippy outside, so I also threw on a wool blazer with patches on the elbow. Right before I left La La's estate in South America, I had gotten some hair extensions put in my hair, so I was back to my normal-looking self. I planned to have Carmine point me in the direction of a good hair stylist because I was overdue for a full makeover.

The Reunion I Will
Never Forget

The distance from the hotel to my grandmother's house was a total of seven miles. From the looks of it, a lot of things had indeed changed since I last visited. I saw that a lot of new high-rise developments had gone up while a lot of the low-income housing projects were torn down. I figured that was a good thing. But while I was driving down Church Street toward Huntersville where my family grew up, I noticed that some of the houses were condemned. The farther I drove into the neighborhood, the more ravaged it became. To make matters worse, there were at least five bums and drug addicts on each corner. The neighborhood small-time drug pushers weren't too far from them, so there was no question that there were hand-to-hand deals in the works.

I wanted so badly to turn around and go back the way I'd come, but I figured that being amongst my people would probably be the only way I could stay clear of the police. No one around here looked like they'd watched the news in a very long time, so they wouldn't recognize me. Continuing my journey to my grandmother's house, I drove about two more blocks before pulling up in front of her domain. The house was exactly how I remembered it, except the vinyl siding was gray instead of white and the front porch was packed with living-room furniture instead of your normal outdoor furniture. The old cloth fabric sofa and love seat were probably filled with mold and mildew from the rain and outside moisture. I knew for sure that I wouldn't be sitting on that godforsaking-looking thing. I was going to keep my visits here to a minimum and carry my ass back to my hotel.

As soon as I got out of the truck and closed the door behind me, the front door to the house opened and Carmine walked out onto the porch. "Oh my God! I can't believe it's you." She smiled and raced toward me.

We embraced each other, then I pulled back from her so I could get a good look at her. I wasn't too pleased with how Carmine was looking. She wasn't pretty like she used to be. She used to have beautiful skin and long and healthy hair. Her figure was the same, but somehow or another she looked like she was at least ten years older than me. She had bags under her eyes that looked like she needed surgery to get rid of them. And her clothes were a mess. She was wearing an old, red, hideous Enyce velour sweat suit with lint balls covering the entire jacket. The Reebok classic sneakers she had on looked a little better than the sweat suit, but not by much. Her hair was combed back into a ponytail, but the edges near her scalp sent a clear message that she needed a relaxer a.s.a.p. I wanted to be the one to tell her, but it was too early in the game for me to be giving her advice without her taking it personal. I wouldn't want us to have a falling out within the first five minutes of us reuniting. That wouldn't be appropriate at all. So, I smiled and said, "I can't believe it's you either."

"You look so good," she said as she circled around me to check me out.

I smiled. "Thanks," I said, then I threw my Prada handbag over my shoulder as if to say, let's proceed into the house, please. Apparently she caught on to the hint, because not even a second later she grabbed my arm and told me to come on in the house. We treaded over the weak wooden planks that were there to support the foundation of the porch and then went inside the house. Carmine walked ahead of me and led me straight to the back room of the house, which was where everyone hung out. It was like the meeting room for the family.

My grandmother was sitting in a recliner facing the television when I walked into the room. I would bet every dime I had stashed away that she was seventy-two years old, but she looked like she was every bit of fifty-five to sixty. She hadn't aged one bit from the last time I saw her. She kind of reminded me of Martin Lawrence's Big Mama character from the movie *Big Mama's House*. When she saw me, she smiled and said, "I see you're not a little girl anymore. Come on over and give me a hug."

I leaned over and hugged her. "How have you been?" I asked her after I stood back up.

"I've been doing fine. Now take a seat," she instructed me, pointing to the sofa next to her.

I sat on the sofa and crossed my legs while Carmine took a seat next to me. "I see you haven't changed anything around here," I commented, looking around the room.

"When you got family living with you, tearing your mess down, how can you keep everything looking like the first day you bought it?" she replied with a disgusted expression. "I've been trying to keep all my kids from coming back in my home for years, but they don't listen. They all get out there in those streets and get on those drugs and forget all about their bills. When they get kicked out of their houses, where do you think they come? Here. And their trifling tails don't ever offer me any money. And on top of that, they come up here and steal me blind."

"Wow! Are you kidding me?" I asked.

"Honey, Grandma Hattie don't do no lying."

"So, who's staying here with you besides Carmine?"

"Carmine's mama Sandra and her little sister Rachael."

"How long have they been living here?" I asked.

"For about six months now, but before they moved back in, your Uncle Reginald was sleeping on that sofa you're sitting on for three years. I just put his butt out a couple of weeks ago because I caught him trying to steal my social security check from out my pocketbook."

"Oh my God! That's awful."

"Child, you ain't seen nothing. Be around here longer than a week and you gon' see what Grandma Hattie be going through."

"You need a vacation."

"I sure do, but I can't go nowhere and leave my house. Shoot, I'd probably mess around and come back and my house will be burned down to the ground. Or it'll be empty from Sandra trying to sell everything out of here."

"Why would she do that?"

"To support her drug habit. What else?"

"Are you serious?"

"Grandma done already told you that she don't do no lying," Carmined blurted out.

"What does she get high off of?"

"She's on that heroin stuff. And that mess got her looking really bad, too."

"I am sorry to hear that."

"Honey, all we can do is pray for her because she ain't gon' stop running them streets until something powerful stops her in her tracks."

I really didn't know what else to say about that situation with Carmine's mother. I mean, who was I to pass judgment? I was a recovering cokehead. Thankfully, I hadn't gotten as bad as my aunt Sandra, but the fact that I used drugs still lingered in my head. So, my best bet was to leave that subject alone.

I was about to extend a dinner invitation to Carmine and Grandma Hattie when the back door burst wide open and the doorknob tore a hole into the wall it smashed into. That shit scared the hell out of me. I thought the police were busting in and I was going to be handcuffed and hauled downtown to Norfolk's jail until an extradition order was processed for me to be sent back to Florida.

While I sat there in stunned silence, my grandmother and Carmine jumped to their feet. "What in the world . . ." my grandmother said, and then her words faded. Two seconds later, I heard loud thumping noises heading toward us, and a man's voice saying, "Bitch, you gon' die this time!"

To my surprise, I witnessed my aunt Sandra being tossed up against the wall outside the den area where we were, and staring down the barrel of a .357 Magnum. Tears were pouring down her face as she pleaded for her life. I honestly couldn't believe my fucking eyes. This young-looking street thug, who looked like he wasn't more than twenty-one years old, seriously had some balls running up in here like this. I sat back in awe and watched the whole scene as it unfolded.

"What in the world is going on?" my grandmother cried out.

"This bitch gave me some fake money for my dope!" he roared, still pointing the pistol directly at her forehead.

"How much does she owe you?" my grandmother pressed on, as she began to dig inside the secret compartment of her bra.

"Forty dollars," he said.

"Please don't kill her. I'll give you the money," she pleaded, then pulled out several five- and ten-dollar bills.

After she counted it to make sure it was the correct amount, she handed it to the guy.

With the gun still at Sandra's head he took the money and counted it to make sure it was all there. Right when he was about to walk off, he mashed Sandra in her face really hard, sending her straight to the floor. "Next time ain't nobody gon' be able to save you," he warned her and then exited the house.

This was too much fucking drama for me. I needed to get out of there and go back to my hotel and regroup before something else happened. Maybe coming to Virginia was the wrong thing to do. I mean, I thought the niggas back in Miami were crazy. But these motherfuckers here aren't playing with a full deck, so I'm definitely going to have to rethink my whole strategy.

But where else could I go without being noticed?

Enjoy the following excerpts from
Kiki Swinson's previous novels

Wifey
I'm Still Wifey
Life After Wifey

Available now wherever books are sold!

From *Wifey*

Tired of the Drama

It's 4:30 am in the morning and I've been pacing back and forth from my bed to my bedroom window, which overlooked the driveway of my six-hundred-thousand-dollar house, waiting for my husband Ricky to bring dat ass home. Who cared about all the plucks he had to make every other night? I kept telling him, all money ain't good money! But he didn't listen. Not to mention, I had to deal with all his hoes on a daily basis. We've been married for seven years now, and since then I've had to spend a whole lot of nights alone in this gorgeous five-bedroom home he got for us two years ago. That's how his three children came into play. All of them were by different chickenheads who lived in the projects. But one of them had a Section Eight crib somewhere in D.C. and she was ghetto as hell. Just like the other two, who lived not too far from here.

Now, Ricky didn't have enough sense to go out and donate his sperm to women with some class. Every last one of them were high school dropouts, holding eighth-grade educations and an ass full of drama. They figured since Ricky had a baby by them, that he was gonna leave me to be with their nasty tails. Oh, but trust me! It won't happen! Not in *this* lifetime. Because all they could offer him was pussy. And the last time I checked, pussy wasn't in high demand these days like them hoes thought. That's why I could say with much confidence—that *Ricky needed me*. I kept his hotheaded ass straight. And not only that, I've got assets. I'm light-skinned and very pretty with a banging ass body! Niggas in the street said I reminded them of the rapper Trina because both of us favored each other and we had small waists and big asses. And to complement all that, I knew how to play most of the games on the street, as well as the ins and outs of running the hair salon I opened a few years back. Not to mention, Ricky gave me the dough to make it happen. Now you see, he was good for something other than screwing other chicks behind my back. This was why I was always trying to find reasons not to leave his ass.

So, after pacing back and forth a few more times, Mr. Good Dick finally pulled his sedan into the driveway. I made my way on downstairs to greet his butt at the front door. "What you doing up?" he asked as soon as he saw me standing in the foyer.

"Ricky, don't ask me no stupid-ass questions! I told him with much attitude. Then I moved backwards two steps, giving him enough room to shut the front door.

"What you upset for?" he responded with uncertainty.

I'm standing dead smack in front of my husband, who is, by the way, very, very handsome with a set of six packs out of this world. I'm wearing one of my newest Victoria's Secret lingerie pieces, looking extra sexy; and all he could do was stand there looking stupid and ask me what I'm upset for? I wanted so badly to smack the hell outta him; but I decided to remain a lady and continue to get him where it hurts, which is his pockets. This dummy had no clue whatsoever that I was robbing his ass blind.

Every time he put some of his dough away in his stash I was right behind him, trimming the fat around the edges.

"Kira, baby don't give me that look," Ricky continued.

"You know I'm out on the grind every night for me and you."

"Ricky, I don't wanna hear your lies," I tell him and walk to the kitchen.

And like I knew he would, he followed in my footsteps.

"Baby!" he started pleading. "Look what I gotcha!"

I knew it. He's always pulling something out of his hat when I'm about to put his ass on the hot seat. He knows I'm a sucker for gifts. "Whatever you got for me, you can take your ass right back out in the streets, find all your babies' mamas, play Spin the Bottle and whoever the fuck wins, just give it to them." I fronted like I wasn't interested.

"Shit, them hoes wouldn't ever be able to get me to cop a bracelet like this for them!" Ricky tells me.

"They weren't hoes when you were screwing 'em."

"Look Kira, I didn't come home to argue wit' you. All I wanna do right now is see how this joint looks on your wrist."

Curious as to how iced out this bracelet was, I turned around with a grit on my face from hell. "You look so sexy when you're mad," he told me.

Hearing him tell me how sexy I looked made me want to smile real bad, but I couldn't put my guard down. I had to show this clown I wasn't playing with his ass and was truly tired of his bullshit. All his baby mama drama, the other hoes he was seeing and the many trips he took out of town, acting like he was taking care of business. Shit, I wasn't stupid! I knew all them trips he took weren't solely for business. But it's all lovely. While he thinks he's playing me, I'm straight playing his ass, too.

"Where you get this from?" I asked, continuing to front like I wasn't at all excited about this H series diamond watch by Chopard.

"Don't worry 'bout that," Ricky told me as he fastened the hook on it. "You like it?"

Trying to be modest, I told him, "Yeah." And then I looked him straight in his eyes with the saddest expression I could muster. I immediately thought about how I lost my mother to a plane crash just hours before I graduated from high school. I tried talking her into taking an earlier flight from her vacation in Venezuela, but she refused to leave her third husband out there alone and wanted to guard him from walking off with one of those young and beautiful women roaming around the beaches. So once again, she allowed her obsession for wealth to dictate her way of life. I hated to admit it but over the years, I had become the spitting image of her. I wanted nothing to do with a man who couldn't give me all the fine things in life. And since my mother had not been married to her third husband long enough, I got stiffed when his will was read. The only two choices I had was to either move in with my uncle and his family or my grandmother Clara, who were my only living relatives. So, guess what? I chose neither. I did this because I just felt like I didn't belong with any of them. I mean, come on. Who wanted to live in a house that always smelled like mothballs? Who wanted to live with an uncle who forced you to be in church every Sunday? Plus, you had to abide by his rules. And he didn't care how old you were, either. So, it had to be fate when Ricky came into my life.

He got me my own apartment not even a week after we met. The fact that he loved to spend his dough on me made it even sweeter. He tried really hard to make sure I got everything I needed, and I let him. Hell yeah! That's why most of the time when I'm upset, I can make him feel really guilty about how he's been treating me lately.

"Why do you keep taking me through all these changes?" I asked as I forced myself to cry.

"What you talkin' 'bout, Kira? What changes?"

"The constant lies and drama!"

"Tell me what you talkin' 'bout, Ma!"

"I'm talking about you coming in this house two, three, and four o'clock in the morning, every damn night, like you got it like that! I'm just plain sick of it!"

"Come off that, baby," Ricky said as he pulled me into his arms. "You know those hours are the best time for me to work. I make mo' money and get less police."

"Who cares about all of that? I just want it to stop!"

"It will."

"But when? I mean, come on, Ricky. You got plenty of dough put away. And I've got some good, consistent money coming in my salon every week. So, we ain't gon' need for nothing."

"Look, I'll tell you what? Let me finish the rest of my pack and make one last run down to Florida, then I'll take a long vacation."

"What you mean, vacation?!" I raised my voice because I needed some clarity.

"It means I'mma chill out for a while."

"What's a while?"

"Shit, Kira! I don't know! Maybe six months. A year."

"You promise?" I asked, giving him my famous pout.

"Yeah. I promise," he told me in a low whisper as he began to kiss my neck and tug on my ear lobe.

That instant, my panties got wet. Ricky pulled me closer to him. He cupped both of my ass cheeks in his hands, gripping 'em hard while he ground his dick up against my kitty cat. I couldn't resist the feelings that were coming over me. So when he picked me up I wrapped my legs around his waist, only leaving him enough room to slide his huge black dick inside my world of passion. I'm so glad I had on my crotchless panties because if I had had to wait another second for him to pull my thong off, I probably would have exploded.

"Hmmm, baby fuck me harder!" I begged him as I used the kitchen sink to help support my weight. His thrusts got harder and more intense.

"You like it when we fuss and make up, huh?" Ricky whispered each word between kisses. But of course, I declined to answer him. Swelling his head up about how I like making love after we have an argument, was not what I deemed to be a solution to our problems. After we got our rocks off, he and I both decided to lay back in our kingsized bed until we both dozed off.

Around 12:30 in the afternoon is about the time Ricky and I woke up. I hopped into the shower and about two minutes later, he hopped in right behind me. I knew what he wanted when he walked in the bathroom. It's not often that he and I take showers together, unless he wants to bend me over so he can hit it from the back. He knows I love giving it to him from the back, especially in the shower. The slapping noise our bodies make together in the water, as he's working himself in and out of me, turns me on.

After Ricky got his rocks off, he left the shower and returned to our bedroom to get dressed. "What you gon' do today?" I asked him as I entered into our bedroom, wrapped in a towel.

'Well, I'mma run by the spot out Norfolk and see why Eric and them can't get my dough straight."

"Please, don't go out there and scream on them like you got something to prove."

"I'm not. I'mma be cool 'til one of them niggas step out of pocket."

"See, that's one of the reasons I want your ass to stop hustling!" I pointed my finger at him.

'Won't you stop stressing yourself? Believe me, most nig-gas out there got nothing but respect for me."

"What about the one who don't?" I continued with my questions as I started to lotion my body down.

"I've got plenty of soldiers out there that'll outweigh that problem."

"Yeah, yeah, yeah!" was my response, hoping he'd catch the hint and shut up.

Unfortunately this wasn't the case. Ricky kept yapping on and on about how good his product was, and how the fiends were loving it. Once I had gotten enough of hearing about his street life, I grabbed a sweatsuit and a pair of Air Force Ones that matched my outfit and threw them both on. I scooped up my car keys and my Chanel handbag, and headed out the front door.

When I pulled up in front of my salon, it was packed. I knew I had at least four, if not five, of my clients waiting on me already. I know they were mad as hell, too, considering I was supposed to have been here three hours ago. My first appointment was at ten o'clock. Hell! I couldn't get up. After waiting up all night for my trifling-assed husband to come home and then after all the fussing I did, I still let him con me outta my drawz. As I made my way through the salon doors, I greeted everyone and told my ten o'clock client to go and sit at the washbowl. "Tasha, girl, please don't be mad wit' me," I began to explain as I threw the cape around her neck.

"Oh, it's alright. I ain't been waiting that long," Tasha replied.

"What you getting?"

"Just a hard wrap. I got two packs of sixteen-inch hair I wantcha to hookup."

"Did you bring a stocking cap?"

"Yep."

"A'ight. Well, lay back so I can get started."

Within the next two hours, I had all four of my clients situated. They were either under the dryer or on their way out the door. Seven more of my clients showed up, but three cancelled. I thanked God for that because I wouldn't be getting out of this shop until around ten or eleven o'clock tonight. That couldn't happen. I had to get home and wash those two loads of clothes I had packed up top of my hamper before I heard Ricky's mouth about it.

He loved for his house to be cleaned at any cost; If his ass wasn't so unfaithful, we could have had a housemaid, because nothing must be out of place. This fetish for absolute cleanliness got on my nerves sometimes. I mean, shit, ain't nothing wrong with leaving a damn dirty glass or a plate and a fork in the sink every now and then. As for certain garments in his wardrobe, I was forbidden to throw them in the washing machine. I was always reminded to read the label instructions for every piece of clothing he had. If it said "Dry Clean Only," then that's where it was going. I got a headache just thinking about it, so, I made a rule to put a big *"H"* on my chest and handle it.

A few more hours flew by and my other stylist's clients started falling out the door, one by one. This meant our time to go home was coming.

"Rhonda," I called out to one of my hair stylists, who happened to be one of the hottest beauticians in the Tidewater area.

"Yeah," she replied.

"You feel like giving me a roller set after I put my last client under the dryer?"

"Girl, you know I don't mind," Rhonda replied as she bopped her head to Lloyd Bank's single, "On Fire."

Rhonda's good people. I knew she was going to tell me yeah, before I attempted to even ask her. That's just her personality. She'd been working with me ever since I opened the doors to this shop four years ago. From day one, she's showed me nothing but love, even through all the drama her kid's father had been giving her. Her kid's father, Tony, is also a ladies' man; just like Ricky. I keep telling Rhonda to get him like I get my husband. Stick him where it hurts: either steal his money or his pack. It can't get any simpler than that. But nah, she ain't hearing me. That's why them hoes Tony's messing with was laughing at her, 'cause she was letting that nigga play her.

Now my other stylist, Sunshine, was working her game *entirely* different. She was your average-looking chick with ghetto-assed booty. Niggas loved her. Every time I turned around she had somebody else's man walking through my salon doors, bringing her shit.

Sunshine was strictly hustler bound. No other kind of man would attract her. You had to be driving a whip, estimating thirty Gs or better. And his dough had to be long. I'm talking like, from V.A. to the state of Rhode Island, to mess with that chick.

Oh, and Sunshine's wardrobe was tight, too. She wasn't gonna wear none of that fake-assed, knock-off Prada and Chanel that these hoes were getting from the Chinese people at the hair stores. No way. Sunshine was a known customer at Saks Fifth Avenue and Macy's.

I've seen the receipts. Sometimes I thought she was trying to be in competition with me, considering I was like a regular at those stores and all. But there can be no contest because when it's all said and done, I am and will always be the baddest bitch.

Since the day had almost come to an end, I sat back in Rhonda's station as she did her magic on my hair. We were in a deep conversation about her man Tony, when Ricky walked through the door. "Good evening," he said.

"What's up, Ricky!" Rhonda greeted him.

"Nothing much," he responded.

"Where you just coming from?" I wanted to know.

"From the crib."

"Our house?"

"Yeah."

"So, what's up?"

"I need to switch cars witcha," he said as he took a seat in one of the booth chairs across from me.

Something must be getting ready to go down. And he wasn't gonna spill the beans while Rhonda was sitting up in here with me. I let her finish my hair and in the meantime, Ricky and I made idle conversation until she left. After she finished my hair, it only took her about ten minutes to clean up her station. Then Rhonda said her goodbyes and left.

"So, what you need my car for this time?" I wasted no time asking Ricky the second Rhonda left out the door.

As I waited for him to respond, I knew he could do one of three things. He could either tell me the truth, which could probably hurt him in some way later down the line. Or he could tell me a lie, which would really piss me off. And then he could throw Rule #7 at me from the *Hustler's Manual,* which insisted that he tell me nothing. A hustler's reason for that was: "The less your girl knows, the better off ya'll be."

"I need it to make a run," he finally said.

"What kind of run?"

"You don't need to know all that!" Ricky snapped.

"Look, don't get no attitude with me because I wanna know where you're taking my car."

"And who bought you the LS 400?"

"I don't care who bought it! The fact remains, it's in my name. Just like the Benz and that cartoon character, Hulk–

painted, 1100 Ninja motorcycle you got parked in the garage."

"And your point?"

"Look, Ricky just be careful. And please don't do nothing stupid."

"I'm not," he assured me with a kiss on my forehead.

"Don't have no bitch in my car," I yelled as he made his way out the door.

While he ignored me like I knew he would, I stood there and watched Ricky unlock my car door and drive off. At the same time, I wondered where he was goin'.

From *I'm Still Wifey*

It Ain't Over

Can you believe it? After all the planning I did to leave my husband Ricky to run off with Russ, it backfired on me. It has been two-and-a-half months since the whole thing went down. Now I'm sitting here all alone, in my hair shop, thinking about what I am going to do about this baby I'm carrying.

Rhonda and Nikki both didn't believe me when I told them that I was pregnant by Russ. But after I pulled out a calendar and counted back the days from the last time we were together, it finally registered through their thick skulls.

"So, what cha' gon' do about it?" Rhonda asked me the day I got the results from a pregnancy test about a month ago. The first thing that came out of her mouth was for me to get an abortion since I ain't gon' have a baby daddy. God knows where he is. But I told her that was the furthest thing from my mind because whether I had Russ in my life or not, I was gon' have this baby. And then she said, "Well, what would you do if he found out you're pregnant and wants to come back with a whole bunch of apologies and shit?"

I told her that shit ain't gon' happen because first of all, Russ ain't gon' find out I'm pregnant 'cause ain't nobody gon' know I'm pregnant by him. And second, after that stunt he pulled on me to rob me for my dough, I know he ain't gon' never show his face around this way ever again. He would be a fool to. I mean, he don't know if I told Ricky that he robbed me or not. So to play it cool, he's gon' do like any other greasy-ass nigga would do after they pull a stick-up move, and that is to disappear. And even though he thinks he got away with it, he hasn't. 'Cause whether Russ knows it or not, karma is coming for his ass. And what will give me much pleasure is to be able to see it hit 'em.

Hopefully my day will come very soon.

Back at my place, which is a step down from my ol' two-story house, I decided to pop myself a bag of popcorn and watch my favorite show, *America's Next Top Model.* Afterward, I began to straighten things up around my two bedroom, two-bath condo until my telephone started ringing.

"Hello," I said without looking at the CallerID.

"Whatcha doing?" Rhonda wanted to know.

"I was just dusting the mantel over my fireplace."

"Girl, sit your butt down. 'Cause if my memory serves me, I do remember you being on your feet all day today."

"I'm fine. But what I wanna know is, why you didn't come back to work today?"

Rhonda sighed heavily and said, "Kira, if I could kill Tony and get away with it, I would do it."

"What happened now?"

"Girl, I caught this nigga talking to some hoe named Letisha on his cell phone."

"Where was he at?"

"He was in the bathroom, sitting on the fucking toilet, taking a shit."

I laughed at Rhonda's comment and asked her what happened next.

"Well, before I busted in on him and smacked him upside his damn head with my shoe, I stood very quiet in the hallway right outside our bedroom and heard this bastard telling that hoe how much he missed her and that he was going to get his hair cut at the barbershop. And right after I heard him say that, that's when I went off."

"So, what did he do?"

"He couldn't do shit with his pants wrapped around his ankles. So, he just sat there and took all them blows I threw at his ass. And then when he dropped his cell phone, I hurled up and snatched it right off the floor and cussed that bitch out royally."

"And what did she say?"

"I ain't let her say, shit. 'Cause after I told her who I was and that if I ever caught her in Tony's face, she was gonna get fucked up, I hung up."

"So, what was Tony doing while you was going off on that hoe?"

"Trying to hurry up and wipe his ass, so he can get up from the toilet and I guess take his phone back. But as soon as the bastard stood up to flush the stool, I threw his phone right up against the wall as hard as I could and broke that bad boy in about ten little pieces."

I laughed again and said, "Damn girl! That's some shit I used to do."

"Well, jackass didn't see it coming. So, it made it all the better."

"Where's he at now?"

"In the kitchen helping Ryan with his homework."

"So, did he ever go out and get his hair cut?"

"Hell nah. Shit, he knew better."

"Well, what kind of lies did he tell you about everything that happened?"

"Girl, that nigga ain't gon' volunteer no information. All he had to say was that I was crazy as hell. And then he went on about his damn business."

"Rhonda," I said before I sighed, "I know you're sick and tired of going through all that bullshit! Because I sure was when Ricky was on the streets."

"Hey wait," Rhonda interjected, "I forgot to tell you that he called the shop today while you was at lunch."

"Did you accept the call?"

"Yeah. But we only talked for a few minutes."

"What did he say?"

"He just wanted to know where you was and when was you coming in. So, I told him that you wasn't. And that's when he asked me to call you on three-way. But I told him the three-way call thing wasn't working."

"I bet he got real mad, didn't he?"

"Hell yeah!"

"So, what did he say after that?"

"Nothing but to tell you he called. And for me to tell you to come down to the county jail and see him before the U.S. Marshal picks him up and takes him off to the Federal Holding Facility in Oklahoma, because he has something very important to talk with you about."

"Well, he should already know that it ain't gon' happen. But, I am wondering what he's got so important to talk to me about."

"Girl, he's just probably saying that so he can get you to come down and see him."

"Yeah. You probably right," I agreed.

"Well, are you going to ever tell him that you're pregnant by Russ?" Rhonda blurted out of the blue.

"Nope. It ain't none of his damn business. All he needs to focus on is signing those divorce papers my lawyer is getting ready to send his ass."

"So, you're serious about that, huh?"

"You damn right!" I commented and then I said, "I'm

gonna get that nigga outta my life once and for all, so I can move on."

"Look, I understand all that. But I wouldn't let his ass get off that easy. Because the next time he calls the shop, I would make it my business to wreck his muthafucking ego and tell him, '*Yeah nigga, while you was running around behind my back with Sunshine's stinking ass, I was fucking your boy Russ right in your bed. And I just found out that I'm pregnant by him.*' "

"Oh my God! That'll kill him!"

"That's the idea," Rhonda told me.

I said, "Girl, that nigga gon' try and come through the phone after I tell him some shit like that."

"Well, no need to worry 'bout that. 'Cause it ain't gon' happen." Before I could comment, she told me to hold on because somebody was beeping in on her other line. When she clicked over, it got real quiet. But just like that, she was right back on the line and said, "Hey girl, one of Tony's homeboys is on the other end trying to holler at him. So, let me call you back."

"A'ight," I told her. Then we both hung up.

From *Life After Wifey*

Choosing Sides

Nikki Speaks

From the time I jumped into my car and left Syncere's house until the time I pulled in front of Kira's apartment building, I wrecked the hell out of my brain trying to rationalize and make sense of the text message I had just read on Syncere's T-Mobile.

The message was clear but I could not bring myself to believe that my man had something to do with Mark's murder, not to mention the fact that Kira had gotten caught up in the crossfire and lost her baby. I didn't want to sound stupid or naïve, but there had to be an explanation behind this whole thing. I needed to find out what it was and how involved Syncere was before Kira blew the whistle on him because whether she realized it or not, I needed my man. So, I was not letting him go that easy.

Immediately after I got out of my car I stood there on the sidewalk and took a deep breath. After I exhaled, I put one foot forward and proceeded toward Kira's apartment to confront the inevitable. Knowing she was going to bite my head off the moment I jumped to Syncere's defense was something I had prepared myself for. As I made my way down the entryway to her building, this fine-ass, older-looking Hispanic guy wearing a dark blue painter's cap and overalls came rushing toward me, so I didn't hesitate to move out of his way. But, what was really odd about him was when I tried to make eye contact and say 'hello' he totally brushed me off and looked the other way. Being the chick I am, I threw my hand up at him and said, "Well, fuck you too! You ol' rude muthafucka!" I kept it moving.

Patting my right thigh, with my hand, to a rhythmic beat as I walked up the last step to Kira's floor, I let out a long sigh and proceeded toward Kira's front door. Upon my arrival, I noticed that her door was slightly ajar so I reached over and pushed it open. "Girl, did you know that your door was open?" I yelled as I walked into the apartment. I didn't get an answer, so I closed the front door behind me and proceeded down the hallway toward her bedroom. When I entered into her room and saw that she was nowhere in sight, I immediately called her name again and I turned to walk toward the master bathroom. "Kira, where you at?" I turned the doorknob and pushed the door open.

"Oh, my God," I screamed at the top of my lungs the second my mind registered the gruesome sight of Kira's body slumped over the edge of the bathtub, while her head lay in a pool of her own blood. I couldn't see her face because of the way her body was positioned. I rushed over to her side, got down on my knees and crawled over next to her. My heart was racing at the speed of light and my emotions were spiraling out of control as I grabbed her body and pulled her toward me.

"Kira, please wake up!" I begged her and began to cry hysterically. She didn't move, so I started shaking her frantically. "Kira, please wake up!" I screamed once again. "Don't die on me like this," I pleaded. Out of nowhere, her eyes fluttered and slowly opened. Overwhelmed by her sudden reaction, my heart skipped a beat and I pulled her body even closer. "Oh my God, thank you," I said in a joyful manner and cradled her head in my lap. "I almost thought I lost you," I told her and wiped the tears away from my eyes. Meanwhile, Kira struggled a bit to swallow the blood in her throat and then she tried to speak. I immediately leaned forward and positioned my ear about two inches away from her mouth so I could hear what it was she had to say.

When she finally moved her lips, the few words she uttered were just above a whisper and barely audible. I was about to ask her to repeat herself and she started choking. I panicked. "Ahh shit! Don't do this to me. Take a deep breath," I instructed her as I began to massage her chest. Then it suddenly hit me that I needed to call an ambulance. I retrieved my cellular phone from the holster on my right side and dialed 911.

"911, what's your emergency?"

"My cousin's been shot," I answered with urgency.

"What's your cousin's name?"

"Her name is Kira Walters."

"And what is your name?"

"My name is Nicole Simpson."

"Okay Nicole, I need for you to stay calm. Can you tell me if Kira is conscious?"

"Yes, she's conscious. I've got her lying in my arms."

"Okay, tell me exactly where Kira's been shot."

"In the left side of her head, right above her temple."

"Is that the only place she's been shot?"

"Yes ma'am."

"Nicole, I'm gonna need you to give me the adress to where you are located. In the meantime, I'm gonna need you to remain calm and grab something like a sheet or a towel and press it against Kira's head to stop some of the bleeding. Has she lost a lot of blood?"

"Yes, she has," I assured the woman. Shortly thereafter I gave her the address.

The operator stayed on the phone with me until the police and the paramedics arrived. Covered from the waist down in Kira's blood, I was ushered out of the bathroom and into the kitchen by this short, white, female police officer who had a ton of questions for me. I only answered the questions l knew the answers to. Once our little session was over, another detective—this time a white male—came in and asked me almost the exact same questions as the female officer did. I found myself repeating everything over again.

My back was turned when the paramedics took Kira out on the stretcher. By the time I realized that she had been taken away, she was already in the ambulance, headed to the nearest emergency room. The white, male detective informed me where they were taking her so I immediately called my family, told them Kira had gotten shot and that they needed to meet me at Bayside Memorial. After they assured me they were on their way, I hung up with them. On my way out, I noticed at least a dozen detectives and forensics investigators combing every inch of the apartment to collect evidence so there was no doubt in my mind that they were going to find her killer.

I got to the hospital in no time at all and to my surprise my mother, my father and my grandmother arrived shortly afterward. We all sat and waited patiently for one of the doctors performing the emergency surgery to come out and give us an update on Kira's condition. In the meantime, my grandmother had a few questions for me to answer.

"Nikki, are you sure Kira was conscious when she left with the paramedics?" she asked as if she was making a desperate attempt to find the answer in my eyes.

"Yes, she was," I replied in a reassuring manner. "She even tried to say something, but I didn't understand her. When I asked her to say it again she started choking and that's when I called the paramedics."

"Well, how was she breathing when they took her out of the house?"

"I don't know, Grandma. I was in the kitchen when they carried her out," I told her and then I put my head down in despair. Knowing that my cousin was in surgery fighting for her life and I couldn't do anything to help her put a huge strain on my heart. Not to mention the fact that if I would've gotten to her apartment a little sooner this probably would not have happened to her. In a sense I felt like her getting shot was partially my fault. Which was why I was feeling so terrible right now.

"What in the world do y'all got going on?" my father interjected as if the sight of me made him cringe.

"What are you talking about?" I looked at him with an expression of uncertainty.

"What kind of people are y'all mixed up with?"

"Come on now, honey, I know you're upset but this is not the time or the place," my mother spoke up.

"Yes, your wife is right," my grandmother agreed trying to keep the peace.

But my father wasn't trying to hear them. Their comments went in one ear and right out the other. "Whatcha trying to do, end up like your cousin in there?"

"What kind of question is that?" I snapped.

"Just answer the question," he commanded.

"No, I'm not," I replied, irritated with his questions.

"It's hard to tell," my father snapped back. "Because every time I turn around, somebody's either getting shot or killed. And if you keep walking around here like you ain't got the sense you were born with, then you're gonna end up just like your cousin back there."

"Alright now, that's enough! I don't want to hear another word," my grandmother whispered harshly with tears in her eyes. Her tone sent a clear message to my father that she was sincerely pissed and he'd better not utter another word.

But, knowing how much my father loathed when people told him what to do, the chances of that happening were slim to none. The moment she closed her mouth and rolled her eyes at him, he parted his lips and said, "You know what, Mama . . ."

But fortunately for us, he couldn't finish the thought because we were interrupted by an Asian doctor dressed in green hospital-issued scrubs, walking toward us. "Are you the family for Kira Walters?"

"Yes, we are," I eagerly replied.

"I'm Dr. Ming and I was called in to perform emergency surgery on Miss Walters."

"How is she?" my grandmother asked.

"Yeah, how is she? Can we go in and see her?" my mother asked.

"I'm sorry to inform you but Miss Walters didn't make it."

"What do you mean, she 'didn't make it'?" I screamed in disbelief.

"Ma'am," the doctor began in the most apologetic manner, "believe me, we did everything in our power but she was nonresponsive."

Hearing this man tell me that my cousin just died hit me like a ton of bricks. I couldn't believe it. I mean, there had to be some kind of mistake. Kira couldn't be dead.

I just had her wrapped up in my arms back at her apartment a couple of hours ago. Whatever this man was talking was pure nonsense and I couldn't accept that.

Meanwhile, as the thoughts of living my life without her started consuming me, my grandmother walked off in another direction, crying her poor little heart out. My parents got a little more in-depth with the complications Kira had